Baby Momma 3

Baby Momma 3

Ni'chelle Genovese

www.urbanbooks.net

Urban Books, LLC
97 N18th Street
Wyandanch, NY 11798

Baby Momma 3 Copyright © 2014 Ni'chelle Genovese

ISBN 13: 978-1-60162-582-3
ISBN 10: 1-60162-582-0

First Printing February 2014
Printed in the United States of America

10 9 8 7 6 5 4 3 2 1

This is a work of fiction. Any references or similarities to actual events, real people, living or dead, or to real locales are intended to give the novel a sense of reality. Any similarity in other names, characters, places, and incidents is entirely coincidental.

Distributed by Kensington Publishing Corp.
Submit Wholesale Orders to:
Kensington Publishing Corp.
C/O Penguin Group (USA) Inc.
Attention: Order Processing
405 Murray Hill Parkway
East Rutherford, NJ 07073-2316
Phone: 1-800-526-0275
Fax: 1-800-227-9604

Baby Momma 3

Ni'chelle Genovese

Acknowledgments

These words, this talent they're not mine but a gift I was given. It had me devouring the works of authors past like termites to fresh wood. We look at the world and try to mold ourselves after it, not understanding that our mold was cast, tested, and fortified specifically after us and in our favor. I give the greatest thanks and all the glory to God. With Him nothing is impossible.

Carl and Natalie thank you for taking a chance on me and the Baby Momma Series. Natalie one of these days I'm flying to NY and we are going to have a Spa day. It'll be my treat for all my questions, comments, and concerns, that's the best way to describe all the e-mails I harass you with. Joylynn you are coming along as well. Thank you for being the wonderful agent that you are. I have the best FB-family in the world Jo'shanda, Dawnsheika , Deirdra, Syrius Ly, & Lana, sisters I never knew I had until now and all because we like the same "funny." Y'all keep me laughing even when I want to pull my hair out. My gurus Judy C, K'wan, Stephanie HL, Nicety, Mr. Lavaba Mallison, Author Harold "H" Williams, Chip at Black Arc Studio, team work is dream work. Thank you for lending an ear or an eye in most cases. Thank you all for your ever growing love and support to Edyie, Lieu, Kellie M, Terri M, Ronnisha, Jerrell, Donna S, Sharaszad, Aisha, Alamaka, Tamika CM, Shadrekka, Nicole NC, Khadijah, Christie R, Jay F, Benefa, Cyntavia, Tera, ShaQuenta, Penny, Stephanie N., Sherron M, Mary S., China, Heather, Hope, Valaria, Myra W, Leslie

Acknowledgments

HJ, Eve K, Michelle C of AAMBC Book Club, DJ Gatsby's Book Club, Alli & Ke'Angela and Angie B's Reading Between the Lines BookClub, Ubawa, Carol Mackey of Black Expressions BookClub, Papaya W and Sistah's on Lit, & The Diamond Divas Book Club. Big bear hugs and <3 I am so thankful for *everyone* that's supported me.

www.nichellegenovese.com
follow me on twitter @nichelleg4

Have you ever ridden a roller coaster backwards? Well get ready and enjoy the ride . . . read, I meant enjoy the read.

-Ni'chelle

Prologue

My fingers were wound up so tight in the belt on my trench coat they were starting to go numb. Bright as day, yield sign yellow was the best way I could describe it. Angelo had taken it upon himself to pick it out for me and I hated it the second I laid eyes on it. *"Think of it like a bombshell meets video vixen look,"* he'd said smiling proudly.

All I could honestly think was 'Where in the world is damn Carmen San Diego.'

Hours ago he came home from an urgent family meeting and after a quick hushed phone call he was draggin' me off to God knows where in the middle of the night. *The better to see you with my dear, that's the only reason why I'd ever pick a glow in the dark jacket. The family probably told him to escort me somewhere secluded so I could be put down like a lame horse.*

The moon was the fullest I'd ever seen it and I couldn't help wondering what Mimi would say it meant. I hadn't thought about my grandma since the night she'd found me unconscious in her bathroom floor. One minute I was fine, listening to Avant in my room. The candied scent of Pear Glace' body splash, my signature fragrance, filled the air. I must have taken some bad oxy, because next thing I know I was retchin' into blue toilet water and then everything went black. When I came to Mimi was hovering over me rambling about a mirror breaking on its own and a bird on the roof making a nest out of hair, both signs of bad luck and death. She was probably still superstitious to the point of insanity; superstition was Mimi's religion of choice.

Angelo looked over at me and the bluish silver light from that moon did un-humanly things to his gray eyes. I knew him, but I ain't really *know him*. You could have the most well-kept pet in the world but if it was dangerous to begin with you always worried about it reverting to its baser instincts and turning on you. Angelo claimed to love me but we never made love. He was a collage of rough rushed sessions that usually ended in me peeling his hand from around my throat before I passed out. Sex was never about me, but I'd just let him get his and consider us since he was helping me stay out of prison.

We'd pulled to a stop in front of foreboding wrought iron gates.

"How are you feeling?" he asked, brushing a cold finger along my cheek, feather-light, faint like the salt in the air from the ocean.

"I'd be better if I knew what was up. And why you so cold all the time? I think your ass is anemic, you need to get seen about that."

He scoffed, "I'm fine. And all yous need to do is play your part. Here, I brought ya' a present." He pulled a little vial of white powder out of his pocket and I looked at his ass like he was crazy.

"You know I don't –"

"I know and that's why I'm not askin'. The family is involved now so ya' gonna have to trust me on some things. Take it, can't have you up in there acting all nervous. *Andiamo.*"

"Well?" the voice called out.

Startled at the interruption, my little imaginary Q-bert who had been hopping around the three-dimensional Parquet wood flooring vanished as I glanced up. Angelo was out in the car and here I was alone with this stranger and probably not supposed to mix coke with pain-killers.

"Well, what?" I asked the pale fiery red-headed man.

"Do you have it? The one in the car said you'd bring it in. I have the money but I'll have to sample it first. You are a funny acting one. You aren't wearing a wire or anything are you?" He lifted his head narrowing his eyes at me suspiciously.

Oh, thanks Angelo, get me high and bring me on one of your drug runs. Appreciate that a bunch.

Sighing, I tried not to zone out again as I stared at the blazing halo of flames on his head. My fingers tingled at the thought of touching his flaming locks. I swore I could almost hear them crackling and sizzling in the air. Instead I reached into one of the pockets of my jacket. Yep, just as I expected little vials clinked and I walked toward the ginger freckled-faced man. He didn't take them as I expected. His rhinestone encrusted smoking slippers were soundless as he padded away. The white satin of his shirt billowed behind him like the sail of a ship. *He's either a Gingy Geenie or a sultan of Satan with all those red flames on his head. And I'm the yellow submarine coke queen.*

There was a blur of shiny wood paneling, marble flooring, bronzed busts on pedestals and winding staircases. The private rooftop patio was dizzily breathtaking, plus all those steps had me realizing how out of shape I'd gotten. Gingy pointed for me to sit down on large chocolate and red cushions in the midst of his rooftop garden. White awnings covered the seating area with yellow and green teacup lights. They twinkled and winked overhead like little Tinker bells.

I handed Gingy his product and frowned when our fingers touched. Static sextricity, I mean like some other-other kind of sexual charge shot all the way down to arches of my feet. The cushion sank beside me as he sat down and I felt like a sensual heat-seeking missile. It wasn't even like he was that fuckin' attractive. The heat coming off of his skin hit me in radiating waves. I naturally leaned closer to warm myself by the hearth of his head fire. *See and this is why I don't mess with this shit. Vicodins don't make me wanna mount a damn stranger. Why would Angelo send me up here high and horny as hell?*

"Woo, you can tell Angelo I agree, he's definitely got the best shit in all of Miami," he shouted. "And your angel-face have a look worth dying for. Why haven't I seen—"

He paused and we both looked down. There it was in the crease of his expensive satiny white lounge pants. The welcome party had come out—the happy tee-pee—and he turned 'bout as bright red as the hair on his head.

"Fuck uh, that doesn't happen like—" He'd started to explain but hell, I understood what he was feeling and I was already pissed Angelo had sent me to do his damn job. We hadn't even discussed the particulars about this shit. *Mmm, might as well earn myself a "tip".* My skirt cinched up as I slid over onto his lap and I didn't know if all Gingy felt was that damn electrifying or if it was just this one in particular. He untied my jacket and reached inside locking his arms around my back. Just grinding against him through my panties had us both gasping and panting. I didn't care if Angelo was outside waiting. This is exactly what the hell he got for forcing my ass into the coke game. I'd make something up. I just needed to get this out of my system and Gingy's lips were gettin' real close to figuring out my kitty's password as he purred along my neck.

Reaching down I unzipped his pants and gasped. *Damn, Gingy lemme find out I picked the wrong other white meat. Big ass dick. Access granted. Thank you for entering your password and pussy ID.* I slid my drenched panties to the side and all but gasped in shock against his ear. Either he was a freak of nature or I'd just been dealing with Angelo so long my ass was a born again virgin.

"Pull my ears, tug my ears, I can't . . . unless you, I need you to," he chanted breathlessly.

The hell, this ain't the time for Simon-fuckin-says, pull on what, and tug what? Ears? Ugh, I just want to cum. I started tugging anyway and he let out this deep guttural moan. The sound traveled through my body like notes vibrating through a harp. All five of my senses were now erogenous senses. Sounds like gasping and moaning, or wet skin sliding even smells like Bonne Belle cotton candy Lip Smackers were all pinging my 'oh em gee' spot dead on. *What the hell kind of Spanish-fly roophie-colada coke did we do?*

"Ally?" Someone shouted from behind me.

Gingy frantically pushed me off his lap. Frustrated, I sniffed my upper lip confused, because I sure as hell didn't wear cotton candy lip gloss.

"Jasper. Jassy, baby it's not what you think I promise." Gingy approached a very pissed off little man with his hands raised apologetically and he was speaking so . . . so *effeminately.*

Completely miffed, I wiped the damn lip gloss off my lips and straightened my skirt and jacket. *He sure as hell didn't have all that flair turned on five seconds ago.*

"Really Al? It isn't what I think? So, you're gonna tell me you weren't just fucking that . . . that hi-ho school bus prosty? She was tugging your ears, Al. *She was tugging your fucking ears!*" Jasper's interrogation ended in a high-pitched shriek and my hands too flew up apologetically when I saw the gun he'd whipped out. *Oh, Bonne Belle and butt-fucks really?*

"I have had enough, Al. You're like a puppy with your little pink lipstick hanging out. Every time I let you out to piss, you're wandering around and you've got your *G-damn lipstick* in or on some . . . . some *tramp*. It's supposed to be *my fucking lipstick*," Jasper wailed at Al and I cringed. Poor little guy, but it was so less dramatic when he kept calling it lipstick. I imagined him crouched in front of Al trying to *put it on* like some lipstick and it almost made me burst out laughing.

The gun exploded and I jumped as Gingy crumpled. Bright red stained his pristine white garments as well as the deck beneath and shit just got so serious.

"You-who, old-yellow, yeah you. I'm gonna help rewrite the manual for all your Stepford-Goldy-Gold Digger, boyfriend fuckers in training. Chapter One: Never Touch Another Bitch's Lipstick."

Jasper turned the gun on me and my eyes widened. I threw my hands out in front of me.

"Angelo wait he didn't know," I shouted.

Jasper turned to see who was there. That was the play I'd chosen out of the split second coke-cocktail induced options that I had to choose from. When the ball snapped in my head, I got low and charged, hitting him with my shoulder in his midsection. His back thudded against the white sandstone of the balcony where he teetered with his arms flailing wildly. We locked eyes and for an instant and I felt sorry for him as he tipped over and fell the four stories onto the rocky private beach below. His neck broke amongst several other things from the way he was unnaturally sprawled on the outcropping rocks.

I walked out the front door and climbed into the car.

"The family needs to know how well you handle certain uh, situations to see how you'll fit in. Was that your gun I heard or do I need to get the boys to clean up?" Angelo asked quietly.

"There's no mess. I didn't even know I had a gun, or that I was supposed to kill or get someone killed. Thanks for the heads up," I replied as sarcastically as possible.

"Anytime, bella. *Anytime.*"

"What do you mean *replacing me?* You don't replace Sadira Nadesche."

Her voice rang through one of the studio monitors where most of what looked like around forty people hovered watching anxiously. They appeared to be in various states of excitement, awe, or shock.

"We're mid-production. I'm the highest paid actress in this industry, voted number one on all the lists. Pick a list. Get me my manager and my lawyer. *Now,*" she said.

The click clack of my electric-blue, peep-toe Badgley Mischka heels echoed loudly across the cement flooring of the set. The camera feed, which must have been another area on set, quickly flickered off. Everyone turned and Angelo, who'd promised to stay by my side the entire time, squeezed my arm gently as what felt like a million eyes focused on me. To the average observer we looked like the perfect couple. He wore a black Henley long-sleeved shirt that clung to his lean thinly muscled frame, Cavalli shades, tousled hair, Diesel jeans, clean, simple, and sexy. Me? My stylist, Sir'Tavius, put me in a little black dress and a Paul Smith blazer that matched my favorite new blue and black Dior purse.

Rumors of a fresh-faced starlet surfaced out of nowhere. A favor Angelo asked from his father. The price for that favor was atrocious. When I made my debut I couldn't show up lookin' like a ragamuffin so Angelo hired me the best stylist in the business.

"Oh, wow, she's gorgable," someone whispered.

"Don't matter how adorable or gorgeous she is, Sadira is going to murder that ass," someone responded.

Ignoring their comments I pressed a tight, nervous smile to my new face and tilted my chin high. Oh yeah, my new face. I guess good things do come from foul circumstances. It'd taken three surgeons, almost a year of healing, and at Angelo's prodding some etiquette and refinement classes to get me ready for the world.

Last August I'd murdered Larissa and tried to kidnap and do the same to Michelle. They were the reasons why both Rasheed and I were sent to prison to begin with. They were also the reasons why I had a daughter who would never know her father, because unfortunately I had to kill his ass, too. Now, because of Michelle my daughter would never know the real me. She would never know my real smile, or how I used to talk. No, when I finally got my baby girl back we'd have to skip over the "how I met your daddy" talks. She couldn't know I was a stripper or even that she was actually born up in a prison maternity ward. Not even how I escaped to get her back. Those memories and facts were deleted the moment Angelo paid his father to help reinvent me. When Michelle broke my nose it gave Angelo the idea of a lifetime. Yes, I was still hiding in a sense; I was just doing it in plain sight and armed with everything from a new identity and credit cards all the way down to a damn near perfect credit score.

A short woman, way shorter than me, with large, thick, square glasses that made her eyes look enormous, walked up to me. She extended a shaky hand, blinking her alien-esque eyes rapidly.

"Desivita Dulce', I presume? I'm awestruck. I mean, my name is Frankie and wow you are a minxer. They didn't show us any pics, which was weird. Not that you're weird, just that it was weird. Directors just said they had a better header, and *ta-da* here you are, and I'm rambling.

Um, we . . . I . . . well, we weren't expecting you until tomorrow. Uh, so your trailer isn't ready yet," she said in a flurry of nervous head nods and hand gestures.

"That's fine," Angelo said, stepping forward to speak on my behalf. "We just wanted to meet everyone. Hone . . . I mean Desi was just curious about the set. It is her first movie. She wanted to get a feel for it, have a look around before the big day. See what her marks are or are there marks on the set or whatever? I mean, I don't know what the fuck it is you call it." Angelo too, blabbered like a nervous idiot. He'd been making me write and say my new name over and over and in the first thirty seconds he almost dropped the ball.

"Oh, well, then let me show you two around. We're really good at adjusting, especially with the way the first producer . . . Uh, hopefully you watched the first movie right?"

I was glad I'd taken one of the extra Vicodin I had left over from my surgery. The movie was a wack-ass horror film called *Revived 2*. The script was easy to memorize because all my parts were "Daisy running," or "Daisy screaming topless." That bullshit made me laugh so much I hurt my new cheeks. Angelo threatened to take it away during my recovery, afraid I'd burst my stitches or whatever he'd said. However, being on set and over-hearing the gaffer and key grip asking the best boy about butt plugs and magic fingers had me thinking I'd walked into a sex shop. *Maybe I'd misread that shit and we were shooting a horror-themed porno?* When Frankie saw my expression she calmly explained that butt plugs were stand adapters for the speakers, and magic fingers were a type of mount.

The first movie was apparently a box office hit. According to Angelo's logic this one would be a good fit for my introduction into the world of bright lights and even brighter stars since it was predicted to do three times better. Angelo already had his own self made fame. He wasn't wanted by U.S. Marshals and on watch lists for escaping prison. Trenisha aka L'il Miss Honey was. With his help and the family pitching in I could covertly push coke as an industry insider and I would be untouchable. Instant fame where I could pick up and go anywhere, do anything I wanted and on top of all that I'd have *star power*.

"So, are you ready for this or what?" Angelo asked once we were back in the car and on our way to get ready for some kind of celebrity all-star party.

I didn't answer immediately. Instead I stared at the face of this almost-famous movie star's reflection in the window. It was weird how little I could see of my old self. Desivita was raised in a group foster home that was paid to doctor up fake records. She graduated from high school in Fayetteville, North Carolina. She'd relocated to LA auditioned for roles and took acting classes and had been working part-time as a Hooters waitress. This stranger stared back at me, with her high, perfectly flushed cheeks and these bright, mysterious eyes. Sir'Tavius had given me a ring to wear and I fidgeted with it anxiously.

"Always wear one accessory," he'd said as he exaggerated a yawn. "That'll make ere'body go snaparazzi with their little camera phones and whatnot." On his finger sat a black angel's wing with Swarovski crystals in the feathers. He'd batted his long, perfectly placed lashes before handing over this ring that engulfed my entire index finger. Twirling it in place I sighed, wondering how I'd get Paris if Honey technically no longer existed. How would I, as this famous actress person, actually approach Michelle and convince her to give her up? Angelo probably hadn't even considered that since he was more concerned with having an "us," and then having us make a family.

It just meant that I'd have to do some creative tinkering on my own damn time and my own damn dime. That's what the hell it sounded like it meant.

Angelo looked over at me. "It's kind of late to be gettin' scared, *bella*."

"I'm fine, baby. You know I stay ready, so I never have to worry about gettin' ready," I told him.

Chapter 1

Self-Destructing Hearts </#

(Six Months Later)

I could probably tell you the time every half hour on the hour throughout the night because I woke up at the slightest thing. Every time I'd shift or turn over, the house settled, or if one of the kids so much as sneezed, my eyes would fly open and my heart rate would shoot to threat level "imminent danger." The only good thing about sleeping as lightly as I did was that I heard everything, which was also the bad part. Something had awakened me and with my sleeping habits a mosquito could have burped, thus sending my brain into panic mode. *Okay, October. I know your signature move is bumps in the night and whatnot but this is not how I want to start things off.*

I'd left my window open and the wind picked up the scent of the gardenias outside. It cooled my face and, as I sat up, made my sweat-soaked sheets feel as though they'd been doused in ice water. It was still unclear if I'd heard feet shuffling or if I'd dreamt about it and immediately my thoughts turned to Larissa. Confused, I'd started to call out but stopped as the hazy, restless cobwebs cleared in my mind. Secretly I wished it were her coming home late. That used to be her usual bullshit reaction to "nothing." Okay, granted what I would call "nothing" was most likely someone or something I'd done. Larissa and I had a long history of drama and an even longer history of unhealthy solutions.

Regardless of how much it hurt, every time I opened my eyes I'd have to remind myself that she was gone. I was a widow now, with a late wife, and there was no changing that. Realization would sink in and my throat would feel like I was trying to swallow a dry handkerchief whole. It didn't matter where I was. I could be lying in bed or at a grocery store with the kids, or just daydreaming. Because, when I say every time I opened my eyes I felt like crying, I meant every time. Since she was gone a noise in the night was definitely not a good thing.

The house alarm was beeping at sixty-second intervals; it only did that when it was running on the backup generator. The power was out; or worse the power had been cut. Just the simple thought of someone cutting the power made me cautious. I reached into the nightstand and grabbed my handgun. It felt cold and foreign to my fingers, but it made me feel safe. The bedroom was painted in a combination of eerie shadows from the battery-powered air freshener in the corner.

Everything always looked strange with shadows attached to them at night, especially people. Some people could stand with a shadow over even a little bit of their face and look like monsters. Rasheed was one of those niggas who could wear a shadow and exude pure sex. Whereas Larissa, my late wife, would look like the very devil himself.

Sometimes I'd slip and absentmindedly think of Rasheed. He was my heartworm for life, even after his death. He'd gnawed his way in, latching on. I'd gotten so used to living with him and the pain and our illusion of love that I felt borderline guilt and misery at having him removed, permanently. He was murdered because of me. Now Honey was trying to murder me over him. Well, over the daughter she had with him. Honey, Danita, Diamond, the list could go on; they were only a few of the many reasons why my heartworm had to go. I shook my head at myself and frowned. You stay with someone for years and over the course of time they seep into your pores little by little, day by day. The craziest thing happens and suddenly, you can't make lasagna anymore because the smell reminds you of one person. You can't drink a certain kind of champagne because the taste reminds you of the other.

It's been said when a relationship is over, you should remain single six months for every year you were with that person. I got with Rah at sixteen, Ris at eighteen, and I was twenty-seven now. Based on that theory I wouldn't be fit to deal with anyone until my ass was damn near thirty-two. Add in the fact that Ris had a drug habit and Rah had children with two different women, one of whom was trying to kill my ass, and I'd probably be better off staying single for the rest of my damn life.

Rasheed was like a drug. I could never tell if I was sprung off good dick or just stuck on dumb love, but we had this hardcore yo-yo "relationshit."

I mean, the harder we fought, the grimier and lower he got with the shit he did. In turn, that's how much higher the highs would be when we bounced back and how much harder his love would seem to be magnified. It was addictive and it was mind-blowing. It's a damn shame that it took me having a baby and some years in order to learn how to tell the difference between ships and shit. Some people are ships and those are the ones you build your relations and connections with. They'll help you carry your burdens and your dreams, and they won't let you drown. Others, as in Rasheed's case, are just shit. Larissa just happened in the middle of all of that. When things

didn't get any better with Rasheed, we decided to set him up using her cousin Honey as a test and bait. He failed.

The only logical answer at the time was for me to marry Ris. That might have been the problem right there. I was thinking logically instead of emotionally. Honey's family didn't want anything to do with the baby so Ris and I adopted her. After investing all of Rah's money we moved to Fort Lauderdale and I opened my own real estate firm. Everything seemed to just blow up in my face when Honey escaped from prison.

I quickly surveyed my things trying to make sure nothing was moving or, worse yet, creeping up on me. I was too damn old for nightlights but with everything going on I could admit that I was too damn scared to sleep without one. Safety light was the best name I could come up with when Trey asked why Mommy's nightlight had "smell goods" in it and his didn't. As far as anyone was concerned I just had it because it smelled nice, and it just so happened to have a safety light on it.

When I heard it, it was faint yet distinct, like "hungry in church and hearing someone trying to sneak a piece of candy out of their pocket" distinct. Someone was trying to get into the house. Throwing the sheets aside, I grabbed my phone and put my Bluetooth in my ear.

I fought back memories of that night that forced me to become a slave to preparation. The night Honey dragged me out of my own house and almost killed me. It made me stay on high alert, always sleeping fully clothed or in my robe over full pajamas. I couldn't remember the last time I'd slept comfortably, let alone the entire night.

I've always had a fear of guns. Guns and cancer, and if you grew up in my house you would as well. My mother passed away from cancer when I was ten and I raised by my father, who was shot in a hunting accident two years later. Even still, I'd never get caught unprepared or unprotected again. If you've never had someone stand over you ready to end your life while your son is crying, calling out, "Mommy", you wouldn't understand.

Weighing the small Luger in my hand, I disengaged the safety and inserted the clip in mechanical motions. The gun range was my weekend getaway. Towanna would watch the kids so I could familiarize myself with my new gun. Some of the folk up in there looked shady; it always made me nervous to be around so many strangers with weapons. Then I'd remind myself I had a weapon too, and was damn lethal with it. Sliding it into the pocket of my robe so it'd be easily accessible, I speed-dialed three. My car keys, credit card, and cash were already in my pajama pocket in case we needed to get on the road. Three packed bags stayed in the trunk of the car in the garage. I kept everything on standby at all times because at any moment someone could come for us or for me and I couldn't risk not being ready.

"Michelle? What's wrong?" Towanna answered on the first ring.

"The power's out and I think someone's outside. It sounds like the bay window downstairs. I'm getting the kids." The words tumbled out of my mouth in a rushed whisper as I padded soundlessly out of the bedroom toward Lataya's and Trey's rooms.

They were like little sponges, soaking up every detail of even the smallest things. I'd just enrolled Trey in what everyone said was the best private school in the area. He'd only been in the school for three days before I was called in over his behavior. On one occasion he told a little girl to sit her ass down before he sat her down and, again, when he tried stabbing a boy with a jumbo pencil over a toy. It was bad enough there were only a handful of black kids in the school to begin with. I couldn't have him being the poster child for the single-parent household.

"Okay, get the kids and go back to your bedroom. I'm on my way right now. Are you all right?" Towanna asked.

"Yeah; scared, but I'm okay."

The kids' rooms were directly across the hall from each other and not more than two feet from mine. Afraid to stay by myself and tired of months in the hotel, when Towanna suggested we stay here with her I was all too eager to accept. Don't get me wrong, I still didn't trust cops, VA cops specifically. However, my choices were staying on my own, or staying with Towanna. Living with a cop was the safest thing I could think of until I could come up with a solid game plan. Towanna'd been more than patient with my "just a little while" that turned into a little over a year, but we split everything and she swore she loved the company. I took the easy way out as opposed to finding a new house right away but, I couldn't help thinking that Honey was out there and eventually she'd be coming for Lataya.

Walking into Lataya's room I gave her a quick once-over. She was sound asleep, her thick lashes fanning over her pudgy little cheeks like delicate dark brown palm fronds. She squirmed a bit but didn't miss a single soft snore as I scooped her up into my arms. She'd been teething and was being all kinds of fussy with the rest of her teeth finally coming in. I eventually had to resort to rubbing the teeniest bit of rum on her gums and, voila, problem solved. She was happy as a jaybird and of course snoring like a drunken sailor not long after that.

I pressed her head full of soft curls onto my shoulder beneath my chin and turned to go get Trey. Even now a shadow of a smile curved my lips and I shook my head, trying to repress a memory of a conversation I'd had with Ris. I'd come home one night and she'd played around saying she'd gotten Trey drunk. Tears burned my eyes and threatened to spill down my cheeks as they always did when I thought about the good times I had with Larissa. They were glowing embers in the fireplace of my mind that never seemed to completely go out. Thinking about something as simple as her laugh, or how she tried to kill Rasheed for me would act as fresh kindling and the fire would—

"Y'all good? I'm not more than five minutes away."

Towanna's voice broke through the silence into my earpiece, almost making me drop my poor baby.

"Shit, woman, you scared the hell out of me. I forgot you were there. I've got Taya, and I'm going to get Trey," I replied in a hurried whisper, hoping I wouldn't wake up Lataya as I tiptoed across the hall.

My mind was a hornet's nest of activity, buzzing with a swarm of thoughts all at once. Aside from thinking about Ris, I was also hoping whoever was downstairs took just long enough to get in for me to get back to my room, even though I'd have rather been heading for the car in the garage.

Think . . . just calm down and think Michelle. There's no way she could have found us. Where have we been, who have we talked to? Stores, parks, work, school, fuck I don't know. It didn't even matter; I was ready to fight until the death for my babies. Would she?

Lord, I hoped Trey wasn't in one of those sleeps that an earthquake couldn't shake him out of and even if one did, he'd move at glacial paces, dragging his feet and whining. As I entered his room his nightlight cast its familiar glow across the floor, illuminating my way. It carved shadowy halos around Ironman and Thor action figures along with his discarded pajama top and half-eaten Oreo cookies. Everything was scattered along the plush beige and brown carpet in a path that ran from his toy chest toward his bed. That mess definitely wasn't there when I tucked his ass in and I made a note to get his behind good for playing and sneaking snacks after I'd put him down for the night.

"Trey, baby, wake up." I spoke his name softly, gently pulling back his comforter. He always slept like a little mole and there was no telling what part of the pile he'd be buried underneath. Something creaked downstairs. It was much louder this time, echoing throughout the house like a cannon blast in an empty auditorium.

"Trey?" I threw the blankets off his bed in a panic. My stomach dropped and I was about three heartbeats away from hyperventilating as I stared down at nothing but The Hulk's animated angry green outline on the sheets.

"Towanna, he's not here. Oh my God." I scrutinized every inch of his room from the toys to his pajama top and immediately my thoughts went to the worst.

"Michelle, calm down. I'm pulling up now." Her voice was calm and controlled.

As comforting as it was knowing Towanna was outside, nothing was gonna reassure me until I could physically see and touch my baby. After all the drama with Honey and Rasheed and even Larissa's murder, I just wanted my kids to have as normal a life as possible. I'd have given anything to make them forget all the bullshit they'd seen. From the petty arguments that I know they'd overheard between Ris an' me all the way down to the bloodshed. Lataya was hopefully too young to be affected by it but Trey worried me the most with his random questions about his daddy and Ris.

It had taken everything in me not to skip the conversation and just kiss all the little confusion lines out of his forehead when I tried explaining the concept of death. He seemed to grasp certain points but his behavior and his anger toward other children made me wonder if some things were indeed hereditary. When it came to Larissa and Rasheed, that boy had a barrage of questions from "do you have to get hurt to go to heaven?" all the way down to "why would Jesus want my daddy if Jesus already has a daddy?" It was definitely a little more than I was cut out to handle. That was the only reason I'd fought every ounce of motherly instinct within me and forced them to sleep in their own rooms instead of in bed with me. My babies needed to not be forever traumatized or afraid of the past. That was for me to lose sleep over, not them, and now I was kicking myself for that decision.

His room faced the front of the house and the blaring red and blue lights from Towanna's police car flashed through his window, turning it into a gut-wrenching crime scene kaleidoscope. Thankfully they were shut off before my imagination could do any more damage.

"Michelle, do you have Trey?"

"No, I . . . I don't know where he is," I replied in a barely audible whisper as I glanced down at his pajama top.

"Then I need you to . . . oh shit . . ."

"Towanna? Hello?"

Tapping the Bluetooth to redial her number, I cursed silently and crept back toward my bedroom. The line wouldn't dial out at all and I could feel the sweat beading on my upper lip as sheer panic set in. Towanna had gone over at least a thousand different scenarios after we'd moved in, but none of them were like this. I went back to my room to put Lataya down in the middle of the bed, piling pillows on either side of her in case she rolled. I'd just started to go check Trey's room one more time—the closet, under the bed—when the hairs on the back of my neck stood up. It was that sixth sense you develop from playing hide and seek in the dark. Where you can just feel when someone or something is around a corner or in a darkened room.

My feet moved in the direction of the Lataya's room, even though my brain said to be still. I was making my way back to Lataya's room.

"Michelle, where y'all at?" Towanna called out from downstairs.

"I'm up here. I don't know where Trey is." I was on the verge of a complete meltdown and my voice cracked.

"Get Taya; come here."

I did as told, making my way toward Towanna. Her heavy-lidded eyes were wide and disturbed, her cheeks flushed. The crisp black uniform she always took so much pride in was wrinkled with dirt on the knees. Gone was the calm and reserved officer I'd spoken with on the phone. She actually looked frazzled and worried with her pistol drawn and her back pressed against the wall by the front door. The domino effect took place. That's when one person freaks out or runs without saying a word and then everyone runs. She looked flustered, so in turn I got even more flustered.

"What is it?" I pleaded with her, "Please don't tell me what I think it is. Did someone take him? Is he okay? Is he outside? Just let me see him," I rambled at her wildly.

"Calm the hell down. The window was pried open around back and the panel box looks like someone fucked with it. Ennis, my partner, is out front calling it in now. Can't figure out why the hell the alarm ain't go off."

"Where's Trey? Towanna, did someone take my child?"

"Calm down, babe. I need you to focus while I sweep the house. Go get in the squad car; you'll be safe while I check shit out. I'ma find him, okay?"

All I could do was nod. My heart was hacking away at my breastplate like a painful pendulum. It banged harder and louder by the second. I watched Towanna do something for me not many people would be willing to do. She was doing her best to stay brave and calm when my own hands were sweaty and shaking. In those quiet, painful seconds I came to the official conclusion that God punished Eve when she bit into that apple, and it wasn't by giving her a monthly cycle or direct knowledge of good and evil. God's specific punishment to Eve and all women was our hearts. Our hearts are our natural defects, our self-destruct buttons. We give our heart to a person and they have the power to destroy us with it or they can bring us back to life. Childbirth is a painful process that bonds us with our children. Yet it's still possible for us to have spiritual, emotional, even heartfelt bonds with children who aren't our own.

Shit, at the moment my heart was damn near imploding from fear and simultaneously melting at the sight of Towanna taking care of me and my kids. I swore whoever or whatever was in the house wasn't gonna have to lay a finger on me. At any moment my heart was gonna bust right out of my chest and kill me in the process. Oh, yes, hearts could also kill hearts. God gave Adam a little this and a little bit of that but he got Eve real good.

My ears rang like a silent fuse and I shook my head trying to clear it as I shuffled past her, trying not to wake up Lataya. A million crickets chirped in greeting as I made my way to the squad car where Officer Ennis sat waiting inside. My senses were on high alert. Everything from the stillness of the air to the lavender baby shampoo that lingered in Lataya's hair bombarded my frazzled nerves. I gave Officer Ennis a soft, nervous smile as I opened the passenger side door of the squad car. It was a little embarrassing to meet him, as we'd never been formally introduced, and here I was in my damn robe with my hair all tied up. He was a cop; he probably met a ton of people looking this way though, if not worse.

He was focused on typing something into the laptop in the patrol car. The scanner in the car was going crazy, blaring so loud I was worried it'd wake Lataya up. She could sleep through a tornado and with the rum I'd given her she wasn't budging, but that shit was overly annoying. Instead of sitting down, I opted to stand beside the car where the door could still shield me. Nervous and fidgety, I tried to make small talk.

"Hi, Officer Ennis. I'm Michelle. Officer Towanna said to come wait out here. Any idea how long before backup arrives?"

Something brushed up against my ankle and my nerves were so shot I screamed, waking Lataya in the process. She instantly started wailing. A white Persian kitten with cotton ball–fluffed fur purred up at me. I glared down, debating on kicking the living daylights out of its little ass. Towanna came running up behind me.

"What the fuck is it? Michelle? Ennis? What's wrong?" she demanded.

I couldn't answer. My eyes were glued on the ribbon tied around the kitten's neck.

"Oh no, Ennis! No. No. No. Michelle, take Trey," Towanna screamed, but her words fell on deaf ears.

There was no way in hell this could be possible. That Persian was Sodom and Gomorrah and at the moment I was Lot's wife. I stood there, nothing but a useless pillar of salt punished for daring to look at it. Attached to the blue ribbon around the damn cat's neck was a little card; even from where I was standing I could see the bright gold letters. Towanna's voice was panicked and frantic in the background; she was in the squad car calling in Ennis's murder. His throat was slit.

Trey quietly scooted past me.

"Ooh a kitty, Mommy." He kneeled down to pet her.

Tears fell down my face as I was motionless, afraid to move, afraid to look around, and even more worried about the fact we were all outside in the open, exposed.

Trey continued to admire the tiny fluff ball. He was determined to pick her up. "Is dis for my birfday tomorrow, Mommy? It says my name, see?" He pointed to the card and went back to cooing at the kitten. "You can sleep with me under Taya's crib. I don't like my new room."

Somewhere in my head I was screaming for him to get away from it, afraid that it'd blow up or try to claw him to death. As if Honey had actually sent some kind of trained attack kitten. How could she possibly even know when Trey's birthday was and how the fuck could she have found us? My knees felt like they were about to give out and my stomach was queasy.

There was no way in hell Rah could be—

"Michelle . . ."

Towanna's strained voice broke through my cluttered thoughts.

"Get Trey; we need to get inside. *Right now.*"

I barely nodded, grabbing Trey by the hand. He cradled his newfound fur ball from hell like he was carrying a football. I didn't feel like arguing with him over that damn cat. There'd be time for me to launch it out the back door or chuck it down the garbage disposal later. Right now, my main concern was getting us inside safely.

Chapter 2

The Miami Blues

The view from the window of our penthouse on the top floor was depressing. It was a "tired after a long day, going to check your mailbox and getting a postcard of a beautiful beach at sunset" depressing. I got the honor of having an upper-level front-row seat to one of the most beautiful attractions in the world. Yet, I wasn't allowed to feel the sun and the sand or smell the salt spray from the ocean on the breeze. This had to be one of hell's third dimensions. It was like baking chocolate chip cookies without eating a single one or hitting a blunt without inhaling.

In my jealous state of envy I'd started calling the little shadowed figures in different stages of beach enjoyment "sheeple." I'd combined the words sheep and people. That's how all the little blotchy outlines looked from where we sat. The sheeple always followed all the rules and did as they were told. The sheeple didn't break laws. The sheeple bought the movie tickets and were instantly in love with me. The movie premiered a week ago and its instant success made me feel almost like being an escaped convict again. Cameras were starting to appear everywhere we went and I had interviews lined up all over the place. Angelo had already accepted another script on my behalf. He didn't ask my opinion or anything. Since the directors didn't want a reading I wasn't sure if he'd paid them off or if they'd requested me. I'd had the script for a month and only half-assed studied my lines. That was pushing it with filming set to start in a day or two. It was whatever; they could fire me for all I cared. I thought I'd be flying around the world actually doin' shit. Here I was *still* stuck up in my glass cage, Angelo's little identity reassignment program sucked. Watching my sheeple be boring sheeple was slowly helping me get over the anger I felt every time I thought about it. Instead of stressin' over movies and appearances I could be making sure Michelle was getting dealt with.

Yeah, but the sheeple's asses are down there enjoying the beach while you up here.

"Jimmy One Side is the only person I got who'll vouch for yous right now. We still need more of the family to speak up in your favor so she'll forget about all this retribution foolishness." Angelo sat across from me at our little dinner table, jabbing his fork in my direction to get his point across.

I hated that fork pointy shit; it made me feel like he was subliminally stabbing me every time he jabbed it into the air. "Why do y'all call him that anyway? Wait, I know. It's because of those burgers that he makes at all the barbeques. They all charred black on one side and still mooing when you flip 'em over?" I giggled at my clever observation.

Every time we went over that fool's house I had to make sure I ate beforehand because nothing that man cooked was edible. The macaroni and cheese would be crisp on top with half-cooked noodles halfway toward the bottom; fried chicken would be smellin' all nice and when you bit into it, ugh. It's a wonder he didn't get married just so he'd have someone to cook for him.

The sound of Angelo's fork clattering to the table made my laughter stop. I'd done gone and pissed him off again.

"No, lucky for yous they call him that because he only gots to hear one side of a story before he decides to body a man or not. The rest of the family ain't been so keen on losing blood over . . ." His sentence trailed off as he sneered at me across the table and my appetite was immediately gone.

"Over what? Go ahead and say it, Angelo. It ain't like I can't figure the shit out. Over a black woman? Because aside from you and Mommy dearest I think eight-tenths of your family's in the system, so I know they can't have a problem with that part of my background."

Sliding my chair out from the table I threw my napkin down on my plate. I'd barely touched my baked ziti and garlic sautéed zucchini I spent half the day making. Yep, I'd learned a thing or two up in the kitchen. Boy, if Mimi could see me now she'd cluck her tongue and ring a bell to get rid of the demon she'd say I was possessed with. The old me would have never stepped foot in a kitchen unless it was to fix myself a plate or look in the fridge. What else did I have to do with my time these days? Once we wrapped filming, if we weren't at a club hosting an event, I was here online socializing and gossiping with Sir'Tavius pointing out who's who. There was only so much of that I could do in one day. Sir'Tavius would then come by and force me into umpteen different outfits and show me what went with what so my look would "stay ahead of the game."

Angelo refused to order out from Olive Garden or IHOP, even though they were still my favorite spots. If it wasn't home cooked he'd scrunch his face up, calling it "overpriced airplane food." The cooking network was my best friend and my ass was getting fluffier by the day. Angelo's ungrateful behind was getting spoiled, too. I never got a "thank you" or "the food's good," nothing. Even now, he just sat there anxiously pushing food around on his plate and when he wasn't doing that he was air forking me to damn death.

I'd learned that you never got up from dinner without being excused. These folk took meals serious as all hell, and walking out in the middle was rude and beyond disrespectful. "I'm gonna take a walk; I need some fresh air, Angelo. We've been up under each other too much. I really just need to get up out of here for a few minutes."

Rumors had started circulating within the family again about Angelo's mom holding his half brother and sister Lania and Key's death over my head and it was absolute bullshit. Angelo got all prune-faced when I asked for details about his last conversation with his mom. It couldn't have been good if he'd actually refused to never speak to her again afterwards. It wasn't my fault. It was Angelo's decisions to solicit their help in dealing with Michelle and then Keyshawn being a typical man had to go get his dick caught up in the spokes of Michelle and Larissa's love triangle. *They* got sloppy doing their part with Michelle, not me. Yeah, some fresh air would really do me good right now.

"And what if someone recognizes you? Been starin' at that TV so long it's done started to addle that brain of yours? You forgetting yous not a regular person anymore, huh? Come back here," he shouted, kicking his chair from under him. He marched over and planted himself in front of me, blocking my path.

Angelo's little temper tantrum didn't mean shit to me. I was undersexed, under stress, and so over his ass at the moment I didn't even care. His eyes were dark and turbulent like the underside of a thundercloud. They always got that way when he was excited or irritated, like right before we fucked or moments before he had to kill someone.

His voice was now cold and unemotional. "So, no talkin', jus' like that? We have a disagreement and this one needs to take a walk, huh?"

I ain't pay him any mind. The only reaction he got from "this one" was an eye roll and a smirk.

I pulled the door closed behind me, tilting the brim of my fitted baseball hat so low it touched the frames of my sunglasses. It felt like I hadn't been outside on my own in ages as I took in the sights and sounds of Miami nightlife like I was seeing it all for the first time. For October it was still humid as hell so I tied my jacket around my waist, loving the feel of the moist air as it kissed my skin.

At least something was kissing my skin. Angelo won't doin' a damn thing for me except workin' my nerves.

All the boutiques on this part of the strip were flashy and crowded. The storefronts all seemed to be fighting with each other for attention. There were plenty of pretty sundresses and heels that caught my eye. But lord knows I had more Michael Kors, Marc Jacobs, and brands in my closet than I knew what to do with. The only reason I stopped at one particular spot was because I wanted to relax and stay low-key. It seemed conducive to both. After debating whether I should go in, I found myself in the small parlor, staring down into a pond filled with the prettiest fish.

"Those are Japanese koi. The gold ones are the most popular. They're called *Yamabuki*. They represent wealth."

I turned to address whoever had spoken to me and froze. He looked familiar as hell, and faces ran through my brain as I tried to remember every man I'd ever seen or spoken to. He narrowed his eyes at me suspiciously.

"Um, Honey?" He pointed at me, waiting.

My mind went blank, like I literally couldn't think of a lie or an alibi, so I slowly started to shake my head no like a mute fool. I began backing away with my heart in my throat.

"Oh, sorry about that. The tattoo on your shoulder, I thought it was your name and um, I knew a stripper with that name. Not that I'm calling you a stripper or anything, ma'am. I'm sorry. Let me shut up."

Oh hell on hot wheels. Does this mothafucka know me from the Hot Spot? Did I dance for his ass or something? The door wasn't but four steps behind me. I could've been out of it and on my way when my adrenaline finally slowed down enough to let his words register. *How the hell could I have overlooked my tattoo?* My mental Rolodex finally kicked in and I was so excited all the refining and training flew right out the window. I debated for a hair of a second on whether or not I should say something, but I was just so excited at seeing a familiar face.

"Hold the fuck up . . . ain't no way," I blurted out, staring up at him in complete shock.

He nodded and smiled in confusion, his rough lumber-jack features softening as he broke into a slow grin.

"Big Baby, what in the hell? I thought you was locked up! It is me; well, a new me. I go by Desi now. But yes." I threw my arms out like I'd just flashed before him like ninja magic. "It's me, Honey, or the actress known as Desivita Dulce'."

"Well, look at yo' li'l escapee superstar self. Congrat-ulations, girl. You've got to tell me how you did it," he responded before scooping me up into a tight bear hug.

It felt so good to see someone from home; hell Big Baby felt good as a bitch, too. The thin fabric of his clothes didn't leave much to the imagination. His body was like a rock wall pressed up against mine. They looked some-thing like doctor's scrubs except they were all black. My mind went to some domination bondage shit. As soon as my feet were back on the ground I took myself back over to look at the damn koi. I needed a dickstraction, as in something to distract me from the "bad touch" thoughts I was suddenly having about Big, even though I needed some kind of distraction from Angelo's sudden lack of not knowing how to put it down at home. *I hope this next movie has some love scenes or something gracious.*

"I'll tell you what I can tell you one of these days. You just have to swear that you'll neva eva eva in your long-legged life say you've seen Honey. You can't remove tattoos up in this shop can you? No, I'm messing, but I wanna hear about you. What happened to you? How'd you get out? You feel goo . . . I mean you look good. You look really good. The beard is mad Paul Bunyanish on you but I kind of like it in a 'chop down some trees' kind of way."

I realized I was nodding nonstop like one of those big-headed bobble thingies on a car dashboard and settled on frowning at him to keep myself still. *Umph, lookin' like thaaat, he could ride all up on this ass. Call me Babe the got-damn Blue Ox . . .*

Big chuckled, thankfully interrupting my cyclone of dirty thoughts, which were probably spinning all over my face. He made his way behind the counter and started fidgeting with some paperwork. "Girl, long story short . . ." He briefly looked up in my direction. "Yo, you okay? You look upset or something."

Ugh, okay, don't frown. Straight face, girl, just keep a straight face. I waved for him to continue. "Keep going, you're . . . I'm fine. Just shocked at seeing you that's all. It's been crazy as hell, but that's another story."

"Well, somehow Rah was the only one who went in. We all got picked up and questioned, of course no one talked, and then all the charges got dropped. Sad shit, my boy took the heat for everybody. Having my life on the line like that, knowing that I could have lost everything . . . it changed me. We all had rainy-day funds; every real hustler does. This what I did with mine. I got my life right, started eating right, working out, meditating. I've got ten of these spots and Miami is lucky number eleven." He waved his arms around the small, dim, jasmine-scented parlor and smiled.

"I'm proud of you. You did good, unlike some of us I guess. So you ain't the massage person, you're actually the owner? Why this, though? That just seems so not you." I stared at him, confused and relieved because he could've been a snitch, thankfully that wasn't the case. This was so not like the Big Baby I remembered. Then again, look at me. We were both in completely opposite directions from where we'd originally started, on some type of yin-yang self-discovery adventures. From the koi pond to the white paper lanterns and dark brown leather sofas, everything looked sophisticated and relaxing.

"Miami won't on the radar. I thought there'd be too much competition, but a couple of investors saw how good I was doing and approached me about this area. Starting was easy; you remember Shiree? Ah man, she used to love my amateur back and ass massages."

"Ass massages, really, what the hell kind of mess is that?" I was cracking up at that one.

"You laughing; why you think she used to fuck with me so hard back then? It wasn't 'cause I was pretty. We both know that." He chuckled. "But nah, your boy is handy. I knew how to do a lot of out of the ordinary shit before I even knew how to cook."

"What the hell? I forgot all about her; where is she now?" I tried to sound nonchalant. I couldn't believe I'd forgotten about her ass. Seeing as how she was Larissa's sister, she might be someone I'd have to check in on for info about Michelle and Paris.

"Aw, I messed up bad with her, ain't never hear from her again after I got picked up. I actually went to school, got my degree and everything because of how good she told me I was with these hands. I don't have any staff in here yet so I'm the staff right now. But Honey . . . I mean um, Des, we were doin' it all wrong. It's to the point now where I don't even use my hands for nothin' but countin' paper. Legit, clean, 'ain't gotta watch my back' paper."

He'd walked over and stood next to me and I couldn't believe how big his ass was. I kept giving him the side eye. He was like Andre the Giant and all I wanted to do was wrestle. He could put me in his sleeper choke hold, million-dollar dream . . .

"You can get a massage on the house if you don't believe me. You ain't gotta get naked or anything like that unless you're comfortable. Trust, I ain't tryin' to lose my license over no foul shit. I've got the hot stones for stress and tension relief. We can start you off with a rosehip oil and lavender mix. Come here see for yourself."

Big led me to an area that smelled like a field of wonderfulness in the springtime and I was impressed. There were so many extracts and infusions, each one smelling better than the last.

"What is this one? Oh my goodness, I kind of like it." It was like those Atomic Fireballs I used to get when I was little with vanilla and a little bit of cherry.

"I make them myself, all natural. You should try this lemongrass and mint oil one for energy. I promise it'll be worth it." He winked.

"Marcus Latharium Bello, oh shit," I whispered in an excited little voice whipping out my phone playfully. "I gotta take a picture. This nigga got a *real name.* Boy you don't even know how we used to bet dollars on you. All them nights where you ran the club the goal was to see how many shots it'd take to get you to tell your real name. This is your business license right?" I laughed.

"Well, as far as you know Ms. Desivita, my name is Big or Big Baby so we're even as far as the name game goes. Now, pick out an oil."

His tone was reassuring as he stared down at me, his expression saying "why not."

Ooh, why had I not done something like this sooner?

A few minutes later I was lying face down in a cozy, dim room, wearing nothing but a soft black cotton towel. My face peeked through a hole in the headrest that Big had adjusted so it cradled my cheeks perfectly. I tried to focus on the small stream that ran under the clear glass tile flooring. Just like the Ritz Hotel, there was something about the people of Miami and their fascination with putting wildlife indoors. Tiny fish darted in and out of the rocks beneath me as the lighting in the water shifted from shades of purple to blue. I'd never seen anything like it. As much as I wanted to enjoy the view, I couldn't have forced my eyes to stay open once Big's hands started working the tension knots in my lower back.

He wasn't lying. If it wasn't the size of his hands, because they were huge, then it had to be their sheer strength. Big could easily break or bruise any part of me if he wanted to but under the heat of his hands I felt myself relaxing. It's a wonder I didn't just slide off the massage table into a melted puddle like a crayon left outside in the middle of summer.

Paris should have crayons now, she is old enough. Those fat jumbo ones and probably some chalk, too, so we could draw on the concrete. I wonder if she can draw?

"You know you're all knotted up right in here," Big grunted, pressing deep into my lower back and it wiped my thoughts completely from my head.

Maybe it was the excitement of having another man touch me with hands that weren't always cold. It might have been the peppery-woodsy smell of the cologne he was wearing that had me wanting to climb off the table and climb him. My stuff was throbbin' and there was probably a puddle up underneath me. He hit what I'd have to call an "oh shit" spot and before I could even think to try to stop him or distract myself, it was done and

I didn't even know how the fuck he did it. I ain't never in my life tried so hard to fight my own body.

"Ooh fuck," escaped through my clenched teeth while I tried to hide and enjoy the small ripples running up and down my legs and through my back.

"What's that, are you okay?" Big paused and leaned down next to my ear.

"Hmm, me? Yeah." I was damn near out of breath. "I thought your li'l fish down there was fuckin' or fightin'. I don't know; it was weird. They stopped though. Whew, I'm good. Get back to rubbin'."

He went back to work and all the while I was damn sure my nails were going to leave little half moon–shaped marks in the leather of the massage chair.

This nigga actually made me cum without dickin' me down or even going near my pussy, what the hell? No wonder white folk fly off and get this shit every damn week.

"You got a frequent flyer card or something like that?" I asked later jokingly but serious as hell.

Big laughed, handing me a shiny gold and white card. "After your fifth massage you get a free deep tissue or a facial with a seaweed wrap. It's up to you."

Mmm hmm, I'll take a free deep anything you're offering. Realizing I was just standing there stuck in a post-climatic-daydream I snapped myself back to reality.

"So how long will you be in town? I ain't trying to let no strangers rub all over me."

"I'm here for another month or so. Winter is probably slow so I'll head back to VA and relax. Come through sometime; we need to catch up. You need to work out or look into some serious stretching. That area around your S4, S5 lower spine felt a little tight."

We exchanged numbers; and to hell with that Big Baby foolishness, I saved his shit under Big Daddy.

Chapter 3

It's All Fake-Believe Anyway

Shame on me for putting my phone on silent, I'd missed a million texts and calls from Angelo's ass. He was just gonna have to learn that I wasn't the one for that whole "text tracking" bullshit. Text tracking is when a nigga calls or texts every ten minutes and then waits to see if you reply in "ain't fuckin' somebody else" amount of time. No, we were not about to play that game. I had enough on my mind as it was.

I Googled S4 and S5 on the way home. Those were discs in the spine that controlled sexual function. The smile that spread across my face was damn near impossible to control from that moment forward. I walked up into our penthouse, trying to erase the smug grin off my face.

Big must have gone and enrolled himself in Game 101 while he was getting that massage degree, because he used to have zero.

Leaning up against the door, inhaling the rose oil and mint still on my skin, I closed my eyes and just stood there for a minute. He'd looked so damn good, and his hands—

"Look who finally decided to waltz in. We've been waiting for you."

My eyes shot open at the sound of Don Cerzulo Campelli's gruff voice. He was actually in our living room, propped up on our couch with a brandy snifter in his hand. I'd have known that voice anywhere. He was one of the most famous actors in the world and he was here, talking to me. Sir'Tavius would kick my ass if he ever found out I met Don Cerzulo Campelli and I didn't have on not one piece of snaparazzi or any makeup. He was probably here to consider me for another role and here I come all sweaty, mismatched, smellin' like straight-up wet padussy. Thanks to Big my panties were soaked, and I wasn't about to walk all the way home like that. They had to come off, so in my jacket pocket was where they sat soppin' wet and everything.

Suddenly feeling embarrassed and beyond self-conscious I looked down and kicked myself. *Out of all the days to wear flip-flops with my polish chipped and lookin' crazy, I'd pick this one. Smooth move, real smooth.*

"Honey, I tried callin' like I don't know how many times." Angelo came in from the kitchen.

"Yeah, my phone died *sweety*." I emphasized that shit and gave him a funky, fake smile stare down, praying Don Cerzulo would think we were just calling each other pet names. Angelo was gonna make me take to burning his ass with cigarettes or something. Maybe the negative association would help him get my damn name right.

"Well, I'd like to introduce you to my father. He helped make all of this happen and now you know why it was easy, but not so easy."

Don Cerzulo's expression was unreadable as he inclined his head gradually in acknowledgment of our introduction. Angelo's father, aka the head of the family, aka the fuckin' Angel of Death in the flesh, was in my living room. His second name was because he stayed on some straight-up hermit shit hiding from every agency on the planet. The story Angelo had told me about his father's name was that the only time anyone ever saw the Angel of Death . . . well, let's just say he was the last person they saw. How he managed to hide that part of his life from the world was a mystery to me, but I guessed that's why he was who he was.

Angelo walked over, his face furrowed up in a frown. "You shouldn't have left the way you did. I was tryin' to—"

"What Angelo is trying to say is money isn't everything, but in this day and age time is our most valuable commodity and sweety, *my time is money.*" The Don's fat fingers slid his suit jacket away from his watch and he tsked at it in disappointment.

"Waiting on you has cost me more than you'll ever be worth in this lifetime."

My throat tightened and I felt lightheaded, my stomach knotted up and that zucchini I'd fixed for dinner wanted out of my stomach but I couldn't tell which end it wanted out of. The Angel of Death didn't make special appearances, and Angelo was just standing quietly, looking pale and sweaty. In the time it would take me to open the door a bullet could be in my head. I ain't escape prison to go out like this. Paris was going to see me and know my name, touch my face. I was a cornered Rottweiler ready to rip their throats out with my teeth if I had to.

"Angelo, son, get over here and be done with this. I told the family I'd see this business through and here I am. So *andiamo.*"

Reaching behind me slowly, I began to pull down on the the door lever. It was the only chance I had. Angelo moved closer to me as Don Cerzulo began to stand.

I twisted the handle, and had barely turned to pull the door open when it hit me like a tidal wave.

"Honey, my Desivita, will you marry me?" Angelo dropped down on one knee and stared up at me through nervous, pleading eyes.

My mind could have been playing tricks on me but I'd have sworn his hands were shaking when my eyes focused on and confirmed what was, in fact, a ring. Wide-eyed and caught off-guard, I quickly looked over at Don Cerzulo in a panic for help, or advice, or I didn't even know.

Marry him? Marry Angelo? I can't, we don't even know each other that well. You're supposed to know a person for years before you marry them. Be in the love, see stars and fireworks, and hear orchestras when you kiss.

Don Cerzulo gave me a quick, tight nod and I'd have been a damn fool if I ain't think he wasn't telling me to say yes or else.

What the hell could I do?

"Of course, baby." I gave Angelo a crazy smile-grimace combo as my thoughts drifted to a man I hadn't seen in ages, with hands that could give me goose bumps and make me moan.

"Mmm, I don't wanna fight. I love you like I've never loved anyone. *Il mio cuore*, you have my heart." Angelo stood and nuzzled my neck before smiling down at me, and I tried to my damndest to smile back.

"What is this on you that smell so good? You buy it today?" he asked.

Still flustered, I could barely piece together a lie. "Uh, just something I saw at one of the boutiques. It was sold out. Um, I just tried it on."

I broke away from him, removing my jacket and setting my things on the stand by the door.

"Tell me which boutique and I'll get it for you; nothing is sold out to us." Angelo was following me like a puppy.

"Never mind all that."

Don Cerzulo smoothed his silver-tipped sideburns as he came up to me. Do you know what money smells like? No, I don't mean them dollars fresh from the bank, but real money. I'm talking about that "wipe your ass with twenty-four-karat gold leaves" kind of money. It smells like sweet cherry pipe tobacco and the Wilson's leather jacket shop at Christmas time. It's Arabian Wood Tom Ford, fox hunting and sky box dinners with truffle oil dressing. There was a time when that smell would have sent me into a "get money" frenzy. Angelo had paper yes, but Don Cerzulo was saturated with it. Some niggas did it on purpose and in the strip club we'd call that shit "asset advertisement", because they got it and they wanted your ass to know.

Don Cerzulo had it unconsciously flowing off of him in waves like some kind of high frequency luxury radiation. I wanted that. My body didn't have a price anymore. No more pullin' the g-string to the side and fuckin' niggas on the low during lap dances. If I played this shit at the right angle Don's paper could easily be my paper.

Don Cerzulo spoke softly. "Just so we's clear on a few things, I don't feel any particular way about the death of the boy's half siblings. His mother's a spiteful cunt; her elevator may not go all the way to the roof." He jabbed his finger into my temple for emphasis. "But, still spiteful. And yes, you're protected now but she's a ruthless bitch. Watch your front, side, back, 'cause she don't respe—"

"Hey now, Pop, nice to see yous two chattin' it up. Feels good."

Angelo walked over grinning, and I damn near screamed at his bad timing.

"Yeah, well, this old man still has to go dig in the dirt. Got a few money trees that need bodies underneath 'em to grow. Finish that drink for me, son. I'm sure you two want to celebrate." Don Cerzulo winked at me, straightening his suit jacket.

"Ah, maybe later. Give me a ride out, Pop. I need to see a man about a horse." Angelo took his glass and handed it to me, smiling mischievously.

Huh, this fool ain't want no ass? What the hell kinda shit is going on up in here?

Confused, I just stood there as he gave me a quick peck on the cheek before grabbing his things and leaving. I stared down at the rock on my finger, admiring it and hating it at the same time.

How the hell did I get myself into this bullshit? I wasn't trying to marry this fool and have his babies. There was only one nigga I thought of like that and it was Rah. Only reason I even entertained Derrick's ass was to show the nigga that somebody else would take care of home if he didn't. I needed a Percocet or a Vicodin, somethin'.

My cell rang on the stand by the door. "Yeah," I answered without looking.

"Are we meeting or not, my dear?" a woman cooed seductively in my ear.

Confused I pulled the phone from my ear. Of course, the number was unavailable.

"Meeting? I ain't meetin' nobody. I think you got the wrong number," I snapped into the phone.

I scrolled through my contact list looking for Big's number. I for real needed to talk to someone about all this marriage foolishness; maybe he could give me some kind of advice.

Psssht. Whatever, you know yo' ass just want that nigga to give you a reason to run away or creep on Angelo. All he gotta do is say the words.

Smiling at the thought I paused, trying to remember what the hell name I saved him under. When I realized I was past the Bs my heart stopped and restarted itself. I cursed so loud the people on the street probably heard my ass. This wasn't my phone. Angelo's dumb ass picked up my phone by accident on his way out. Why did we have to have the same exact fucking model? I gulped down the drink in my hand. When that ain't make me feel any better I launched the empty glass against the wall.

He never left out this late at night, and he never mentioned a meeting with no damn woman. Cheatin'-ass motherfucka. We could have gotten a third wheel if he wanted to play. I'd done a couple girl-on-girl strip parties back in the day. It'd been nothin' to get a cute plaything for a few nights; hell, it'd take some of the boring sex stress off me. But this . . . this mistress shit wasn't happenin', not on my watch.

Even though you was ready to let Big get it, that's ironic. Karma maybe?

No, Angelo was fuckin' with the wrong one.

Chapter 4

Warm Kitty, Soft Kitty, Little Ball of Fur . . .

The house had been buzzing with activity and the last officer had finally come and gone. Trey was upstairs in my bed. He'd finally worn himself out crying over not being able to keep that damn cat. I'd have to go find him a puppy or a goldfish as soon as possible to make up for it. The chance of that thing being microchipped with a tracker or something crazy was too much of a risk. It was almost four in the morning and Towanna was about as frazzled as I was, if not more so.

"Towanna, you gonna be okay?" I approached her timidly. She was sitting in the darkened kitchen, nursing a drink. She rarely drank but you'd never know that from looking at the half-empty vodka bottles on the table.

"Fuck if I know. Been in damn near twelve years and I ain't never lost a partner before."

She wouldn't even look at me and it made me feel a hundred times worse. I'd forewarned her about taking us in. Death and danger had been my damn best friends these last few years.

"What's in the glass?" I nodded, trying to move to something lighter since I was too choked up to apologize for her loss and too stressed to think of more to say.

"Pixy Stix. Cherry, grape, and watermelon. Three Olives. One and some change parts each."

"Damn, that sounds a little too potent for me; can I just tap one of your bottles?"

She scooted one toward me and I tipped it to my lips, frowning and gasping because that mess tasted like straight-up Robitussin.

"You such a fuckin' lightweight. Go get ya ass one of the kids' juice boxes out the got-damn fridge. Wastin' my shit," she growled, snatching the bottle right out of my hand.

"The hell I am; you just an angry-ass somebody when you drink." I snatched the bottle back, ready to smack her ass with it one good time if she kept this bullshit up. Her anger set off my own temper and I went from sad to furious in a heartbeat. "You can't hold this shit against me, Towanna. Yes . . . I'm sorry about your partner, I really am. But don't you go turning into no asshole over something you volunteered for. I ain't come to you for help, you came to me." I scowled at her and took a long swig. Visions of glass shattering all up the side of her head made me feel a little better as I imagined using it to literally knock some sense into her. How dare she cop that kind of attitude with me?

"Michelle, why you gotta be so damn selfish and shit?" Towanna sprang up out of her seat. Her hands were fisted at her sides and I gripped that bottle ready to go to war. Everybody handles death and alcohol differently and in my opinion she wasn't handling either one well.

She was fast. Even intoxicated she managed to lash out and get the upper hand. The heffa moved with Bruce Leroy—esque lightning speed. The bottle was wrestled from my fingers before I could even raise it. She was also stronger than I imagined. A picture of me in the emergency room trying to explain two broken wrists flashed through my head as she bent my wrists back in a painful vise grip, wrapping her arms around me, pinning my arms behind my back. Tears welled up in the corners of my eyes from the pain.

"I risked my life and Ennis gave his!" she yelled in my face, spraying tiny speckles of Pixy Stix–scented spit onto my skin.

"Really, you think I don't know that shit. Let me the fuck go, Towanna. You have a right to be upset, but you need to shut up. The officer they've got posted outside might hear you and you're gonna wake up the kids," I replied quietly, setting my own anger aside to give her a wide-eyed look of warning.

Towanna didn't pay me any mind; she just replied in outrage, "You think you the only one with kids? What about Ennis's kids?" She shook me, her face twisted in anger before pulling me into a tight python death squeeze of a hug. "Man, you so damn selfish. He could have kept that kitten. You can't even see when someone in love with your ass. When someone would do anything for you, risk they life for you and your kids." Towanna's voice had transformed into a warm whisper against the side of my neck.

Her grip loosened on my wrists but she kept my arms pinned behind me. My breath caught in my chest. I struggled to wrap my angry mind around her avalanche of words and feelings.

Just keep piling it on there, buddy. I already feel like shit about Ennis and now we're gonna add love into the equation, too.

"Towanna, you don't even know me well enough to be in love. If so then you'd know my auntie had a black cat named Lucky that tormented the hell out of me when I was little. He could open doors and everything, would pee on me when I was asleep. I hate cats. My favorite color is sky blue. And I like girly drinks that make me feel pretty when I say them: Bellini, Tequila Sunrise, piña colada . . ."

The liquor, the drama, her closeness were all overwhelming. How was I even supposed to respond to something like that? Who the hell dropped a love confession in the middle of an argument? Confused and tired I dropped my head onto her shoulder for lack of anything else to say. I wasn't ready to think about love or talk about love. When the time was right I just wanted to fall and have them fall right back.

Larissa could barely reach my neck unless she was standing on something or I was sitting down. Those were my exact thoughts as surprisingly soft lips brushed against the side of my neck.

You can't cheat on the dead right? Then why did this feel so wrong?

Her fingers massaged my wrists in the places that she'd most likely bruised. I was still a little pissed off, and scared, definitely frustrated beyond reason.

I shook my head against her shoulder. "Pin them back like you had them and bite my neck."

Maybe it won't feel like cheating or I won't feel as bad if it hurts.

My breath hissed from in between my teeth as she did as directed. I closed my eyes, the world went spinning, and I let myself enjoy that sinfully erotic feeling that comes with a little bit of pain. When she alternated sides I moaned and bit her back, smiling against her neck when she gasped in shock. Towanna leaned back and looked at me, surprised at my brazenness.

Yes, sweetheart, momma can get rough too. Don't let the look fool you.

My expression was guarded but my thoughts were X-rated. She was so close I could see the light dusting of freckles along her cheeks, and the copper flecks in her eyes. I made the mistake of letting my gaze drop down to her lips. I had the worst weakness for some pretty-ass lips.

Completely giving up and giving in, I kissed her. She tasted like plums and Pixy Stix, and if I wasn't tipsy yet her lips were getting me the rest of the way.

"Fuck all the misery out of me." I actually moaned that into her lips. I didn't mean to say it. That wonderful thought bubble slipped out of my head and hung in between us like a fog cloud.

I might as well have said "abracadabra." No sooner had the words left my mouth, than my robe came off, her belt buckle clinked, and our clothes vanished.

She sat down in one of the wooden kitchen chairs, pulling me down to straddle her lap. We both giggled when it teetered under our weight. The legs were uneven thanks to Trey's handiness. He'd taken all the screws out of the thing one day when he was supposed to be taking a nap. I'd put it back together but it just wasn't exactly the same after that.

The giggling stopped when Towanna's lips made a journey from my earlobe down my neck. She blazed a hiking trail with her tongue. Goose bumps rose like the tiny marks hikers leave on trees. If she lost her way in the dark she could always follow the trail back to my lips. I couldn't stay still, and I damn sure couldn't be quiet. Parts of me were waking up that had been lying dormant for months. She went from my neck to my nipples as her hand slid down in between us.

Fuck, when was the last time I shaved? She's probably gonna think I'm some kind of hippie cavewoman.

"Mommy?"

The sound of Trey's voice snuffed all of the flames in a small whisper of cold water. Thankfully the power was still out so the kitchen was dark. I got dressed with lightning speed and snatched up my robe before scooping him up, heading toward my room.

"What's the matter, baby?" We were almost fully up the stairwell.

He was already dozing off on my shoulder. His voice was quiet and groggy from sleep. "I woke up an' you were gone. Da man in my room said go find you."

My foot slipped and I almost missed a step. Fear shot through my chest, stopping me like a brick wall. "Trey? Baby, were you having a dream?" I whispered shakily next to his ear as I stood frozen in place one step away from the landing.

"No," he whispered, shaking his head into my neck.

A chill ran down my spine and my ears rang from straining against the silence in the house. Warning bells chimed in my head. In those seconds it felt like I was torn in half.

Get Lataya or go get Towanna? Pull the gun out of my robe pocket or leave it concealed just in case?

Something rustled at the bottom of the stairs and I turned slightly, thankful Towanna had pulled it together. The warning was on the tip of my tongue when those warning bells jumped out of my head and manifested in front of me.

"Snowball." Trey squirmed, suddenly wide awake as we both laid eyes on the kitten. It tiptoed out of the shadows of my bedroom, and instinctively I backed down a step. We'd sent that cat off with the cops. There was no way it could have gotten into the house. The blue ribbon had been replaced with a small golden bell attached to a red collar. It jingled softly but in my mind it was as loud as bells ringing from a church tower.

"Towan—"

I called for help but it was too late. Pain exploded in the back of my head and the world lit up in a burst of bright flashes before everything went dark.

Chapter 5

Houdini Who?

"Chelle? Michelle . . ."

Towanna's voice was a faint murmur against the jack-hammer trying to crack through my skull as I came to. Something, a pillowcase maybe, was thrown over my head. Panic flooded back over me. My hands were tied together behind me and from the sting in my ankles my feet were bound too.

"Did you see who did this? Where are they and where are the kids? Please don't tell me they got the kids," I whispered anxiously into the darkness.

"Don't know. Someone must have come up behind me right after you left. One sec I'm watching you walk away, man, and then it was dark and shit. I heard voices earlier, been quiet for a minute though."

"If they hurt my babies I swear . . ." My words were cut off by the tortured wail building up in my throat. I groaned as an alternative to screaming my frustration.

"You been out for a good while. I started countin' when I heard the front door close. 1,320 seconds. That's about twenty-somethin' minutes right? "

I waited for her to say more, and when she didn't, I prepared myself for the worst. No one would go through this much trouble just to tie us up and leave. Trey was in my arms what seemed like moments ago and now this.

"Michelle, I need you to stay calm okay?"

"Towanna, am I not sittin' here calmly right now? You ever seen a woman get assaulted, wake up with a sack over her head, kids MIA and be as fuckin' calm as I am right now?" I'd been clenching my teeth and fightin' one hell of a headache. The harder my heart beat the more it hurt.

"No, see, I kind of overheard some shit. They was whisperin' about you comin' up off some drug money you stole or somethin' like that. Man, I think the plan is to hold the kids and ask for a ransom."

Did she just say stolen money and ransom in the same sentence? I ain't steal a dime of what I took from Rah. That was my money; hell most of it was even in my name. I worked, cried, and bled for that money.

"There wasn't no drug money. I don't know where they would have gotten that info from."

She sighed from somewhere beside me and I could tell she was frustrated and probably more scared than I was. Her partner had already given his life and she was probably worrying about following in his footsteps.

"Shit, Michelle, man. If there ain't any money you're . . . we're gonna have to come up with something. I can't do this by myself, yo. Think about it, is there anywhere that nigga might have hid the money?" She sounded frazzled and on the verge of panicking.

"No, not that I can think of. I've got my own money. I can pay damn near whatever they ask."

I sure won't about to tell her what I'd done. Those grimy little details went to the grave with Larissa and Rah, and I wasn't about to unbury them for anyone. Not even Towanna.

She got quiet for a minute, so quiet that I thought she might have passed out or died on me.

"You hurt? You are okay right? I didn't even think to ask you earlier. I'm just so worried about my babies. I'm sorry." Speaking into the pitch black, not being able to see her reaction or condition, felt awkward as hell.

"It's cool, I understand. Think I'm still tipsy and that knock upside the head ain't help. Everything's catchin' up with me. Gonna close my eyes for a sec."

"You can't go to sleep. What if you have a concussion? You might not wake up. They might come back any second and—"

"And, I ain't gonna be any good if I'm tired. Just too much adrenaline for one day, man. Count to a thousand and then whisper or something. That'll wake me up."

I'd started to tell her again that sleep wasn't a good idea but she had a point. If we couldn't do anything at the moment, she could at least get some rest. Straining against the silence I contended with counting the beeps from the alarm system every sixty seconds. Somewhere around 319, the front door opened.

"Oh shit, Towanna, I think they're back."

My heart was in my throat and I squeezed my eyes shut to block out the feeling of helplessness. There was a presence beside me. I could feel it there staring down at me. It didn't make a sound and I felt lightheaded from holding my breath listening. The air around me shifted and I could tell it'd moved away. The beeping from the alarm system felt like sonar. It pinged crystal clear and whenever the person moved in front of me the sound was deadened just slightly.

If they gonna kill me let 'em do it and get it over with. All this waiting was pissing me off just as much as it was scaring me.

"Hey, hey don't fuckin' touch me! Get your hands off me. I ain't got nothin' for you and neither does she." Towanna's shouts went silent with the sickening thud of something connecting with flesh.

*Lord, let her be unconscious and not dead. This isn't
going to end this way; it can't. Not after everything I've
been through.*

It was so still and quiet in the house. I couldn't stop
the scream that shot out of my throat as rough hands dug
into my skin. The small metal buttons from my pajama
top sounded like jacks as they scattered across the floor.
It might as well have been ten degrees in the house from
the way I was shaking. Air whooshed against my exposed
skin as my shirt and robe were slid off my shoulders.

*Is a gun on me right now? Stay calm, gotta stay calm.
The worst they can do is hurt the kids. I can handle
anything anyone does to me as long as they're safe.*

I bit the inside of my cheek so hard I tasted blood as my
bottoms were yanked down to my ankles. Bracing myself,
I waited for what I knew was coming.

*These niggas won't gettin' the satisfaction of seeing or
hearing me beg for mercy or my life. I'll scream and cry
in my head before I do it out loud. God, why couldn't I
just have a fair fight at least once in my life?*

My chair was tilted back and I could hear the rustle of
plastic being slid underneath me before I was lowered to
the floor.

I could see the headlines in the papers already: MICHELLE
LAUREL FOUND BRUTALLY RAPED AND MURDERED IN POLICE OFFICER'S
KITCHEN. All the years I'd lived secretly fearing how or when
I'd die. Wondering what day God stamped over my life like
an expiration label. It wasn't like in the movies. There's no
superhero or heroic neighbor who bursts in to save your
ass at the last second. No bomb goes off and no fights break
out. There's no random act of kindness by your captor that
suddenly sets you free. It's all you, and for the first time
through the entire ordeal I quietly cried.

Something feather soft brushed up against my cheek,
sliding around my shoulders and across my back. There

was a soft meow beside my ear and I knew they had Trey. Something moved along my feet in the plastic. They were teasing me with a damn kitten, really? I was hurled back into bed at my aunt's, trapped staring up into Lucky's demonic yellow-orange eyes while he sat on-top of my chest growling. The sound of plastic over my head had me waiting for a knife, gunshot, or the raping to start.

The air was starting to get stifling hot all around me and I thought I'd suffocate when I heard Trey's voice beside me.

"Mommy, where is the money?" His little singsong voice made my chest heave.

Pinned beneath my own body weight, my arms began to throb and ache.

"Mommy, they don't like closed bags." Someone had to be coaching him. There was a click and I thanked God it was some kind of recording and he wasn't there in person seeing me like this as the first question was played back for me. Shaking my head, I refused to answer. *They might as well kill me now.*

And then, a hiss split the air so close to my ribs I could feel it on my bare skin. Another hiss responded on the opposite side of me, like one you'd hear at the zoo or on National Geographic. It was very distinct unmistakable and sheer, absolute terror set in.

Oh, dear God, please help me. Please don't let that be a snake, it couldn't be. I could barely breathe. Fear sent tiny darts of pain to the center of my chest every time I tried to inhale. I was so tense I flinched out of reflex. Something moved, making the plastic crackle underneath it as it brushed up against my side. It slithered against me with cool rubbery winding motions touching and moving away as it traveled along my body. *There are snakes in here! God, get them out, get me out. Please don't let them be poisonous.*

"Mommy, they don't like closed bags." Trey's voice was almost my undoing. It was an eerily familiar and loving soundtrack to my gruesome execution.

His voice played over and over, yet I still didn't speak. I couldn't make a sound; terror had frozen my vocal chords, capsized my lungs, and locked all my muscles. My worst nightmare had come true and the living hell of reality made my dream seem like a fairy tale in comparison. The bag rustled like someone'd hit or kicked it and I jumped as if I'd been shocked. Pain tore through my side as my skin was slashed open. I screamed. The snakes were . . .

"Mommy, where is the money?"

There were at least three different hisses. There was so much movement on either side of me and I screamed again as something slid across my chest and something else . . .

My arms were going numb beneath me. All the danger, the slithering and hissing was getting closer and closer to my neck and shoulders. There was more movement around my feet. Fur brushed against my toes.

Snakes and cats? What the fuck? Who the fuck does something like this?

Hyperventilation set in when there was slithering across my neck and shoulders as well as in between my legs. Without my clothes I was vulnerable, exposed to every claw and strike. The cat hissed, or it could have been the snake as my shoulder was ripped open. Stress made my body heat rise. It turned the inside of that plastic bubble into a plastic hell as Trey's voice resonated all around me.

"I took the money. I did." I sobbed softly, afraid the cats would taunt the snakes and I'd get clawed or bitten again. "Invested it into my business and put the rest away. It'll take me at least a day to withdraw it all from the different accounts."

Gut-wrenching sobs shook me down to my soul. The bag was cut open and my chair was pulled up off the floor. My skin stung from where I was bitten or clawed and my arms felt like they'd been stomped on repeatedly.

"I luh you, Mommy. See you later." Treys voice clicked off and the front door closed. There's no telling how long I'd sat there, scared a snake or something would still be coiled up at my feet. Towanna was possibly dead. I had no idea which animal attacked me, if it was poisonous or anything. My nose started bleeding. The blood trickled down to my upper lip, tickling my face. My nose itched and it wasn't one of those nice easy-to-ignore itches either. I squirmed uncomfortably, trying to lean my head so I could rub my nose across my shoulder. The chair rocked and hope swelled up in my chest, making me forget all about my injuries and the snakes.

Bending my wrist as far as I could I grabbed one of the rungs on the back of the chair and twisted. It yielded quietly and I almost shouted to the rooftop. This was the chair I'd half-assed put back together. I'd managed to twist both rungs off and was holding them behind my back when I realized I needed to let them bitches go in order to untie my hands. Excitement and trepidation coursed through my veins. Hopefully I could get out before they got back. With any luck they didn't leave a watchdog or a guard out there.

I let the chair rungs slide down my hands slowly until they stopped moving. Giving up a silent prayer I let them go and they fell soundlessly. My chair must have been just on the edge of the area rug under the kitchen table.

After undoing my wrist I yanked what I discovered was in fact a pillowcase off my head in a "swish moment." That's what I call it when you celebrate with yourself for doing something extraordinary. It could be catching your phone midair before it hits the floor or tripping on stairs and keeping your balance. My celebration was short-lived as the familiar ocean of dread swept in and washed away my smile. Towanna wasn't sitting beside me anymore. She was nowhere to be found. I pulled my clothes back on as best I could and I crept into the living room on wobbly legs. She protected me when I needed it, welcomed me and my kids into her home. It was my turn to return the favor and find and protect Towanna.

Chapter 6

Always Beware of the Jellyfish

The streetlights filtered in through the blinds in the living room, making yellow-orange slashes across the floor. The clock on the wall ticked like it was attached to an amplifier. Relieved there were no blood trails on the carpet, I looked for any other signs of Towanna as I made my way toward the main window. Her eyes followed me as I passed pictures of her with her family. The bright gold R for "Respect" winked at me at the bottom of the frame. It was her mother's favorite song Towanna told me. She and her brothers didn't look anything like their father. They were all replicas of her mom; she was beautiful.

My plan was simple: find out if these assholes were still around and how many of them were in between Towanna, me, and the kids. Okay, so maybe that really wasn't a plan. It was more of an outline because I wasn't exactly sure how I'd get to or past anyone, but it was a start.

I parted one of the blinds with shaky fingers. The sky was turning violet-blue and birds were just beginning to chirp here and there. I guessed I was expecting to see black SUVs and BMWs lining the driveway. Yet they must have rolled out pretty quick because there wasn't a single car—

"Michelle? What the hell you doing out here?"

Jumping at the sound of my name I turned, excited and alarmed at the same time. Towanna was sitting up on the couch looking perfectly fine and confused as hell. I hobbled over, intent on giving her a hug.

"Towanna, I was worried as hell about you, woman. When I heard you get hit and then I got loose and you were gone . . ."

I stopped not five feet from her as my brain caught up with what I was seeing. We analyzed each other, both of us trying to sum up all of the events.

"How did you get out here, Towanna?" There was no point in even trying to hide the suspicion in my voice.

Her shoes were off and tucked side by side neatly beside the couch, there wasn't even a visible bruise or scratch anywhere on her.

"Man, I just woke up on the couch out here and saw you over there lookin' out the damn window and shit." She shrugged. "Head hurts like a bitch though."

"Why would you be out here all cozy on the damn couch, when you were just tied up in the kitchen with me, Towanna?"

"Man, what the hell you tryin' to say?" Towanna threw her hands up in frustration and sat back, glowering at me.

It wasn't like we just went through hell together and I was giving her the fifth degree. No, no, no. I went through hell and walked in on what looked like her taking a nap. Something was up and it was making me want to throw furniture at her ass. *Ten, nine, eight.* I counted down to keep myself from trying to choke her ass out. I knew I was being irrational especially since she could take me down with a wrist-grab. If she had anything to do with what I just went through on my life I'd make her pay. My insides shook as I paced the couch in front of her staring her down out the corner of my eye.

"Towanna, where the fuck are my kids? I'm not playing with you."

"Man, Michelle—"

I was so over this shit. "Trey!" I shouted his name at the top of my lungs and headed for the stairs.

There was a noise behind me. It was a mixture between a war cry and a bloodcurdling howl. The full brunt of Towanna's weight crashed into my back, knocking me off balance with the impact of a battering ram. She must have built up a ton of momentum because I swear she collided with me in a thunderous crash. The sound ricocheted throughout the house. It left me dazed and knocked the breath out of my lungs. Pinned beneath her weight with my face pressed into the carpet I could hear the kids crying for me from upstairs.

It was all over faster than a knife fight in a phone booth. Towanna didn't seem to be moving. My gun had gone off when she knocked me down. I pulled myself from underneath her and she moaned softly.

"Anyone up there wit' them I need to know about?" I asked, my voice breathless and shaky from fury and fear.

I kicked her when she didn't answer, but she didn't move. In the future I'd have to remember to be a better judge of people. Nobody's willing to help you for free. She probably knew about Rah's money the entire time. I should have known better than to put my trust in someone in law enforcement. The world is full of jellyfish and even though you think you'll be able to see right through their fake asses, you still have to be careful. They'll sting the hell out of your ass the second you let them get too close.

I stepped over her lying ass and I couldn't even feel sorry for her. I'd lived with her for a year now and not once had she used "man," "shit," and "yo" more times than when she was obviously lying to me. I tsked at her like I couldn't believe she'd killed her own partner and tried to play me for a damn fool.

No one would have ever believed what happened up in here. Not in a million years. It was time for me and the kids to make moves.

Chapter 7

Listen, Time Will Tell Every Time

The sky outside was fading from black into the soft blues of morning. It was almost five a.m. when Angelo crept in. I'd gone through his entire phone, e-mails, voicemails, texts, and all. Either he was overly cautious or actually up to something because everything was empty or deleted. His contact list didn't even have real names. I'd searched for my number first and it was listed under Acts 5. Jimmy One Side was the only other number I knew because I'd called him a few times. He was under 2 Judges 16. The list went on and the more I scrolled the more creeped out I got. Angelo didn't even own a Bible. He was raised Catholic but never went to Mass.

Reluctantly I'd given up and set his phone back on the stand by the door. I prayed Angelo hadn't gone through my texts. Hopefully Big hadn't tried to call or anything while he was out with my phone. It would have been easy to cover up the text he sent earlier if that shit ain't come from "Big Daddy."

It took everything I had not to get up and go off on his ass. He'd gone straight to the bathroom and gotten in the shower. Suspect. When he finally decided to ease his ass up in the bed I pretended to be sleep. As expected, Angelo wrapped his frigid limbs around me, tryin' to steal my body heat. He started grindin' on my ass and I rolled my eyes to myself. I knew he ain't think he was about to hump all up on me after he'd been who knew where.

"Where'd you go? You never stay out this late," I quietly grilled him.

"Nowhere for you to be worried about. I had to take care of some things."

He nuzzled my neck and I brushed him off.

"We can't right now, think my cycle's about to start. I got cramps."

"Want me to go get the towel?" He winked at me, and I just rolled my eyes and rolled over. No, I didn't want him to go get no damn towel. I don't know how much time passed before he finally fell asleep. But it was the only thing ticking down in my head with the clock on the mantel piece in front of the bed as I waited. I slid out of the bed and found his pants. This fool had the pocket mentality of a five-year-old. It took me four tries to find my phone among the clutter of a pocket knife, casino token, zip ties, screws, a slip of paper that listed every poisonous plant in Florida and its side effects, and spare gun clip.

Add a dump truck, Yoo-hoo cap, and a lucky dinosaur and I got two kids . . .

He shifted in his sleep and I flattened myself out on the floor, not even taking a breath. I was on straight-up ninja assassin mode trying to get to that damn phone.

I went into the kitchen and checked my texts, e-mails, and incoming and outgoing calls. Thankfully there was nothing there from Big Daddy, and Sir'Tavius had sent thousands of outfits that he wanted me to consider for my next public appearance. I did a double take as a new messages came through.

Desivita, picking you up at eight p.m. Wear a nice skirt or dress and heels. We are going to an audition. I will meet you downstairs. Don

Des Call Time 8am check your email for directions
Do Not Be Late

It was cool outside and felt more like early spring instead of late fall. Since all they were going to do was take me out of my clothes and throw me in wardrobe, I just threw on a sweatshirt with some jeans and my winged high-top Adidas. Angelo threw on an instant attitude at having to be up so soon after getting his "sneaking around doing what the fuck ever" self in the bed. I'd told him to give me the keys. I didn't need him chauffeuring me all over the place. As a matter of fact it was time I got a car of my own anyway. *It would be easier for me to deal with Michelle, among other things, without my real-life stunt double following me around.* Angelo acted all kinds of insulted, offered to get me a driver and whatever kind of car I wanted. He wasn't fooling anyone though; he was paranoid about who or what I'd do if I could get around without him and it was obvious. We didn't speak the rest of the way to the set.

The set was a warehouse beside a boat marina that they'd transformed into several scenes. We passed through a club dance floor, next to a back alley that looked like it was plucked right up from outside with manhole covers and a dumpster. There were swarms of actors, extras, and stagehands all over the place.

"My Queen Midas has graced us with her golden glemmied presence. You will win me a Globe and an Emmy? You will glemmy my movie?"

I could only nod yes at this mountain of a woman who reminded me of an Amazonian warrior goddess. I immediately regretted not studying my script because she looked like she had a bull-whip or a cattle prod hidden somewhere to torture disobedient actors. And she'd enjoy it too.

"Don't feel special, newbie, she says that shit to everyone," Sadira called out.

She prowled toward us like a wanton alley cat. Angelo's scent, shit any man's scent probably, grabbed her attention within a ten-mile radius. It took all the refinement and etiquette training I had not to whoop her ass right then and there as she basically eye-fucked my fiancé. Angelo tensed beside me before letting my hand go and that almost sent me over the edge. I rolled my eyes behind her back as we fake hugged one another.

"The two of you need to go get into hair and makeup. Your first scene is dirty dancing and a boat chase," the director called out as she went to speak to a cameraman.

Angelo had all but vanished into thin air by the time I turned around, and I wasn't about to ask Sadira any damn questions. Sir'Tavius showed up just in time and we almost broke our necks simultaneously. The cause was about six feet three inches in bright yellow swimming trunks. His nomadic desert skin was oiled up and down, covering every muscle, divot, and dip. I didn't even know I was holdin' my breath until his large, bushy, barely tamed ponytail was out of sight and I exhaled.

"Uh, two questions. What the hell was the director talking about dirty dancing for, and who was that?"

"Bye, girl, because I see you ain't read ya script. A: twerkin'; and B: Kai, your stupafine costar, the one you lockin' lips with on the speedboat." Sir'Tavius gave me an "I love you, bitch, but I'm so jealous I hate you" twisted glare.

Oh wow. The twerkin', strippin', dancing, whatever they want me to do won't be a problem, but um, Kai and that body, oh, my damn. Did Angelo read my script and know about this kiss? He couldn't have.

My nerves were all over the place while I looked around for Angelo, who was still nowhere to be found. We were in such a rush I'd left my purse in the car, and my phone and my pills, everything was out there.

"What's the matter, Desi? You lookin' a little flustered, boo," Sir'Tavius asked, patting my arm.

"Nothing, I just need to calm down. Too much stress and it's too early to drink."

He nodded like he understood and took off, leaving me stranded.

"We'll be ready for you on set in an hour, Des."

The director sailed past with that announcement as Sir'Tavius reappeared, pulling me into my dressing room. He looked like he had a mouthful of feathers and was gonna burst if he didn't get to tell someone something and fast.

"Girl, I got you some happy pills." He handed me two long oval-shaped pills.

"What are they?"

He looked down at his hand and then back up at me without blinking. I took them, swallowing those things without water like we used to do back in the day. I quickly dressed in a red cocktail dress and sat myself down. Sir'Tavius quietly worked on my hair and makeup while I watched in the mirror. Even with all the surgery movie makeup still made me look like a completely different, different person. *Michelle would never recognize me like this. Never in a million years.*

"That's better; now you look you an actress. Um, is everything going okay? You ain't goin' over your lines or doing vocal exercises. Things all right with you and the boo?" His hands stilled in my hair and he locked eyes with me in the mirror.

I wanted a real friend outside of Big. Someone I could tell about Paris's and Angelo's funny ways.

"It's all right, he might be cheatin' he might not. Life will go on."

"Karma kicks ass. Oh, and you ain't get those from me. I stole them bitches from Sadira's purse."

"What the hell? You gave me somethin' her crazy ass takes?" I swiveled around and glared at him. "What if she saw you?"

"Pssst, please, she too busy fuckin' your man to seesaw anythang but that dang-a-lang."

"Too busy doin' what?"

I was up out that seat and dressing room so fast it's a wonder I ain't create a spark and combust from all the spritz in my hair. I planted a tight-lipped smile that said "go to hell" on my face as I marched past faces I didn't know. They all knew me and spoke or nodded in greeting.

"The director and everyone's down there; you're going the wrong way," someone pointed out.

I just nodded and kept going. The opposite of where everyone was meant I was going exactly the right way. If I'd have been thinking I might have asked Sir'Tavius exactly where he'd seen them and why he'd waited so damn long to say something. Maybe he was waiting to see if I knew or wanted to know first; that's how some folk do. They feel you out before they give you dirt, because all they're really worried about is being held responsible if you have a complete meltdown after you find out.

I knew I had to be going full speed ahead, but the floor and even the air around me seemed to be in negative warp speed. Blinking felt like I was taking these erotic micro-naps where even though I was pissed the fuck off, my angry pulse felt good. Every time my eyes closed my heart would send a thump that shimmied down my entire body. I had to lean up against a wall for a moment to get my bearings. My ears picked up the sounds of low gasps and whispering.

Peeking around the corner I could see Sadira and Angelo on a couch. *Maybe I should let her have him and*

then I can get more of whatever the hell these pills are.
No, I'd just have to remind myself to ask who her supplier
was after I whooped that ass. It took everything in me
because gravity was working against me, but I grabbed a
metal bar leaning against the wall and charged.

That's how it happened in my head anyway. What
really happened is I was too woozy and uncoordinated to
actually charge or attack anything. One time I'd bought
this bag of apples that was stuffed beyond maximum
ca-fuckin-pacity. When I tried to open the bag it split at
the bottom and they just clumsily bumbled out. I'm sure
that's the effect I had as I tripped over my own feet and
ferociously spilled out onto the floor in a slow-motion
tumble of big hair and bright red.

"What the fuc—" Sadira shrieked.

"Cut. Cut. Did I say improvise? I didn't tell anyone to
improvise. Why is she improvising? Is this how she glem-
mies? Someone tell her to turn her fucking glemmy off
and stick to the script before I come out there and knock
it out of her. Ruining my fucking money shots." The
director's voice boomed through an overhead intercom.

I looked up as the room swayed and Kai climbed off the
couch from where he was lying to help me up to my feet.
Not about to be upstaged, Sadira rushed over and started
making a big deal out of having her scene interrupted.
They were on a closed-off portion of the set that had
cameras in the ceilings, so the director could watch off
screen. It was perfect for love scenes or really emotional
moments. Mmm, and Kai had a mole on the left side of
his neck. The lighting made his pulse flicker under his
skin, and he had these teeny tiny sun brightened hairs all
over his body. He seemed to be quietly studying me just
as closely as I was studying him.

"We're all hanging out in my suite later. You should
come by when we wrap." My eyes floated toward that fine

mouth of his and I nodded. What I wouldn't give just to be that nigga's teeth. I'd get to spend all mothafuckin' day in between his lips and his tongue; you couldn't convince me that wasn't heaven.

I was about to unleash my so-called exorcised inner demon named Honey all over his fine ass. "Only if you let me climb that—"

"Um, Desi, come here, boo." Sir'Tavius snatched me up, putting his arm around my waist, quickly twirling me in the direction of my dressing room.

"I thought you said she was with my man." I glared at him out the corner of my eye.

"Okay, um if you don't know how to get in character or read scripts that's your own fault. He's your man in this movie, heffa; she tries to steal him."

"Mmm, Sir'Tavius, I don't know how or when but I'm gonna get his ass," I shouted, suddenly amped about my new mission. *Go, team, get that ass.*

"Is that so? And who might this be?"

Sir'Tavius and I had the same exact look on our face at the same damn time, when we heard Angelo's voice. He'd been MIA all this time and of course he'd show up now.

"She jus' going over some lines, Angelo; don't pay us no mind." Sir'Tavius to the damn rescue.

Angelo looked between the two of us with an eyebrow raised before chuckling and wandering toward the catering area.

"Tavius, I need you to help me get that ass. I'm gettin' that ass. Look at me. I grabbed him by his shoulders and stared past the swooping silver tipped lashes he was wearing. "Look in my eyes, you see this? This is my serious face, I need that ass. I need *some ass*, or I'm gonna take it from someone." I gave him a good up and down glance for emphasis. "Your legs lookin' a little muscular in them jeans Tay. You been workin' out?" I teased him.

"Ho', no. We gonna make sure you have your purse and all the fixings from now on, because them pills got you somewhere else."

"You see what I'm stuck with though?" I pouted.

We turned and examined Angelo's departing frame, both of our heads tilting to the side.

"Ugh, him just so skinty. Do he even have a booty girl, what do you grab? Ain't no meat on the chicken. I'd break that all to pieces. Wouldn't be no more good."

"Tay, he's already been broken." I giggled, pointing myself out as the guilty, skinty boy breaker.

Chapter 8

Red Box

Sir'Tavius promised to take me home once we finished shooting for the day and Angelo reluctantly left. We were actually done by four and it gave me more than enough time to relax before meeting Don Cerzulo later. I borrowed a form fitting green cowl-neck dress from wardrobe to change into since I didn't have time to go home.

"Tavius, I just want you to know that I'm like five feet two-ish and my knees are in the dashboard. I still love you and your mini, golf-cart car."

"It's a Fiat, bitch. Recline the seat. I can't help that I'm always hauling Queen Etheria's wardrobe across the damn state."

We laughed and joked all the way to the hotel. By the time we got there the crowd that had gathered out front was an apparent sign most of the cast was already inside. Sir'Tavius got me as close to the main lobby doors as possible. The last thing I needed was for Angelo to see my picture popping up all over tabloids.

"You're here, your boy Tavius hit me and said you were outside." Kai walked over, smiling. I immediately decided whatever trouble I was getting into was going to be so worth it.

He led me to a reserved elevator with double wide golden doors. It needed a key card just to get them to open. It was strictly for access to the wing with the suites and penthouses. We went up to the one just beneath the top floor and the elevator opened up to the devil's playground.

The shades were all drawn so that even during the day it looked like it could have been midnight. In the center of his suite was a large glass room. It glowed in a dull red. That red-room wasn't as fascinating as the people inside it.

"They can't see us. It's a sauna. Inside there's music and they're watching themselves in mirrored glass," Kai informed me in a soft whisper.

He grabbed my hand and led me toward it. My heels sank into the carpet and I passed ivory furnishings with violet lighting underneath. Whoever designed this room needed to design some strip clubs, fertility clinics, and marriage counseling offices, because from the second the elevator opened I'd been on ten.

I stood less than four inches from Sadira, the world's number one actress. Her face was pressed down into the marble bench. Some big-ass football playing looking nigga with shoulder muscles on top of his shoulder muscles had her pinned down by the back of her neck. My eyebrow shot up when I thought about how bad I wanted that to be me. Kai had walked over to the counter and it was like watching a calendar model twenty-four-seven.

He walked in sexy confident steps, stopped and that sexy unruly man ponytail of his swayed as he winked and smiled at me. His thick pink lips wrapped around a neon green pipe and he exhaled, ab muscles flexing as he took off his shirt. Rewind. The nigga was behind the counter, hitting something out of a pipe. It definitely wasn't marijuana. I'd never smelled anything like that before. Not crack, or that fake weed salvia shit. I had no idea what he was smoking.

I glanced back into the red room, and almost walked myself right up in there. Shit, they wouldn't notice. There were like four different couples going at it and at the moment I didn't know if Sadira even knew she was eatin' a nigga's ass and not pussy. No, no, she definitely looked up at him. Smiled and stroked him with one and sucked her finger to get it nice wet and wow.

"Kai, come here, boy. What the hell you in there doing?"

He jogged his ass over to me. "DMT, baby. I had to get ready for you. You should try it."

I ain't have time to be playin' with his uber-high ass. I was on a schedule. I wrapped my fingers in all that damn hair and pulled him down. *Mmmm, damn.* He felt good and I backed him up against the glass so I could watch everyone else at the same time. I licked a salty layer of sweat off his skin and he groaned. I did the same thing to the opposite side of his neck and he slammed his fist back hard against the glass.

"Shut the fuck up. I can't focus," Kai yelled, and I jumped my ass the hell back.

What the hell was this fool on? Real talk, you could practically hear grass growing out here; that booth was damn near soundproof.

He looked at me apologetically, rocking back and forth on the balls of his feet. "Not you, it's not you. They wanna show me God, Honey. He knows everything. Sees everything."

"What did you call me?" I stared at him, frozen, confused and paranoid. This had to be a joke or a set-up. *Did Angelo put him up to this?*

"I'll get one for you."

Kai walked back toward the counter and I just stood there staring at the red box in front of me. They looked

like one of those paintings from Dante's *Inferno,* minus
the demons. They didn't need demons to torture them.
Sadira, Kai, me, we tortured ourselves. I squinted when
the lights came on and waited for Kai to explain whatever
he'd found to show me. The panicked screams made my
feet move before my brain could process what the fuck
was happening.

"Look, look up there. Who is that? She pushed Kai,"
people were screaming.

I quickly ducked back into the room, trying to blot the
image of Kai's body sprawled across the pavement from
my mind. I didn't push him. I wasn't anywhere near him.
There was no way in hell I'd go down for a murder I didn't
commit when I'd been getting away with real fucking
murder. Panicked beyond reason I called the only person
I knew could help me.

Don Cerzulo was reclining in the back of a luxury car
with limo-black windows. He gave me a warm smile as I
climbed in.

"Desi, stuff like this happens all the time. DMT is some
hard shit, makes you hallucinate and all kinds of stuff.
Everything will be fine. I've handled it. Forget about
it, okay? It's done. We have bigger things to deal with,
not even going to ask why you were at one of Kai's hotel
orgies."

My eyes almost bulged out of my head. As if it wasn't
bad enough that I had to call my fiancé's father to help
me, the dude I was with was known for throwing shit like
that.

"I had no idea, that's what it was. The cast was going
and I went too, Don. That was it." I shrugged, and
helped myself to a glass of champagne. Twirling the
stem between my nervous fingers, I stared off into space,
thinking about everything and nothing at once.

"It's a sad thing," Don said quietly.

I looked away from the palm trees and whirring lights of the city flying by my window. "What's a sad thing?"

"That you can be anyone, go anywhere, and do anything. People do anything to get it and just as much to protect it. But, after a while, it all gets boring."

He looked out his window and I gulped down the rest of my champagne. *It sounds to me like someone has way too much money and too much damn free time on their hands.*

"Let's make this game interesting." Don Cerzulo sat up with a clap, rubbing his hands together. "It's time that face of yours earns its keep."

I waited as the car slowed to a stop. We were somewhere near downtown Miami, but I couldn't figure out where. I had an eerie feeling that this was going to be a little more than an acting class.

"The best actors are method actors, Desivita. They get into their roles; they live them."

The driver opened Don Cerzulo's door before I could ask him to explain and I was speechless after that. We walked along carpet that was such a bright shade of red I was surprised a flock of jealous cardinals didn't swoop down and attack. It led us up stark white steps into an Italian-style villa that had to be the set of one of Don Cerzulo's latest movies. This romantic storybook palace had majestic arched ceilings with glistening antique chandeliers and ornate tapestries. I was in awe and Paris would have loved it; any girl would. My ass was in love with it. All I needed was a princess dress and I'd be in business. There were a few men wandering here and there in expensive suits, looking at the art in different areas.

"All of this was done by hand. It took one man two years to duplicate the paintings from the Sistine Chapel," Don Cerzulo remarked.

I hadn't even noticed that the walls were painted and not wallpapered. Every inch was covered with an angel, cherub, or a cloud. Marble staircases with intricate gold and black leaf carvings on the railings divided the massive foyer in half.

"What in the God's name is going on in here?"

A wizened little gray-haired man came rushing in, looking around frantically. He took one glance at us, stopped cold in his tracks, and tried to turn and leave. All the men who seemed to have been so preoccupied earlier were immediately occupied with dragging him over toward me and Don Cerzulo.

"You're supposed to offer me a drink. Ask how I'm doin'. But no, thanks, and I'm doing a lot better than you're lookin' right now." Don Cerzulo chuckled.

"Business is business, Campelli. You don't break into a man's house over what goes on in the meeting room. I—"

"You, my friend, are going to make the news tomorrow. Producer slash movie director Raul Scanetti commits suicide in Miami home. They're gonna find you upstairs in your little dick-complex, California king-sized bed. Pea-sized brain matter splattered all over the ceiling. Your movie is now my movie. I am the next bidder who can actually afford to produce it. By the way, this is the new star. Say hi to the man, sweetheart."

Scanetti sputtered unintelligible, gut-churning, "about to die" pity moans and I was a nice brewing medley of "shock and what the fuck" stew. Don Cerzulo glared at me, nudging my arm, urging me to actually speak when I honestly ain't have a clue what to say. I managed to squeak out a weak "Hey," without making eye contact.

"We can fifty-fifty, seventy-thirty? Anything, it's yours," Scanetti pleaded.

Don Cerzulo nodded to one of the men, who pulled out a pistol with a suppressor on it and a set of gloves.

"Desivita, take the man upstairs. One bullet in the temple, arm fully extended or you'll get blood splatter on you. Don't touch anything on the way up or down. You will earn your keep in this family. Now go." He nodded toward the stairs.

"No, wait, please no. I've got kids and my wi . . . wife, what about her? Desivita, don't do this; you don't have to do this. I can help you." Scarletti fell to his knees, pleading with me and crying.

I looked at Don Cerzulo and shook my head no. I couldn't do this kind of shit. There wasn't any reason for me to kill this man. If it had been Rah or . . .

Don Cerzulo's face twisted into an angry snarl as he leered down at me.

"What do you thinks gonna happen to you if I don't have a use for you? Either you work for me or you die here with him and be all over the news tomorrow as a junkie actress turnin' tricks for work."

Don Cerzulo's voice made my blood run cold and I could feel the winds whirring of some dark, malevolent storm in my chest. It's a wonder my teeth didn't break from grinding them as hard as I was. Two men pulled Scanetti to his feet in front of me. He stood with his shoulders shaking, tears and snot hanging from his quivering chapped lips. The stench of coffee tinged urine hit my nose full on as he pissed himself right there. I slapped on the black latex gloves while Don and his men in black snickered and laughed at him.

What I wouldn't give to be regular-ass, catching a ride to the Hot Spot Honey right about now.

Chapter 9

There's No Place Like Home

"Mommy, who's house is this?" Trey wandered aimlessly around the small, modestly furnished front porch, touching everything. Two wicker chairs sat on either side of a tiny wooden table. An old-fashioned flower can filled with dirt sat on top of it. He had that look that all little boys get when they're seriously searchin' for something to unintentionally fuck up or break. He'd settled on poking a rotting cantaloupe with a stick.

"Trey, get over here and be still. And don't you touch nothin' when we get inside or I'm wearin' that behind out. You understand me?"

He nodded, trudging over to stand beside me just as the front door opened.

I smiled my brightest smile. "Hey, Momma."

"Da hell are you? Another one of them Jehovah's Witnesses? 'Cause I told the last ones not to come back 'less they was bringin' red wine and tata chips. Look like you ain't get the message."

"Momma, it's me, Michelle. Rasheed's, um, ex-fiancée. Um, you remember our son, Trey? Your grandson?"

"Oh, Lawd, hey, baby. I'm so sorry. Time's been hard on this ol' mind. You heard what happened to my boy? Them county folk came through here askin' all kinds of questions. Couldn't even have an open casket." She sulked while looking at me through cataract-clouded eyes.

I almost broke down, apologized, and begged forgiveness for everything I'd done. It never crossed my mind how Rasheed's momma would suffer without him. I didn't kill him, but I may as well have for getting him locked up. Her nightgown was stained and frayed around the edges and her hair was haloed around her head in a short salt-and-pepper afro. Momma had always kept at least three fancy wigs with a special one for church. Without Rah paying for her medications and her bills, and left to live off the system, she looked the worse for wear. My ass should have been sending her something, even if it was anonymously.

Unfortunately, this was the only game plan I could come up with. It was a long shot. A pitch-black, blindfolded, "with no wind to guide me" type of shot but I was taking it. Virginia wasn't even on my list of relocation options but that meant it would also be the last place anyone would ever think to look for us. If anyone did come looking, Rasheed's Momma wasn't one of the first people they'd question, and I highly doubted Honey would even risk the trip. She was, after all, a wanted woman.

For every mile I put between myself and Florida a new question formed concerning Towanna. Things just weren't adding up, like why she'd wait over a year of establishing a fake friendship if she was after Rah's money. After I'd shot her there'd been no news on the radio; I hadn't gotten any phone calls. I should have checked her body. Trey needed to be in school and my business couldn't run itself. I could probably home-school him. *And strangle him in the process.* It wouldn't take long to find an acting manager to run my real estate company. I could hold web conferences to manage and check in on the manager once I got one in place. I just needed to keep my head down until I could find Honey and get her locked up again or taken out for good.

"Child, you gonna stand there and stare me down or you and my grandbaby . . . wait, you had another one?" She was staring down at Lataya, who'd just woken up in her car seat sitting near my feet.

"No. Well, I mean Rasheed did. Just not with me."

"That little red heffa ain't come from my son. Yella an' cocoa, yella an' yella, hell yella an' pitch black don't make no red baby. Was the heffa a white girl?" She furled her face up and I almost laughed out loud.

I chuckled. "Her momma is a little reddish yellow if I recall correctly."

"That ain't Rasheed baby. I know what a White look like. Done birthed, burped, an' outlived 'em. She ain't got the White nose or the ears." She sighed heavily before continuing, "Come on in anyhow. Wit' your imposter crumb snatcher." That last part was a grumpy mumble under her breath.

"Um, Momma? Why is that rotten cantaloupe on your porch over there? You want me to throw it away for you?" I couldn't help offering; flies were buzzing around the thing and it was stinking up the entire corner where it sat.

"Hell no. It showed up one day. Don't know where it came from because I damn sure ain't ask for it. I ain't touchin' it, and don't you go touchin' it neither." She leaned in so close I could see the gray rings around her cataracts as she whispered, "I think it's a body snatcher."

All I could do was stare at her, waiting for a laugh or the punch line but she just turned and hobbled inside ahead of us. She was dead-ass serious.

The carpet was so worn down I could barely tell the difference from being outdoors to stepping inside. It was as if I'd stepped into a Dumpster with ambient lighting. I sidestepped empty soda cartons, stacks of newspapers, and piles of old lottery scratchers and empty bingo markers.

Trey tugged at my leg, put his hand around his mouth, and whispered, "Mommy, is this Oscar the Grouch's house?" His little face was all scrunched up in confusion.

I couldn't even get mad; that was a better description than what I was thinking. At least he'd asked quietly. Aside from the old newspapers and cardboard there was the overwhelming smell of cigarette butts. It was a wonder the woman didn't have a Newport 100s testing facility in her kitchen. Something along the lines of "there was an old woman who lived in an ashtray" came to mind from how strong the place smelled.

She closed the door behind us, whispering, "Child, I don't know if it's safe. Ever since they told me my baby passed I been sensing things. Hearin' folk creepin' around outside. They are tryin' to get in my house. You saw it. They leavin' pods out there, hoping one'll snatch me up. Body snatchers and peepin' Toms. The Illustration been watchin' me."

I needed a damn minute. Here I was worried about real people and real-life threats and Momma was worried about . . .

"Wait. Momma White, are you talkin' about the Illuminati?" Our situation was bewildering enough as it was. I needed to get this craziness nipped in the bud, fast.

"Shhh. You know that pod can hear you, girl. That's exactly who I'm talkin' about."

She waddled her way through the clutter and sat down in the only clear spot on the couch. I couldn't figure out where to set Lataya's car seat and I for damn sure wasn't about to take her out of it. It was hard enough keepin' an eye on Trey's busy little fingers.

"Now, lemme see the baby toes. All the White babies have stubby, fat, li'l Flintstone-looking feet wit' a ba-by-dick second toe," she said matter-of-factly, crossing her arms across her chest.

Trey gasped. It was too late to cover his ears and I seriously debated sending him off to explore.

No, that wouldn't turn out well; who knows what this woman has where up in here? Trey is liable to wander off and come back with a cat that's been dead up in here for five years and she'd probably say he killed it.

Shaking my head at him, my eyes silently said, "Boy, you'd bet' not repeat that." He'd better not add any of this to his already-colorful vocabulary. We'd have to get a child-friendly filter on Momma White's mouth and soon. I was sure I'd heard her and scared to ask for clarification.

I cleared my suddenly dry throat and asked, "A . . . a what for a second toe?"

She snorted in irritation. "A baby dick, like a monkey finger, a damn cobra-clutch grabbits long as hell second toe," Momma White responded and with an attitude on top of that.

She even added terms for toes that I'd never even heard used in reference to a toe in all my adult life, as if they were medically defined terms I should know.

"Mommy, do I have monkey fingers?" Trey questioned.

Shit, he definitely had a long as hell second toe but I wasn't about to give him a complex about it. Rasheed was always funny about his own feet. Kids teased him so much about his toes when he was younger that he rarely walked around barefoot even with me. I ran my fingers across my eyebrows, mentally wiping away all this toe business.

"Okay, yes, Momma, she has a long toe. Now, how about we get you away from the Illustration, and go to a nice hotel? I'll let you hold Lataya and you can examine her for yourself all you want."

"No. I ain't goin' anywhere. Mona be done came up in here and took all my shit. Shit I worked for. I've got to be a vigilante."

I sighed, wondering what on earth I'd walked into. "Vigilant, Momma?"

"And that too," she replied, twisting her mouth up at me.

Lord, please build up my patient side because I'm sure there ain't nothin' right about chokin' out an old woman.

Chapter 10

Shot at and Missed, Shit at and Hit

Me and the kids spent the night at the Hilton. I'd been doing all kinds of mental gymnastics trying to come up with ways to get Rah's momma up out the house. Aside from setting fire to it or flooding it, she wasn't budging. The least I could do was get off my bourgeois-ass and pitch in with cleaning it up. There was no way I could leave her with it like that. She'd have these hacking painful sounding coughing fits that would leave her doubled over wheezing for air. It was probably from years of smoking and I'm pretty sure there were all kinds of dust mites and mold spores making it worse. I couldn't help but feel sorry for her, my own momma sounded somethin' like that when the doctors said they couldn't do anything more for her. They just sent her home telling my Daddy to make her as comfy as possible.

"Michelle, you're ten now that means you can be a big girl and help out around here okay?" My father was sitting on the edge of the bed. I stood in the doorway of my parent's bedroom staring down at my red Jellies and nodded. The sound of my name made me look up as my momma weakly tried to call me over. The action sent her into coughing spasms that shook her entire body. I stared at sallow grayish-brown skin covering a skeleton with sunken in hollow eyes; she didn't look anything like my momma.

I felt bad because as much as I loved her, I was a little bit scared of her. My nose wrinkled as the room filled with the smell of shit and I covered my face with my sleeve.

"Go get the nurse, and stop acting like that. She cleaned your little ass for years. Be respectful," my dad scolded me.

My mother withered away in her bedroom and as bad as it sounds I tried to spend as little time in there as possible. It was hard seeing her leave for the hospital kissing me and telling me she'd be fine and then coming back with the scent of death all over her. My daddy started looking for comfort in the bottom of liquor bottles and he only came home after the bars closed. I didn't care for Nurse Faye at all. She wore too much perfume and popped her gum all the time. She kept her hair gelled up in a bun on top of her head, and stayed digging up in it with a rat tail comb.

I'd left school early one day because I'd started my first period in the middle of class. The school nurse calmed me down assuring me I wouldn't bleed to death before sending me home with some extra pads. Nurse Faye was in the den watching the soaps and rubbin' her feet. She stopped and jabbed herself in the head with that damn comb before digging her hand all in my box of Cinnamon Toast Crunch. I knew it was disappearing fast as hell, nasty ass heffa.

I went straight to momma, she was medicated and in a deep sleep. I checked the padding underneath her to make sure she didn't have an accident before scooting it over so I could snuggle up next to her. I pulled the covers over my head and dozed off with my face buried into her side wishing I could make her better.

"Ahhh, right there. You are so, so bad Mr. Roberts."

"Shhh you'll wake her up."

"She ain't waking up no time soon. She had her mor-phine shot early, now hurry up before Michelle gets out of school."

Still groggy I could hear my daddy and the nurse talking in hushed tones. Momma's door was wide open and I peeked out from under the cover. He was standing in between the nurses legs with his pants around his an-kles and she was sitting up on the kitchen counter naked from the waist down. He took a chug from a bottle and then went back to grinding into her. They went on like that for I don't know how long moaning and sighing. I shook my head into momma's side as angry hurt tears fell into her gown.

"He a man baby don't be mad at him, he still got needs."

The sound of my momma's low whisper made me jump.

"But it's not right momma."

She sighed, or at least I thought it was a sigh. Her chest made a rattling sound and the alarm beside her bed went off as her heart stopped.

The timer on the oven went off and I opened it to see the oven cleaner eating through all the black crud on the racks. I'd nearly asphyxiated myself with bleach and scrubbed through a whole box of Brillo Pads. I don't know what I was thinking when I'd decided to tackle this cleaning job by myself. Momma White needed Molly-maid, Super-nanny, and an extraction team up in here. We could finally see a hairline of a dent in all of the filth she'd accumulated. For every spot I'd managed to clean, she'd be right behind me, taking something out of the trash or pulling an item or two back out of boxes.

It took a carton of Newports and a bottle of Merlot but I'd managed to bribe her into letting me clear one of the bedrooms for me and the kids. All we really ended up doing was shuffling items from that room to other parts of the house. The woman was a bona fide hoarder of empty cigarette cartons, cup noodle cases, and little else. There were no pictures from when she was growing up or when Rah was little. Nothing was left of value because her sister had squandered all of that for heroin or whatever else.

This particular morning I found Momma staring out of the kitchen window.

"Momma White? What are you doing?"

She was so still she could have been a wax sculpture. I'd have named it *Rebellious Domestication*. Momma White was holding her coffee mug full of wine with a lit cigarette perched carefully between her fingers. The ash hanging off the end looked almost as long as the cigarette itself. She was staring intently at the trees in the backyard. Thankfully the kids were still asleep, but I wanted to get to the sink and wash dishes before they were up and all in my way. She didn't seem to be paying me or the dishes any mind.

"Momma? Are you all right? Is something wrong?" I gently tapped her shoulder.

"Shush, girl. He gonna hear your loud ass, and then we all gonna be dead."

My pulse raced as a memory of my last night at Towanna's created a massive pileup of emotion in my throat. I swallowed past the lump. "Who are you talking about? Who's gonna hear me?" I whispered cooperatively.

She gave me an annoyed glance, briefly curling her lip in disgust before pointing at a tree closest to the house. "Right there in the corner. He got that shit turned on though, guess he call himself hidin'. Damn Predator sitting right there. I see him. Camouflage don't fool me. See the leaves movin'?"

I followed her withered finger through the smoke burning my eyes and stared at the few remaining Reese's

Pieces—colored leaves that were barely hanging on the tree branch. I was looking and thinking, you know, hunter, apex predator, and then my shoulders slumped. I rubbed my eyes in aggravation and looked at Momma White, who was still staring, fascinated with this tree.

"You mean *Predator*, like on TV?" I couldn't keep the disbelief out of my voice.

"He obviously ain't on the TV if he in my damn tree spying," she snapped back, taking a sip from her mug.

Left with nowhere to go and stuck with my ex's bat-shit crazy momma.

This had to be God's way of punishing me for all the fucked-up shit I'd done in my past. I'd have pointed out the fact that it was just a squirrel but that would turn into another one of her "Illustration" arguments and I wasn't even in the mood for it right now. On more than one occasion I'd started to ask her if she was on something. I was thinking maybe Mona wasn't the only one doing "the hard stuff." The house would be dead silent and Momma would start yelling for everyone to shut up. She even had Trey convinced the walls melted every day when the sun came up. He'd sit on her lap and they'd whisper about where they thought the drywall came from when it grew back at night and what color it might be.

I noticed a trickle of blood down the back of her leg.

"Momma, did you cut yourself?" I asked her.

"Hmm? Oh no girl. It's a boil. Put fatback on it and a few home remedies. It's fine."

"Oh, okay. Well, let me have a look then, you don't want it to get infected."

I'd already figured it was infected because it was the leg she'd been limping on. She reluctantly walked over and slightly lifted her house dress. She had a huge mean looking hole on the back of her thigh about the size of a soda bottle cap. I'd gotten a rag and some peroxide to clean it with.

"Momma, you've got to go to the doctor. Um . . ."

"Spit it out child."

"You have maggots, in your leg Momma."

"Oh, girl tell me something I don't know. They only eat the bad parts. They making it healthy. How you think they got there. That's why I let you look. Do you think they done yet? You gonna need some tweezers to take 'em out, some of them little buzzards'll latch on good and won't wash out."

There weren't too many options since I wasn't exactly her kin. Momma wasn't going to be happy with me but hopefully she'd thank me one day.

The hospital wasn't exactly what I expected for a mental institution. After seeing Trey and Lataya settled into a quiet, guarded play area on the main floor I checked in and went to see how Momma was handling herself. You'd have thought we were sentencing her to life in prison when they came by the house to speak with her and diagnose her condition. Her stay in here was completely contingent upon her cooperation. Turned out she was schizophrenic and in the early stages of Alzheimer's. I'd already agreed to take care of her once she agreed to get with the program. I'd found a ton of unopened Risperdal prescription bottles littered around the house. At some point she'd decided to start boycotting her meds. It made me wonder if that mess was a dominant or recessive trait in the gene pool. I'd need to start watching Trey and Lataya's asses because shit like that always skipped generations.

I was escorted through at least five different checkpoints by a well-mannered, broad-shouldered guard. My cell, keys, and belongings were left at check-in, as nothing could be taken inside. Hate to say it, but it was all very reminiscent of visiting Rah in prison. There was a rundown of do's and do not's. Such as "do not leave the visiting area, do sit quietly, and do not be alarmed if other patients randomly join your conversation." Oh, and "do not stare."

All the visitors were corralled into a large dining area with bare ocean-blue walls. A row of barred windows let in sunlight, greeting us with a view of the concrete walls. They surrounded the entire building.

Well, isn't that a cozy sight to see. They could at least put up some shrubs or rose bushes; these folk already depressed enough as it is.

Momma wasn't at the stage in treatment yet where she could have unsupervised visits in her room. That would come later. I sat down at a long cafeteria-style table and waited. A few patients were already seated in the area. It wasn't like on TV where you'd see people wandering around in raggedy hospital gowns. I was instructed to pack warm, comfy clothes for Momma, and to be sure not to put any belts, razors, or mouthwash in her suitcase. All the patients wore brightly colored hospital bands and clothes of their own choosing.

I questioned that logic when I saw an awkward-looking, pale, middle-aged man sitting slouched in a corner. He wore nothing but biking shorts and brown penny loafers with no socks. Blinking seemed to take a conscious effort as if he were snapping himself awake from a quick nap. He was giving me the thousand-yard stare down with his dark, beady eyes in between blinky jerks.

Humph, but it isn't okay for me to stare though?

The guy seated next to him slid out of his seat and began holding an intense conversation with the chair. He started crawling and sliding it around the dining area. His sister or wife sat by, watching sadly, and I gave his crazy behind a cautious side eye.

Momma was finally led in, strolling like a regal mafia matriarch. A short, stocky woman, who made a Shih

Tzu come to mind from looking at her, bounced along beside Momma. She had a pinched face and stubby little legs with a pink bow in her hair. They were followed by a hunchbacked old man with graying hair, and a towering, serial-killer Green Mile–looking somebody.

Shit, I should have been allowed to at least keep my cell phone, my Mace, something. Momma rolled her eyes at me and sat clear at the opposite end of the table. She promptly folded her arms across her chest and sat gripping her upper arms with a sour look on her face. Sighing, I got up and walked around to pull out the chair beside her. If she wasn't going to come to me I'd just have to go to her. Regardless of what she thought, putting her in here was my way of helping, not hurting.

Green Mile had been giving me his version of the thousand-yard stare from where he stood. Before I could plant my ass firmly in the seat I gasped as something cold and wet splattered across the front of my blazer. The room erupted into chaos as Green Mile decided it was just time to go ape shit ballistic. He flipped the table and started launching chairs at the orderlies with missile-like precision. I was literally watching *King Kong* live and direct. If there'd have been something in there for him to climb, he'd have scaled it and been roof bound in a matter of seconds. Panic alarms went off and a squadron of orderlies, guards, or whatever you call them stormed in. I stared down in disgust at the brown ooze ruining my cream Marc blazer, and I shut my mind off.

Lord, please don't let this be what I think it is.

I fought back a gag. Figure the odds. I'd been shot at and missed, shit at and fucking hit. Momma glanced up at me with a smirk on her face.

"Ms. Laurel, I am so terribly sorry. Please come with me we'll get you cleaned up."

A gorgeous, thick-hipped nurse with dimple piercings manifested in a mango sugar-scented cloud. Giving me a reassuring smile, she took me by my elbow and led me through one of the side doors into a maze of hallways.

I will not ask for her number. I will not ask for her number. Hmm . . .

But, what if she asks for my number? No. I will not give out my number.

We are on a break. Mentally chastising myself for even thinking about cheating on my sexual diet I continued to follow along and keep my eyes above hip level. I was sure these were the areas they left off the tours when they solicited you for your money. The friendly dark blue walls gave way to a more institutional-feeling, split-pea, soup-colored green. We passed rows of rooms with "fit your face" sized square windows. They lined the hallway on either side. People screamed or cried nonstop like they were being tortured behind the stark white doors. My nosey ass tried to peek in and every now and again I could see people curled up in their beds; sometimes they were strapped down.

And this is supposed to be the place where we send depression and mental illness to be cured? When I went through shit with Rah, I'd tried to sleep the pain away, sometimes for days at a time. And then Ris would save me. Bowling, jogging, drinking, dancing, and fucki—

I could hear what sounded like a life-sized bug zapper humming at the end of the hall. "Is that . . . ?"

"Electroshock therapy? Yes, some people actually need it," she answered before I could even get my question out.

She led me into the women's locker room. "You can get yourself cleaned up in here." She smiled sweetly and disappeared around the side of the lockers to go get me a fresh shirt.

Stripping down to my bra I did my best not to smell or come in contact with the filth on my jacket and blouse.

"Mmmph, aren't we nice."

That either had to be the fastest trip in history or this locker room was the size of a broom closet. I bit my bottom lip as she brushed the towel across my shoulders and down the center of my back. She walked around and stood in front of me, pursing her lips as she handed me the towel, staring down at my barely covered breasts. I couldn't remember the last time I'd bought a new bra and the cups weren't exactly a perfect fit anymore.

So much for covertly checkin' out another female, Michelle. No more looking at anything for you. Ever.

Thankfully she just handed me the towel, giving me another calculated up and down with her eyes that I read like an erotica novel.

"Unless you need some help, I'll let you to get cleaned up. And again I'm sorry." She quietly added under her breath, "But, I'm not."

I gave her a tight-lipped smile. "I'll be fine. It's okay, it wasn't your fault."

I hated to be the reason for the look of disappointment on her face as she walked out of the locker room but, oh well. My hiatus had just barely begun and after Keyshawn and Ris I needed to do some serious soul searching. I was only happy with Larissa when Rasheed was acting up, and I was happy with Keshawn when Ris was stuck on stupid.

Maybe I need to look into that polyamourous stuff, get myself a . . . No, I need to look into my own place. Where did I pack that damn vibrator? All this Honey business . . .

Honey probably needed to be up in a place just like this. From what I could remember and from what I'd seen she was always a little off. Maybe something like this would be better for her than prison. I rinsed myself off and toweled dry quickly over the sink. There was a gray T-shirt lying on the bench beside the lockers and I aimlessly slipped it over my head. I didn't see her bring it

back in. *She had better not be watching me wash.* Pulling
the collar to my nose I sniffed it just to make sure it was
clean. They weren't about to have me walking around
in a funky, dirty T-shirt. It smelled wonderful, like Gain
detergent, warm vanilla, and cardamom.

They needed to knock some dollars off Momma's bill,
that's what they needed to do.

"So do you always sneak around locker rooms, sniffing
and stealing things that don't belong to you?"

I jumped and whirled around, my eyebrows raised in
shock and embarrassment. I'd been so lost in thought I
hadn't even heard anyone come in. My mouth plopped
open and I was pretty sure it was stuck in the shape of
either "oh, shit" or "oh, no."

I'll take "oh, shit" for $800, Alex.

Old King Kong himself was standing calmly just inside
the doorway of the locker room.

*Now you already know this fool's crazy. Do you do or
do you don't make eye contact?*

Clearing my throat, I brought my eyes up no higher than
neck level, and then I chickened out and looked off at the
lockers to the left of him, focusing on them instead. "Do
you always walk up in women's locker rooms? Because,
thanks to your king-sized temper tantrum back there I
needed a new shirt, so I'm adopting this one. And just so
you know I'd have plucked my son's face clean off his head
if he ever pulled what I watched you pull out there and
he's only five." I prayed I could keep up the small talk long
enough for the nurse to come back.

"Well, I apologize for the unfavorable first impression
that I'm sure I made. It's nice to meet you," he replied
casually. His voice had a husky deepness to it that made
it seem bottomless.

*Why, oh, why do the crazy niggas always gotta be the
ones with them deep-ass voices? And you know this fool*

can probably back that shit up with some crazy deep-ass dick, too. Girl, shut up!

He gave me a large, beaming smile as he came over, extending his hand toward mine. Timidly I returned the gesture, afraid my ass was about to get yoked up as his baseball mitt of a hand engulfed mine.

Aww hell, here we go. I can see this headline now: WOMAN MURDERED IN AN ASYLUM LOCKER ROOM BY KING KONG PSYCHO MOTHERFUCKA.

Satisfied he nodded down at me and sauntered over to one of the lockers.

"I don't think you should be messing with that. Are you even supposed to be um, roaming around at your leisure? I'm Michelle by the way."

Um, hello? Why you tell this fool your name? What if his crazy ass done killed everybody and now he's trying to escape? This shit happens on TV all the time. He threw shit and lost his damn mind up there not even five minutes ago. Why isn't he in the crazy solitary? This can't be good.

His long, tapered fingers maneuvered the combination on the lock until it popped open with a click. "We do drills twice a month to see how well the orderlies are following procedure. Patients are supposed to get checked before each visitation to make sure something like today doesn't happen. Darren will lose a day's worth of pay. It could have been real fecal matter instead of chocolate pudding and peanut butter. I'm Dr. Harrington by the way."

He turned from rummaging around in the locker and handed me his badge. A smug smile lingered on his thick, full lips. Embarrassed at reacting the way I reacted to some damn chocolate pudding I couldn't help blushing.

Now you know you've been elbow deep in diapers worse than that. You should've known better, woman.

"Oh, yeah, and the locker rooms are unisex. It's a psychology thing. The hospital will gladly compensate you for your clothing, and I'd be more than honored if you'd let me take you to dinner, as my way of apologizing for scaring you." He'd turned on that bottomless-pit voice of his again and there I was teetering on the edge.

Oh, no, no, no. I'm not ready for this dating nonsense. And he seems too sweet and way too stable to even fit into my crazy-ass lifestyle.

"I . . . I'm sorry, but I can't. I just moved here and I've got a lot going on. Like a lot. Don't get me wrong, you seem really sweet. You just really don't want to get mixed up in my life."

He gave me an inquiring look, like I was something to be queried or studied on his couch. "Thirty-two seconds ago you looked like you were praying I wouldn't chop you up and stuff your little ass in one of these here lockers."

I scoffed. "I did no such thing. You obviously imagined the hell out of that look." We both chuckled at my obvious lie.

"Riiiight. You were up in here subliminally threatening to slap off faces and now you think I'm too sweet? You do remember me saying I'm a doctor? A damn good one, too. I can fix anything." He winked, and I felt my cheeks flush variations of pink and red that Crayola probably hadn't even invented yet.

"I don't need fixing. I just need a damn break." My wistful reply was a combo-meal whisper of hopelessness and hopefulness. It could've gone either way.

"Oh . . . Dr. Harrington, I didn't know you'd be in here. I found Ms. Laurel something to wear." The nurse came barging in, holding a scraggly looking set of old, used scrubs.

"She's fine, Denise. She uh, 'adopted' my T-shirt. Show her how to get back to the dining hall."

Giving Nurse Denise a smile, I then nodded good-bye to the fine doctor.

How the hell was I supposed to know the T-shirt was his? And on top of that he caught me smelling it. I can't lie; if it were up to me this shirt would never see the inside of a washin' machine. It smelled like a bald, honey bun–hued King Kong of a bottomless pit. And all worries aside, I wanted to fall in that bitch fifty ways from Sunday.

Chapter 11

No Harm, Your Foal . . . Fowl . . . Foul

I stared at the umpteen-whatever-count threads in the pillowcase so long my eyes started to cross. This was the second time he'd pulled that coming in late shit and I was fed up. When Don Cerzulo dropped me off, as much as I didn't want to see Angelo I kind of needed to. We'd never discussed the terms of my surgery, fame, hell, my life for that matter. It was one thing when it came to doing shit to get Paris back, but this was . . . was slavery. Do or die. How long would I have to be Don Cerzulo's puppet before we were all squared away and what if I got caught in the process?

It couldn't be that hard to suffocate his snorin' ass. Angelo snorted and sawed logs in his sleep. That's exactly what it sounded like. *Them hoes on* Snapped *do that shit, hold the pillow over his face and—no, wait—they shoot the niggas through the pillow. Men suffocate hoes with pillows. Must take a lot of muscle to do that shit. Look at my ass, already tryin' to murk every-damn-body for no reason. The Don's methods already rubbin' off on me.*

When I couldn't take the sound of the air whistling out of his nostrils anymore I quietly eased out of bed. My bare toes touched the cool gray marble tile, sending rivulets of pain from my backside down my legs and I cursed him. Angelo came home, took his "wash away the evidence" shower, and got in bed. I pretended to be asleep just like

I always did, even though I'd just had a really good Skype call with Big. Angelo started kissin' on my shoulders, grindin' on my ass, and I just refused to react. I ain't sign up for this shit. Who wanted a relationship with an absent man and some bullshit no foreplay quickie morning sex all the damn time?

So what did Angelo do? He decided he's just gonna lick his hand to lube up and slide in. Shit, I still ain't move. If he was hoping that was gonna get me in the mood he missed the mark. Askin' if I could feel it, and if I loved him. He was breathing his hot-ass toothpaste breath all up the side of my head. He eventually wore himself out and my skin was cracked and dry. Dumb ass, I guessed he was one of those kids who liked to hit the Slip 'n Slide without water.

Talking to Big definitely made me reassess things. He wasn't gonna be in the area for much longer and I was feeling pressed to find Paris and haul ass. Marriage to Angelo was sounding less and less appealing the more I thought about it. After pacing a hole in the living room carpet I finally made up my mind. It was always easier to ask forgiveness than to ask permission.

A woman in a sweaty red tank top jogged past me as I made my way down the street. Pulling my hoodie tighter over my head I looked around to make sure I wasn't being followed or recognized by anyone and quickened my pace. Granted, Don Cerzulo's ass said don't touch anything; something good did come out of that situation.

Scarletti's wife had a pharmacy of pills beside the bed. I didn't even read the labels. I just emptied a bunch into one bottle. I shook out a light pink one and a pretty light yellow one. They'd either wake me up or make me calm; either way it'd be interesting.

Walk through a deserted carnival ground in any state and it'd feel just like Miami at seven a.m., minus all the beautiful joggers of course. I'd decided to press my luck and text Big to meet me for coffee. He was actually awake and agreed to meet me at a spot close to his shop.

"Look at you, looking all good this early in the morning."

I got up from the table to give him a hug, again amazed at how big he was.

"They got some bomb-ass chai tea up in here; it's better for you than coffee," he told me.

"I have a confession to make: my ass don't even like coffee. I jus' wanted a reason to see you. But, I'll try your tea."

"So what has you out and about this early in the day, unaccompanied by your man?"

His tone went dry when he added the last part and I wondered if I'd said too much in our Skype conversations.

"It's hard to explain. On like one side I'm grateful to him for his help but that shouldn't mean I owe him shit forever. He proposed and his daddy was there and I ain't know what else to say. And now I feel stuck, when all I really want to do is find my baby and be happy."

"And Michelle got her right?" He reached over and rubbed my shoulder. I nodded. "Would I be your favoritest Big hero if I told you I think I know where Michelle is?"

I couldn't tell if he was serious or playing. "I'll stab you in the eye with this spoon if you fuckin' with me right now." I grabbed one of the spoons off the table, giving him my version of Angelo's pointy stabby, poking his hand for emphasis.

"Damn, okay, Tonto, calm down. Yes, I'm serious, I wouldn't play with you about something like that."

My hand started shaking as I set the spoon down on the table. The room swayed and I blinked several times. I looked Big directly in the eye and slid my hand up his leg under the table. Honey was officially back, well, mentally anyway, and she was ready to handle business. I was the baby-voiced seductress with the womanly curves that drove niggas insane and now I had this silver screen siren's face to complete the picture. They'd do anything to make my pouty lips smile and hear me say, "Yes, daddy." And in that moment I turned it all on for Big.

"If you tell me where Michelle is and where my daughter is, you would be my Big Daddy and I'd do anything for you."

He swallowed hard and shifted in the booth. "My homeboy looks in on Rah's ma every now and again. We all know she always been a little off so he make sure she got food and smokes. Just leaves stuff on the porch most of the time because you catch her on a bad day and you liable to get taken hostage or shot if you can't convince her why you there. Said he rode past last week and saw a woman with a little boy and a little girl in a car seat up on the porch. The car been there every day since."

I couldn't believe my ears. Even if we were sitting in the middle of ten o'clock service on Sunday, it wouldn't have kept me from climbing on his lap and kissing him. Up until that moment I didn't have the slightest clue where to even start looking for Michelle. I'd have asked Angelo what he thought if he were ever home long enough. I was pretty sure he'd seem more interested in making a baby than finding mine.

I leaned back and smiled; my chin was probably red as hell from Big's beard but I ain't care. "Let's go back to your shop; you can give me a celebratory massage." I winked. The number one rule of runnin' any man is to keep they asses working for you. As long as they feel like they earnin' something you hold all the power. Because, everyone knows that anything worth working for has value.

Big grinned and paid our tab; he even offered to carry my backpack but I declined. My emergency cash and a pistol were in it as always and it never left my hands.

"You know I'm leavin' in a few days right?" he said over his shoulder as he fed his fish.

"I thought it was gonna be at least a few weeks."

"Nah, the season here is slower than I thought it'd be. I wanted to tell you in person."

Good news and bad news. Up and down in the same day. I was instantly depressed as hell. Big wiped his hands on his jeans and turned to face me. Worry lines creased his forehead.

"What do you plan on doin' about your baby girl?" he asked.

I shrugged suddenly realizing how overwhelmingly hopelessly possibly impossible my situation seemed. She was right there and I had the means and everything. Except flying to Virginia and just taking her wasn't really an option. Anything I did now would draw tons of media attention so I had to be careful about how I got her. Angelo and all this murder, death, kill business was a hurdle I wasn't ready to jump over or knock down just yet. I didn't need to tell Big any of that though. I was pretty sure he could tell from the bags under my eyes, or from the way my skin was starting to break out. My ass ain't never been big on wearing a bunch of makeup, but at this rate I'd have to look into some foundation or face powder. Eyeliner and lip gloss wasn't really cutting it for me anymore.

Big's arms circled around me and he somehow managed to duck down, propping his chin on top of my head. He sighed and it pretty much summed up the moment.

This is damn nice. My very own live-action teddy bear and he's leaving me. What am I gonna do?

Big felt solid and safe; he was an invincible pillow fort against all my believed and make-believe monsters. He even came equipped with his own extra-large black Maglite.

"We gonna figure this out, Little Bit, okay?"

I buried my nose into his chest and nodded. He always smelled so damn good, too. I just wanted to breathe him in so I could remember it later. I inhaled warmth and sandalwood.

"Girl, you makin' my nipples sweat." Big broke my concentration, sounding like he needed a dang church fan.

I actually stopped breathing and leaned back to stare up at him, scrunch-faced and everything. "What in the world are you talking about, boy?" I asked him.

"All that nose breathing. What in the hell are you doing? It's makin' my chest hot."

Big scowled at his shirt, then leaned down, grabbing me by the shoulders. This fool started rubbing me back and forth across his chest so vigorously I was surprised we ain't catch fire.

I yelped, "Negro, what the—"

"You was tryin' to wipe a damn booger on me. I know how y'all women folk do."

We both busted out laughing.

Somehow laughing turned into us kissing. And, kissing turned into me in the air with my legs wrapped around his waist moaning against his lips.

This is what the fuck passion is supposed to feel like. This feels like front-row seats to a fireworks show over the ocean with an orchestra playing dramatic music in the background. And this is the kind of feeling I'd be more than happy to settle with for the rest of my life.

He held me up with one hand, pulling my hair from its ponytail with his free hand. Fingers in my hair never felt so damn good. I groaned. Every part of my body was alive and begging for his undivided attention like it was all jealous of my hair and my lips. We'd backed up against the far wall. How or when he got my shirt and bra off I didn't know. I'd never wanted to be out of my clothes so bad while trying to stay in them.

Of all the days for Big to make a move and then tell me he has to go somewhere. We can't do this, not today. Not after Angelo done ran and splashed himself all up in there no condom no nothing. That would just be nasty.

We could do this any day except today. Intent on telling him just that, I broke my lips free, placing my hands on his shoulders. "Big, I need you to lis—"

He pinned me back against the wall and made figure eights, grazing my bare skin with his course beard. I'd just gotten my mouth tooted up to call a time out when he decided to go all hungry wolf cub on my ass. Big growled and bit me on my side. I squealed and pinched him. It wasn't bad, he just caught me off-guard. Before I could do more damage his mouth made a swirling ball of heat around my nipples. I didn't want to breathe anymore. Air in meant my chest would expand, drawing him closer, but eventually I'd have to let that air out. I didn't want my skin to be any farther from his lips than it had to be. Forgetting where I was, I had one of those "throw my head back and be cute" moments. My head smacked the wall and I squeezed my eyes shut, hoping Big didn't catch that very unsexy Kodak moment.

"Um, was our meeting cancelled? Because, I didn't get the message."

My eyes fluttered open and were met with Big's. He gave me an irritated "get you later" stare down as he slid me gently down the wall. Standing behind him for cover I clumsily put my top back on. I didn't hear the door open or anything.

"Nah. My bad, T. I got sidetracked. You know how it goes. Why you ain't hit the cell?"

"I did, several times actually. Figured, what the hell, I'd just roll through."

"Shit. Um, Desivita." Grinning, he glanced back to see if I was dressed. "Let me introduce you to my business partner."

I nodded at Big, but I couldn't bring myself to look Angelo in the eyes. It was easier to talk to the floor in between us. "We already know each other, Big. That's my fiancé, Angelo."

"Wait, Testa is ya man? King, the boss of Miami. Oh, fuck." Big ran his hand over his forehead and sat down hard on the leather couch.

I glanced at Angelo. It was like looking at a shipwreck survivor, well, a rich one anyway. He'd rolled through all right. His ass rolled right out of bed, into his wrinkled-ass man capris, Ralph Lauren button down, and them preppy boat shoes that I hated. He could have rolled through a shower and a brush first.

"Yes, King Angelo Testa, *the* Boss of Miami," Angelo snapped at Big.

I looked down and rolled my eyes. Was he really standing here in his Carrera shades, looking like a spoiled brat, spouting his name, when he won't nothin' but a daddy's boy?

Angelo leered at me. "All I've done for you and you'd cheat on me?"

"You're mad, because I'm out here doin' exactly what you've been doin'? Late nights and early mornings, huh? That's not what the lyrics mean, Angelo, you were doing it all wrong. Climbin' in our bed from Lord knows where for what? Some stale-ass morning dry humps. Fuck outta here with that."

There's always that point in an argument when you know you've gone too far. The words leave your mouth and you know they should have stayed in your head. They hit the air and the other person's ears and they're the kind of words that change your life forever. Yeah, his dick game was wack but I didn't have to actually say it out loud, especially not with Big right there. I'd heard Angelo and his boys say that "get outta here" or "fuck outta here" line at least a hundred times a day. Hearing it from me was just salt and vinegar in an open wound.

"I ain't been doing anything, Honey, except meeting with this one"—he nodded at Big—"to go over investment business models, and then catching red eyes back and forth to Key West. I've been spending money planning a surprise wedding so you'd be able to walk around for a weekend without feeling like a fish in a fishbowl." Angelo reached into his pocket and threw hotel reservations, snippets of cake pictures, and business cards onto the floor in front of me.

He was really serious about that marriage thing. Why wouldn't he be? You said yes to the man, in front of his daddy, and you're wearing his ring. What the hell did you think would happen? Maybe one of us would die first and I wouldn't have to be bothered for real. Or something like what's happening right now would happen.

Why couldn't the floor have just opened up and swallowed me. His lips were drawn in a grim, thin line, as his nostrils flared angrily and tears ran down his cheeks. There wasn't even a "sorry" I could give him because I wasn't sorry. I just wasn't in love and had never been in love with him. If anything I was sorry he'd fallen in love and had decided to go all in with me.

Time felt as though someone had laid an hourglass on its side, stopping the sand all together. The room seemed quiet—too quiet. Waiting for Angelo to react was like watching lightning and counting the seconds waiting for the thunder. I couldn't tell if the storm was going to move on or just quietly building up energy.

"Desivita?" a woman's voice called out from the shop door.

The muscle in Angelo's jaw was ticking. I looked around him to see who or how someone had even seen me. Either them pills were kicking in and I was hallucinatin' or there was an entire fucking studio of paparazzi outside. Big got up and stormed over, locking the door to keep more of them from getting in.

"Hi, Desivita, so is it true? Are you the Angel of Death?" she asked, waiting for me to answer her dumb-ass question.

"No, and this is not a good time for any kind of an interview. I'm sorry." I tried to sound polite but her question rattled me to my core.

"You made your movie debut in *Revived 2* after the original producer, Albert Meekins, was found murdered by his lover who committed suicide. Sadira Nadeshce had already completed over eighty percent of the movie when you replaced her under mysterious and unexplained circumstances. There were even tweets about you trying to attack Sadira, the star of your current film on set with a metal bar during a scene with your on screen love interest."

I gasped and looked at Angelo, who surprisingly hadn't stormed off yet. No way? Al and Jasper weren't a drug deal? But, I'd never heard anything about a producer dying; no one ever made a peep about it during filming. *Unless they were too scared or threatened not to talk. Fuck, Don Cerzulo, what the fuck did you start?*

The woman continued, "First there were sketchy rumors of you being spotted on the balcony and leaving the hotel of co-star Kai Nimako after his alleged "fall" from the sixteenth floor. Now, not moments after the release of Scanetti's alleged suicide, Sadira announced via Twitter that she's being replaced on yet another film. Her replacement in the leading role is none other than you, Desivita Dulce'. So again I ask are you the Angel of Death? Is that nefariously dark angel ring more than a fashion statement? Is America's new 'it girl' killing her way into our living rooms? What kind of woman are you?"

Angelo spoke this time without looking at me. "I'ma tell you something my pop told me. He said a woman can only be one of three things: foal, fowl, or foul. What that means is she's either gonna be a bird, always waitin' on you to throw her some crumbs, with no real values, flyin' from coop to fuckin' coop because she don't know better; or she gonna be a fuckin' thoroughbred, loyal 'til the day she dies. You might have to put that crop to her ass to show her who's the boss. But, end of the day, she a winner." His voice got scratchy and he cleared his throat. "Or she foul. Fouler than . . . fouler than the stench of a slaughterhouse, in the middle of a heat wave, with a jilted freezer, and no power.."

With that, Angelo turned on his heel and strode out, letting in the mass of people who had been dying to hear what was being said. His insults lingered, burning my ears, weighing down the atmosphere. They always say angry words are the truest words. They just don't say how much it'll hurt to actually hear them. Both rings on my fingers felt heavier than usual; one was suddenly an ugly, embarrassing reminder of my fake-believe engagement.

The other sparked my fear that Don Cerzulo Campelli was using me for something else, something big and wrong as fuck. Now that I didn't have Angelo in my corner I had no way to predict or defend myself against him. I had to have done something, said something; maybe

Angelo found the texts from Big that very first night. None of it mattered; what did matter was getting myself away from Miami and this fairy tale bullshit. People were yelling and snapping pictures all around me and all I was thinking about was how long it would take me to get to my little girl.

Chapter 12

All of Y'all Crazy

(Back in VA)

I was sitting at the kitchen table leaving a voicemail for the office. I needed to get a few properties sold and I needed someone to start sending me listings so I could find something somewhere that felt safe. The kids were down for their afternoon nap when I heard a floorboard creak behind me.

"Trey?" I quietly called his name before stuffing the rest of the chocolate chip cookie I was trying to enjoy in private in my mouth. I folded the bag back up as quietly as possible and slipped it back in the cabinet. These were mine and yes, I snuck and ate them. Sometimes I even hid them in my clothes and took them in the bathroom. Trey and Lataya had enough snacks to fight over. It was probably selfish of me but I couldn't help it. Mommy had to share everything from her bed to a cup of water, which became their cup of water after they'd put backwash in it. The only things I wanted right now were peace and quiet, and my damn cookie.

The house actually felt like a home again. Without Momma there to clutter it up I was able to throw everything away that didn't have a social security number on it. If we could just keep her on her meds maybe it would stay this way. I peeked in the living room; seeing nothing

I went down the hall. The door to the kid's room was cracked.

If that boy is wandering around not answering me I am gonna wear him out. I know he heard me calling him.

Both of the kids were still in the bed sound asleep. Poor Trey, my baby ain't have no covers on his behind. Kissing each of their foreheads, I carefully unraveled the blankets from around Lataya. I didn't know how that girl did it. To be so tiny she always managed to burrito herself up, stealing every inch of the comforters and sheets. I made sure the pillows beside the bed were still stacked nice and high and left just as quietly as I went in, pulling the door closed tight behind me.

The wind made the branches scrape wildly against the siding on the house and I tried to familiarize myself with the sound. I'd pulled my gun on that sound the first few nights when I'd heard it in the middle of the night. It reminded me of the sound I'd heard that night I was tortured.

Counting down no longer worked when I was anxious or afraid. Not after being nearly suffocated with snakes slithering all over my neck and in between my legs. Sample a small piece of your worst nightmare, and see if it doesn't change you. Because, in the beginning I always thought the worst that would happen was they'd kill me. I never considered all of the sick and twisted things that a person would do just out of revenge before the killing actually happened. Things that I'd have no control over if I got caught off-guard, and the thought alone made me feel frustrated, angry, and nervous.

Making my way back toward the kitchen I choked on a scream as we collided in the hallway. Something hard and metal slammed hard into my chest and rattled loudly. I fell back, checking myself for a stab wound or blood.

"Shiiiiiit. You can't see where da hellllll you goin'?"

If Wild Irish Rose, blunt smoke, and fried chicken grease could talk, it would look exactly like the little withered woman croaking up at me in the dim hallway. The voice belonged to a skeleton-thin, slightly older version of Momma White. I did a mental up, down, and sideways double take on her. This heffa was actually wearing skin-tight pleather leggings with a tube top. She was busy adjusting the tangled 1B/27 bird's nest propped on top of her head, giving me an irritated look. If you asked me, I might've knocked it straight because she repositioned it into some kind of crooked craziness.

"I'm Michelle; um, how did you get in? I mean, I didn't hear the doorbell or anything like that. Do you have a key or something?" I asked as politely as I possibly could.

Where the hell did I put my purse and car keys? Rah always said his auntie was a crackhead and even Momma said she comes in here takin' . . . Hold up, is that my toaster she's holding?

"Don't need no key. Mona ain' neva nee' a key. Keys are why y'alls is slaves to the sys'em now. Stop believin' in keys an' you can go anywhere you wanna go. Like me." She slurred all her words together as she stumbled, turned, and began walking in the complete opposite direction of the front door.

"Where are you going, Mona?" I called after her, worried she was about to march herself through the kids' room. The only thing in that direction was Momma's room and the bathroom.

Let me find out I need to hide the shower rings and soap dishes, too.

I got up and followed to see where she was headed. She mumbled as she walked into Momma White's room, crawling across the bed toward the open window that I knew was closed and locked.

"Goin' out the way I came. An', let my Reena know I'ma see if I can borrow 'bout ten dolla's from her damn illegal natives."

Her illegal natives?

"Umm. You're talking about the Illustration?" The fact that I even knew the right wrong name to correct Mona with almost irritated me a little.

"Mmm hmm. An' her toaster," she muttered as she shimmied out the window.

I sighed, calling down out the window after her, "Ah, that's my toaster, Mona."

It wasn't like I was expecting her to say, "Oh sorry," and bring it back or anything. I could always buy another toaster. Guessed that's why Momma was adamant about staying. Mona would get in somehow and someone needed to be vigilant, or "a vigilante" as Momma had put it. I could see Mona coming back with a shopping cart next time.

"Oh. Well I'm borrowin' yo' toaster, honey. Tell the 'ministration to pay me for you. I mean you for me. Ah, hell ask for yourself, they parked right there on the corner," Mona called out over her shoulder, pointing as she jogged down the street, toting my brand new toaster under her arm. She stopped at the corner next to a black Altima and I watched her tap frantically on the window. It rolled down and a woman threw out a few bills that fluttered wildly into the street. I ran to get a better look out the front door but it sped off with the tires squealing and smoking. Mona was there and gone so fast I thought I might have imagined her.

If Mona could get in and out, hell, anybody and they damn momma could. Lord, I needed help some kind of bad right now. Who the hell was that in the car? It had VA plates; she could have rented a car, it couldn't have been her. Did Mona tell her anything? Who would believe

Mona? That woman acted about as nutty as Momma. Nutty or fiending and willing to sell someone out . . .

I went back to Momma's room and closed and latched the window. When I pulled to make sure it was secure, it wouldn't budge.

She must've used something to get it open. This house, this arrangement, just wasn't gonna work. I needed to find us all a place fast.

"Trey, baby, don't slurp the noodles; you're gettin' sauce everywhere. And eat your toast. You asked for it, so eat it."

I'd made spaghetti for dinner because it was quick and easy, but with the mess the kids were making I immediately regretted it.

"This not toast, Mommy. You put it in the stove, and toast go in the toaster. Oun't like it," he whined, dropping it square in the middle of the table.

"No nost. No. no. no nost, No no no no no," Lataya chimed in singing and banging her empty sippy cup on the table. She was all grins with spaghetti sauce all over her little cheeks and chin. I tried to get her to at least stop clanking the cup. Trey was frowning tapping the table with his fork.

He'd barely taken one bite out of it and was already complaining. I always made garlic bread in the oven, which he didn't like, so I'd make him buttered toast instead. Without my damn toaster I had to make Trey's buttered toast the old-fashioned way.

"Boy, it's still butter on a piece of bread. So eat it before I butter that ass. Your sister's eatin' hers without a problem."

"Eat, eat, eat. Eat . . ." she sang, silencing herself with a fistful of spaghetti.

Trey dropped his fork and slumped back in his chair. "G-ma and the walls said she not my sister and when my daddy—"

"Lord, help me," I actually groaned out loud. This boy and all his G-ma talk; and when did he decide to shorten grandma to G-ma? I didn't even know. I wanted to wring both her and Trey's necks at the moment. He was saved by my phone.

"Ms. Laurel? It's Dr. Harrington."

I smiled into the phone, thankful for the distraction before I snatched Trey up from the table. I'd been secretly hoping he'd call and ask if I'd reconsidered. My nerves were still on edge from dealing with Mona and that car. An adult conversation would take my mind off things, even a brief one; it would make me feel so happy right about now. Even though I'd coached myself over and over to tell him no, I could feel the cogs spinning in my brain.

"Yes, this is she," I replied sweetly.

Damn, I'd need a sitter. Maybe he'd consider a child-friendly date. No, that would be awkward. Trey would ask too many questions and Lataya would get fidgety. We wouldn't get any kind of conversation in. I didn't have anything to wear. We couldn't even do happy hour anywhere because I didn't know who to trust with the kids. Not after that car earlier. No one knew I was back in town. I could have called one of my girls from the bank. But if Honey was having me followed they wouldn't know what to do if confronted—

"Your mother's had a small stroke. She's stable and asking for you."

His words sank into my ears and settled in the pit of my stomach with the rest of the gloom that seemed to be hovering over my life, and my shoulders slumped. "I'll be right there," I replied, disappointed and worried about Momma.

The hospital took up the first two floors. They'd obviously had enough drama with patients self-inflicting wounds, having heart attacks, and enough seizures to require one on site and for that I was thankful. It was also a relief not to go through half the security I went through on my last visit. I felt naked leaving my gun in car and if I'd known it was going to be so lax I would have kept it in my purse.

Dr. Harrington was waiting beside the front desk when I arrived. I had to admit he handled the transition from rugged brute to sexy intelligence extremely well. His lab coat was most likely a size too small on purpose. His biceps completely filled out the sleeves and I was pretty sure if the man so much as sneezed he'd completely rip his way out of it.

When he glanced down at the floor clearing his throat I realized I'd been staring and I finally opened my mouth. "How . . . How's Momma doing? Is she gonna be okay?"

"She's asleep now. It was minor; they don't see any permanent damage. She was lucky she was here taking it easy and not at home alone."

"Good. Well, I don't wanna wake her up. I'll just get the kids—"

"The kids will be fine in the playroom. Come sit with me, have a drink. Someone gave me a bottle of Cîroc Amaretto. It's been sitting in my office and you are gonna be my guinea pig. You can even talk my head off for free."

"Who says I want to talk? And I have to drive. Plus I've got the kids."

He flashed that disarming smile of his before answering me. "You show me a woman who doesn't like to talk and I can guarantee it's because she's mad, or she can't stand the person she's sitting next to."

I was trying hard to keep from laughing. Call it a control thing, but I knew he wanted to make me laugh and I was just refusing to do it. The result was a crooked, twisted-mouth smile. He did have a point, because I couldn't count how many silent dinners I'd sat through because I was mad or Larissa was pissed off. I finally answered once I had my humor fully contained. "Touché, you got me. I will drink to that. Just one though."

The sound of ice clinking into two crystal glasses was the background music to the look of me in awe. His office was impressive. It was about half the size of a hotel ballroom and breathtakingly masculine. Several rich walnut bookcases lined one of the deep blue diamond-patterned walls. One was filled with volumes of psychology books and journals; the other one had a signed football by Redskins players, and his various degrees. Two large flat-screen TVs were mounted to the far back wall facing his desk, which was made of the same cherry finish as the bookcases.

That would be just like a man. Who in the world needed two TVs?

The sun shot golden glittered arrows off the corners of buildings as it set. I stood in front of monstrous floor-to-ceiling windows overlooking a view of downtown from the top floor. He handed me a glass and leaned beside me on his oversized mahogany desk.

I smirked. "So what kind of doctor doesn't need a computer?"

"Aren't we the observant one. It's all wireless and the flat screen on the right is my computer screen; the one on the left is my TV. Even though I will have two games goin' if I'm stuck in here on a slow day, don't tell anyone though."

He nodded toward them and I was in "wow" for a moment. I needed that all up in my life; working with the guys and staging the houses usually kept me up to date on those types of things.

*I have definitely been slacking on my techie game
something serious, and that is so not like me.*

"So, Harrington, what's your first name? And don't tell
me it's Doctor."

"That's a good one. I'll have to remember to use that.
It's Devon."

I sighed. "Well, Devon, I'm in the wrong damn line of
business. I've got a company in Florida and my view was
just the Realtor's ass in front of me." I pouted. "It wasn't a
good look, trust me. He was a big boy, always managed to
have a 'man camel toe.'" Seeing Devon's confused look I
clarified, "You ever seen a fat guy in really tiiiiight pants?
Now imagine him bending over and his balls—"

"No! I refuse to picture any dude's sac in any format."
Devon made the "blech" face along with sound effects.

"I'm just sayin'. I looked directly at it once by accident.
It's like a freaking solar eclipse. You know you shouldn't
stare but you can't look away. The vision still hasn't been
fully restored in my left eye." I did a dramatic hiccup sigh.

"Aww, there there. I'm a doctor remember. Let me
have a look at it." He playfully took my chin in between
his thick fingers and stared curiously into my eyes.

Our gaze locked and I instantly became hypersensitive
to everything. Heat waves rose from his hand, radiating
into my skin, making me wonder if they could do that
everywhere. He had the thickest curliest lashes I'd ever
seen on a man. I wanted to laugh and ask if they came
that way out the pack, insinuating that they were fake,
but I couldn't stop looking at them . . . at him.

Mmm, and what gorgeous eyes you have, Doctor . . .

Suddenly uncomfortable I blinked, ending the trans-
mission and locking him out of my head. *Oh no, sir, you
ain't about to glamour me googly-eyed with your Dr.
Wonder Sex Care Bear stare down. Tighten up, girl. One
drink and carry your ass.*

Frowning, I shooed his hand away, clearing my throat. "You ain't even an eye doctor. You might break it."

"Why are you so guarded?" His voice was low and pensive.

"I'm not guarded. I'm just careful. If I told you even half of what I've done or what I've been through, you'd probably have me thrown out of the hospital." I took a sip from my drink to try to cool me down. He needed to turn on some AC.

"And she actually murdered my wife. Did you hear me? Murdered her and the guy I was seeing. Not seeing like cheating, because we were about to divorce anyway, I think. It was bad. But, honestly, would you ever drug your own wife?"

His drink stopped midway to his lips and he stared at me, wide-eyed.

"Don't answer that you're a damn head doctor. You'd probably have just as well had us all strapped to your bug zapper downstairs." With the attitude of a queen dismissing her court, I waved off any excuse he was about to try pitching in my direction. "Anyway, so this cop comes along; next thing I know I'm tied up living out my worst nightmare. Traumatized me, trust no one."

I'd started with how I met Rasheed all the way to how I ended up staying with his mom. Devon sat completely motionless. The only things that moved on the man were his eyelids. He blinked, and finally sat up like he was coming out of a trance.

I gasped. "Oh fuck, you're probably thinking I'm like the worst kind of person. I'm really not. I can't believe I told you all of that. Am I gonna have to kill you now? The way my luck has been going you're probably gonna try to kill me or just randomly die and I . . . I don't even know." I sobbed into my hands.

A sip had obviously turned into me having a drunken meltdown moment. I could hear him laughing and I frowned, peeking at him from between my wet, teary fingers. This fool was sitting there just grinning, running his index finger back and forth across his bottom lip, looking conceited as hell.

"So, I take it that you like me, huh? Because that was quite a bit of talking," he asked in between grinning and biting his bottom lip. He was referring to our conversation downstairs.

I shot daggers at him with my eyes.

Devon looked down at his watch. "Why don't we take the kids out and do something fun while Mommy sobers up? I'm sure they're hungry by now and unless a DUI is on your bucket list? I don't know. Let me see if I can remember you saying anything about that in your adventures." He couldn't stop laughing, and I couldn't stop feeling mortified.

Okay, so I could add funny and disarming to the list. I had to give him points. He could have taken advantage of my emotional breakdown and tried to get me butt-ass naked on his desk. Hell, he could have let me sober up in the visiting area with a pot of stale coffee and pretzels after everything I'd told him. Maybe there were some good guys out there, because not once had he been anything less than a gentleman when I'd been doing all the mental Olympics.

Even if he is a good guy, then what? Ugh! I think I think too damn much. Sloths are fast but choose to move slowly. Maybe it's time to stop being so damn smart all the time.

Chapter 13

Almost Doesn't Count

"You sure this is Rasheed momma house?" I asked, looking out the corner of my eye at Big, trying not to get irritated. He hadn't stopped eating since we got in the car. This fool was the textbook definition of a stress eater. It took all of my willpower not to open my mouth and point out that that's probably how his butt got big in the first place. If he wasn't stressing about how much money he might lose without Angelo as an investor in Miami, it was only because his mouth was full. Every time we passed a rest stop or a gas station, he was out the car looking for tuna salad, Swiss Cake Rolls, and Jujubes. It didn't matter how many times I explained and re-explained, Angelo was not worried about him. If anything, I needed to be worried. I'd managed to get on everyone's list on both sides of Angelo's family. He wasn't gonna want anything more to do with Big and had enough money to not be pressed about the chump change he'd loaned him.

"Yeah, girl, I'm sure. All the homies pretty much grew up here hanging out with him. It's the one right there with the burgundy shutters." He spoke around a mouth full of Hot Pocket.

"Why ain't the porch lights on? There ain't even a car in the driveway. What time is it? eight forty-three p.m. on a Thursday; someone should be home this late, Big."

"Maybe she took her to Bingo. His ma was always crazy about that shit."

The car was smellin' like a stuffy mobile canteen.
Since it was last minute the only thing at the rental place
was a compact Prius hybrid. I'd had to do most of the
driving since Big was obviously on his man cycle. Y'all
ain't know men had cycles? Shit, they get moody, pissy,
sentimental, and be all touch me, touch me not. At one
point he actually tried talking me into turning around
because he didn't properly tell his fish good-bye. We
made it to VA just in time. He would've contracted some
kind of deadly food poisoning eating all those random gas
station snacks, or I'd have killed his ass. We could have
flown but the chance of being spotted by Don Cerzulo or
any of Angelo's people was just too risky. Besides, I didn't
want any more people questioning me about that Angel
of Death business.

I gave Big a wary look, patting his shoulder. "Okay so,
you just stay in the car and um, guard your snacks. I'm
gonna go look inside and see if they've been here."

I parked far enough away that no one would notice the
car and got out, pulling the hood of my jacket over my
head. I walked around the side of the house, glad all the
windows were low to the ground. There was one around
the back of the house that didn't have a screen on it. I
pressed in and pushed up on the glass. When it slid up I
celebrated and waited to see if an alarm or anything went
off. When nothing happened I pushed the window up and
climbed through, landing on an old, musky quilted bed.
The house was pitch black. Sliding my phone out of my
pocket I used the flashlight app for light and cracked the
bedroom door open. If I'd had a weak heart I'd have died
on the spot. She was standing there like a damn ghost.
Reflexes made me drop to the floor drawing my little
handgun out of my pants leg.

"Who the fuck are you?" she whispered down at me
with her pistol aimed at my nose.

"Desivita, and your ass?" I snapped back, my gun pointed at her gut.

"Oh shit, the little murder actress. I'm Towanna." She put her gun away, reaching out her hand to help me up.

I took it, brushing myself off, looking at her warily, and asked, "Why are you hiding in here in the dark, Michelle fuck you over too?"

Hey eyebrow went up and I realized where I'd messed up before I could even fix it.

"Too? How does Michelle know Desivita Dulce' and how she fuck you over?" she asked, and I wasn't answering I'd already said too much.

"A'ight, well I think she saw me. I was out in front watchin' the house and a crackhead come out the house through the window you just came in, and straight out to my car. Carryin' a damn toaster. Anyway, Michelle came to the door so I pulled off in a panic. When I came back the house was empty."

No, no, no. I started shaking my head back and forth. This hit-or-miss, "a day late and a dollar short" bullshit had to stop eventually. Tears shimmered in my eyes and I sat down right there in the hallway. I actually had a breakdown in somebody else's house. I couldn't think of what I was supposed to do next or where I was supposed to go. My life was all fucked up and the only thing I wanted was with the one person who fucked everything up in the first place.

"She's mine, Towanna, and I'll miss her first words. I ain't never heard her laugh or kissed her check and it's tearing me up inside. How do I walk away? If someone could just tell me how, I'd do it. Michelle took her from me, and I just want her back."

Towanna surprised me when she didn't ask any questions. She just sat down beside me and wrapped her arms around my shoulders. She leaned her head against mine and rocked back and forth with me.

I leaned my head back against the wall, staring up at the dark ceiling. Teenage Rasheed probably had all kinds of nasty little girls up in this house when his momma wasn't home. The metal upper half of a pull-up bar was stuck to one of the doorframes and I immediately knew that was his bedroom.

My chest got tight and the hole in my heart with Rah's name carved around it slowly started to ache. I had to get my mind off him and on to something else. What me and Rah had won't nothin' but a stripper's dumb fantasy. When I got him out of prison, I saw him for what he really was with my own eyes. I took a deep breath to calm my thoughts but something Towanna said made me pause.

"Towanna? Why would Michelle and Rah's momma leave the house if she thought she saw you?" Wiping my tears on my sleeve I turned to look at her. My eyes were adjusted to the darkness, but now I felt like I was literally in the dark about something. I knew Michelle couldn't have possibly made a new stalker ex-girlfriend already.

Towanna let out a long sigh. She dropped her forehead down to rest on her forearms, which were propped up on her knees. The short poofy ponytail at the back of her head swayed a few times like she was wiping her eyes or her nose before she quietly confessed to the floor.

"I can't help this shit. I'm a protector. And, she got this thing where it seem like she's cold and invincible, but she's not. It makes you feel like Atlas. Like you could do or be anything for her when you finally get Superwoman to take off her damn cape. I fucked up though, on some other shit. Trying to be fast, rushing shit. Anyway, long story short, Chelle's gun went off, it was an accident, just hit me in my vest. She ain't know and I was stunned. She thought she'd killed a cop and she ran."

Towanna was sniffling and wiping her eyes, her head still down.

I couldn't believe my damn ears. She could have said she hated Michelle. That the girl gave bad head, had stank-ass garbage-truck pussy and gave her the herp. Anything would have been better than what the hell she'd actually said.

Hitting her in the back of the head with my gun I pulled hers from her waistband and stood over her. The blow should have knocked her out and I cursed when it only stunned her. She rubbed the back of her head and looked at her hand to see if there was blood on it.

"The fuck you do that for?"

I didn't answer her. My gun was aimed between her eyes while I called Big. "I need you in here now!"

I was motioning for Towanna to walk so I could go unlock the front door when this nigga decided to just Donkey Kong barrel crash his ass through it.

"Yo, where you at?" His voice boomed through the house.

So much for being covert.

I rolled my eyes, calling out to him, "Back here, just follow my voice."

He fee-fi-fo crashed through the house, knocking shit over in the process.

"Big, this is Officer Towanna. Officer Towanna, this is Big," I introduced them.

"You ain't say you had a cop."

"Because if I'd said that, Big Daddy, would you have gone all Mighty Joe Young on that door to get to me like you just did?"

The "Big Daddy" and doe-eyes routine wasn't gonna work for this. He was not happy.

"What the hell you think you gonna do with a cop? I can't get in this kind of shit right now. I'm a business-man." Big's tone was short and sharp while he scowled down at me.

I shrugged. "She's not just any cop; she's Michelle's ex–fuck buddy super cop or something. She'll probably come in handy."

Chapter 14

Knights Like This . . .

"And you call yourself a what kind of doctor?" I scolded Devon on the drive back, thankful the kids had fallen asleep in the back seat.

"I'm sorry. A haunted hayride sounded like something fun. I didn't know we'd get chased by axe murderers and zombies. I was thinking more like spooky ghosts and goblins." "As if that's any better. You definitely don't get to pick anymore child-friendly activities. Your administrative privileges have been revoked. They're probably gonna have nightmares about this." I giggled, unable to stay completely serious.

"Ah, anymore? So that means I get a do over date. In that case, I'd suggest we expose them to gambling and mass amounts of junk food there's a Chuck-E-Cheese somewhere around here," he laughed.

I slapped his arm playfully.

After my "never to be spoken of again" meltdown in his office, we'd grabbed Lataya's car seat out of the car and I was able to sneak and grab my gun case from underneath the seat. I'd have felt vulnerable without it in my purse. We'd driven all the way out to Podunk middle of nowhere to ride on a haystack through a "haunted" cornfield. Even though the kids were scared shitless, I did have fun.

"Michelle, wake up."

I didn't even know I'd dozed off. I looked around, trying to get my bearings.

"Are we at Momma's? How'd you know how to get here?"

"GPS; her address is on all her records. It's late. I was gonna drop y'all off and just pick you up in the morning to get your car but you might have a problem."

I looked past him at the front door standing wide open. I sat back quickly and stared straight ahead. "Go, now. Just drive, please."

You've got to be kidding me. What makes this so bad is I don't know if it's Mona or someone else. If they're waiting in there for us or if it was a robbery, good thing my laptop is in my car. Shit, it's a good thing we aren't pulling up in my car right now.

"Shouldn't you be calling the police right now?" He gave me a concerned look.

"No, you don't ever go to the police unless you know which ones are dirty. My ex had half of them on his payroll back in the day. If they're dirty and the person who did this wants to get away with it, there's nothing you can do about it. I don't know why I even bothered coming back here." I wanted to angry-slap myself repeatedly in the forehead in frustration but I settled on rubbing my eyebrows.

We rode with me lost in my thoughts for what seemed like hours before the car stopped. There was no way in hell Honey could have possibly been able to find me. I hadn't seen anyone, hadn't talked to anyone.

Did she have a tracking device implanted up my ass? If I were her I'd never in a million years think to look for me with Rasheed's momma of all people.

The sad part was that I couldn't even sit down and rationalize with Honey. What she and Rasheed did was between them. I didn't get Honey locked up, but she was so hell-bent on revenge and avenging Rah's murder that she couldn't see the forest for the trees. She could visit Taya, call her, talk to her, but as long as she was a wanted felon, giving Lataya up was not an option.

We'd pulled into an oversized garage filled with four-wheelers, dirt bikes on one side, tools, toolboxes, and a couple of motorcycles on the other.

Assuming this is his place, no one will ever find us here that's for sure.

"I've got four guest rooms upstairs that I never use. This is the kitchen." He pointed quietly so as to not wake up Trey, before turning on the alarm at a panel on the wall.

I nodded and followed along, carrying Lataya's car seat. There were several doors that were bathrooms on the first floor before a laundry room that also somehow connected to the kitchen. I was just relieved when I saw stairs. It meant I could finally lay my tired ass down.

After seeing the kids tucked in I told Devon I'd be fine sleeping with them after I showered. They would most likely wake up and have a fit at being in a new place otherwise. I wanted to be nearby.

We were standing in the hallway outside a bathroom. The recess lighting was dimmed enough to keep you from running into the cream-colored walls in the middle of the night. Devon pulled me into a hug and was telling me everything would be fine. And there it was, that cardamom, warm vanilla, masculine scent that was all him. Devon started to draw back but I didn't want to let go. I needed to be comforted and I needed to hear exactly what he was saying. His warmth and closeness . . . *ten, nine, koalas' fingerprints* . . . I couldn't mentally block myself this time. Instead I directed all that fear, anxiety, and panic into pulling him back, burying my face into his neck and letting him hold me. I was probably squeezing the breath out of his lungs and he didn't complain or protest. His hands stroked methodically up and down my back until I relaxed against him, drawing in deep, even, Devon-scented breaths.

I wanted that smell all over my skin, like his T-shirt I secretly slept in every night since we'd met. I loved my babies to death but I was tired of technically sleeping by myself. My brain decided to shut down that section that thinks and worries too much. All thrusters set to go and umpteen thousand volts of pent-up "get him, girl" energy surged in between my legs. I'd worry about tomorrow, tomorrow.

Lightly pressing my lips against the side of his neck, I paused, waiting to see if he'd object. I had to know what that smell tasted like and I flecked my tongue over his skin. He drew in a sharp, quick breath and my own breathing sped up. I lifted my head, waiting for my kiss, because that's how it works. He let me hover there not more than a breath away. Thinking he was playing some kind of game, I frowned and started to pull away and he shook his head at me. Those oversized hands of his slid down my hips, igniting my skin underneath my jeans. When he roughly palmed my ass I gasped.

Our lips weren't more than a hair apart and that's where he kept me, suspended on the edge. One of his fingers slid a little lower than the rest. Instinctively I arched, wanting to feel more of it, grinding against him and he smiled teasing me. We were in some kind of psychological war that I didn't know the rules for.

I reached down the front of his slacks and we bit our bottom lips at the same time. It wasn't too big and it wasn't invisible. He was perfect and I was so excited I forgot all about his Jedi mind fuck or whatever he was trying to prove. I started stroking him through the fabric of his pants and he closed his eyes and moaned in response. That's what I was used to: being able to break a man down with one hand. All the staring games to see who blinks first or breaks first, that wasn't my territory. It was the thrill of making anyone, man or woman, bend, melt, cave in, react at my will. For the first time in my life, I said, *fuck it,* and I made the first move.

Soft red and yellow lights refracted off the ceiling and walls. Walking into the bedroom was like getting away from the city and standing beside a gently churning creek in the forest. I'd seen them in the lobbies of hotels and restaurants but never in someone's house. There were two massive marble wall fountains that had to be at least six feet tall on either side of the bed. Water slowly trickled down the slate, rust, and auburn-colored surface gently splashing into the basin at the bottom.

"Devon, that's crazy . . . beautiful," I whispered, awe-struck.

He walked over and posed beside one and my jaw dropped. All this fool's clothes had vanished, and he was crazy beautiful too. The bedroom door was wide open and I shook my head. Poor thing definitely wasn't used to having kids around.

"You gonna need to close that, lock it, too." I pointed at the door and undressed.

We met in the middle of the bedroom, our naked bodies collided, and his skin felt like smooth, searing heat and muscle over steel. He kissed me and a surge of intense want and need went through me. Biting his bottom lip I moaned and reached down to stroke him into action but he stopped me.

"No. I've already figured out Michelle's problem. Michelle always wants to be in control." He went to get something from underneath the bed. I stood there completely confused and suddenly a little nervous.

It was hard to see with the meager light from the fountain so I had no idea what he had until he'd slipped some kind of Velcro handcuffs around my wrists. In a single motion he simply lifted my arms and had my wrists attached to a little thingamajigger hanging from the ceiling before I could even say the word thingamajigger. It was low enough that my feet were still planted firmly on the floor.

"Devon?" His name was a whispered plea from my lips.

Aww hell, I've gone and done it now. Sure, Michelle, go home with the resident Dr. Psycho serial killer and decide to do something you never do. Oh worry about tomorrow, tomorrow. What the fuck about tonight?

When he didn't answer me I became a human cocktail of random emotions. It consisted of about 2 parts scared, with equal amounts of frantic and pissed as I started yanking at my wrists. There might have been a dash of hope somewhere in there but it wasn't enough to keep me calm. "Devon? What the fuck is this? We ain't even on this kind of level. I don't even know who else's wrists been in these nasty-ass things. I will kick the fuck out of you, just step over here. I swear if you don't let me out," I hissed at him swingin' one of my legs in his direction for emphasis. He easily side-stepped it.

He started laughing. "I do my sit-ups with that. My ankles go in there."

I scoffed and he moved behind me, pulling me back until I could feel his skin pressed against every inch of mine. He wrapped his arm around my waist, filling his hands with my breasts, spreading out his fingers so they touched all but my nipples. When he placed himself in between my legs, my pussy turned traitor to my brain and she throbbed, aching for more attention. It was all the sweetest torture and not being able to do anything, or anticipate what he was going to do next, was making me feel crazy.

"You are so beautiful to me. Do you know, I thought about you every day until I saw you again?" His words were a warm caress against the back of my neck.

My eyes closed and I rested my head back on his shoulder. I rocked slightly, rolling my ass back into his hips, simultaneously sliding the length of him against my clit, and I all but purred. My eyes damn near crossed when he rolled my nipples in between the heat of his fingers. Without any warning he pressed upward. Clamping his hand over my mouth he buried every inch of himself so deep I instinctively bit into the fleshy part of his palm. If it weren't for his hand I would have screamed.

Damn, I must have forgotten what this felt like. Try to swear off what for how long? My knees felt shaky as hell. Devon was stroking it so good I'd have been on the floor if I weren't attached to the ceiling. Devon had me up off the floor and I didn't even know what that shit was called, but I just wrapped the back of my legs around his thighs and held on. I did my best to be quiet but it'd been a minute and I was right there. My pussy started to clench up, and I held my breath because I knew I'd yell or scream. All the pressure, and aching, was building up in that one spot and he then just stopped.

What the fuckin' fuck kind of bullshit . . .

"Devon, please," I begged him.

He reached above my head and undid my hands and carried me over to the bed. I was breathless, shaky, and getting more pissed off by the second. He smiled down at me and I couldn't see why. I wanted to explain that he was supposed to let me finish before he did all that damn cheesing. Then I saw the light; how many colors are in a fireworks display? Devon kissed his way up my body like he was saying hello all over again, and then he went in. Like "choking me so good I forgot I changed my last name" went in. "I'm marrying this Nigga" went in. I'd already made up my damn mind and everything.

Exhausted, I snuggled into his side and started falling asleep, listening to the water splash in the fountains beside us. I had to admit that shit was extremely relaxing, and sexy.

"You and the kids will stay with me for now. I've got more than enough room and I feel like it's time to have my life disrupted by two little people and their mother's craziness." Devon's voice loomed in the darkness.

I quietly rolled his words over in my head. *How would a new house and a new person affect the kids? Especially Trey? Could I actually trust this man with my kids under his roof?*

Releasing a long, drawn-out sigh, I looked up at him, trying to figure out his character, worth, and values at a glance. It was one thing when it came to me; it was a completely different matter when the kids were concerned. I considered getting Jim Bartow and the security team but that shit had cost me an arm and a leg and at the end of the day more people had died, Honey had lived, and I still wound up getting abducted.

Suddenly anxious from thinking about Honey I squeezed Devon. I needed to get settled into a routine with the kids and fast. The image of Momma's front door kicked in quickly made me switch from long-term safe to right-now safe.

"I don't like being told what to do." I huffed against his chest.

Devon shifted and leaned over me. "I can always make you beg."

He was giving me a sly, sneaky grin and I quickly shook my head. I was too damn tired for any more of that; he'd completely worn me out.

Chapter 15

All Good-byes Ain't Gone

"My nigga? Man, I know you ain't cryin'."

I climbed in the car and Angelo was sniffling like a little bitch. He called himself mannin' up or whatever, flying through the city on some Nascar shit. If I had to hem this fool up and get behind the wheel so be it. My ass was Makavelli right now. We couldn't afford any heat from a speeding ticket.

"Rah, man, she was fuckin' him. I mean, about to fuck him. Right there in broad daylight. Anyone could have walked in. I walked right in. Then the fuckin' bloggers, paparazzi walked right in like they were supposed to. No, I'm not . . . yes. Yes, I'm good, man."

Angelo slammed his hands against the steering wheel before wiping his nose on his sleeve. I looked away and focused my attention on my phone, acting like I didn't even see that nastiness. He wasn't taking this as well as I thought he would.

I asked him, "When I was locked up, I sent you kite. And if I recall correctly, my exact words to you in that letter was that—"

"Your exact words were that I had what you'd call an' anybody getta. That I shouldn't feel special for having her because anybody could get her. And, Honey would fuck me over if I wasn't careful," Angelo sounded off. He squared up his shoulders like he was getting some of his bravado back.

"Right, right. Remember, I told you, she did the same bullshit to me. Had me thinkin' she was locked up with my seed, knowing her ass was Triple H. I'm just glad you seen it before you wifed her up." I dapped him on the shoulder. The kid definitely needed to toughen the hell up before we hit these streets hard and moved into VA.

He snickered, glancing over at me through his pretty boy shades. "Triple H, man, what the hell is this, a code for somethin'? I'm lost," he muttered in his Guido Italian-American "run all the words together" accent.

"Triple H? You know, three Hs? Honey the homie humper. That's her MO, her title. She went from me, to my boy, to my other boy. Need to get her some embroidered panties wit' a big-ass H on them shits like a . . . a damn super she-ho." I slapped the dashboard, cracking up.

I could see Honey's little ass bustin' up in bedrooms. Her hands on her hips, wearing one of her barely there lace pieces from the Hot Spot and some knee-high boots. That image sent me through a slideshow of forgotten memories. Memories that I thought died the day Michelle turned her back on me and walked out of that prison. Smiles, steak sauce, hotel rooms, Trey's first word, and—

"What about your boy Big though? You needs to let me get Dirty Moe or Bad Apple Sims to handle him," Angelo pressed impatiently, pulling me from my somber thoughts.

"Angelo, man, I know y'all probably talk about us wit' our nicknames but, what is it with these names Bad Apple Sims, my dude? What the hell?"

Frustrated, Angelo jabbed his fingers through his hair. "Honey used to say the sa . . . They're twins. We kept getting them mixed up. Then one of 'em pushes his own grandmother down the stairs. It was over like twenty bucks or somethin'. Pennies really. He did hard time behind it, too. Came out tatted up and we could look at him and see he was different. But, when he went in it was just so absurd. Like, kid, your own grandmother though, really? Everyone kept saying, 'that's one bad apple.' So now we have Sims and Bad Apple Sims, and he can handle Big Baby for half of what anyone else would cost. And he can do it just as good."

I definitely didn't need TV or the Internet with Angelo around.

"Ah, man, Big, he ain't know better. He thinks I'm dead like everybody else. It's guy code. Man law. I'm out the picture. I mean, who could blame him? She cute, probably called him 'daddy' wit' the baby voice. Y'all gave her that fame power. She still got that fat ass?"

"Shut the fuck up already! It ain't power it's quicksand. Had she stayed in line, she'd have floated. She acted up and started moving around, trying to creep and be a sneaky whore. She stirred up the muck and now she's gettin' pulled under by her own actions."

Angelo swerved across the lane and I let it go. Ain't nobody tell him to go pull that whole bended-knee routine. All it did was made him feel worse when the real deal came to light. I'd been in that boat myself. My baby momma found out and stole my paddles, life jacket, and she drilled holes in it, knowing my ass couldn't swim. In my little black book payback was definitely a bitch, and her name was Michelle.

They put niggas in prison not realizing it's concentrated criminology, gangland, and law school combined. You learn who's who, how to do what better, smarter, and more efficiently, because if there's one thing we all have down to a science it's how to get caught.. When I found out Honey was mixed up with the Miami Italians, I heard an easy way out. There was so much talk about Angelo bein' nothing but a pussy-whipped shadow of his father.

They called his ass "the joke wit' good coke in Miami." Shit, it ain't take me long to realize the perfect storm would knock his boat right out the water and into my dry dock of a jail cell.

I planted small seeds, sent him a letter telling him about Honey and how she was messing with my master at arms. He was like second in command of my team and my best friend, Derrick. Mind you I was just lookin' to earn his trust so I could push product inside. Imagine my shock and awe when I found out Honey was on a vigilante mission to get me out. So I did the unthinkable. I let old boy know if I escaped, his first mate Honey would jump ship. It was a no-brainer to a calculatin' nigga like myself. I got Angelo on the phone and flat-out told him what the dudes inside thought about his cartel, his fam, shit, kids he ain't even had yet. Dead ass, I even put a couple of Guidos on the phone for validation. He was probably heartbroken, hugged his pillow, cried, I don't know.

But, if there's one thing I did know, you never dead-end a man's ego without offering him a road to redemption. In return for my freedom, I'd be Angelo's redeemer, his savior, so to speak.

He got the official braggin' rights for murkin' my ass; it was a start. It only cost me a few teeth and a burnt-up body. Now all we needed to do was erase the Angel of Death's shadow and handle business. Yeah, payback's a bitch all right, but I was about to play her and everybody else so hard for this paper. My new fake ID needed to say Parker & Parker. The game I was about to run would put the Parker Brothers to shame and make me five times richer. No more living hand to mouth, hustling to get rich. Angelo's people rolled in that old-world money that got inherited and trust-funded.

I met a few dudes on the inside who told me how some of the biggest movie production companies began with startup money from Angelo's pops. This kid didn't even have a row of the Rubik's Cube figured out. In my book he wasn't anything more than a glorified distributor.

"Get your head together. The best way to get over a ho is to get under a better one. You need to throw a party. Invite only, password to get in is 'wet dream.'"

He started to protest but I kept going; this was my show. "Make sure all the somebodies who push product are there, including your pops. I don't care if you pay him to show up; just make sure he's there. I'll handle the rest. Drop me off at the barber shop. I need to get cleaned up for this shit."

Back home I could walk in any shop from Campostella to Five Points, E.O.V. to Berkley Commons, sit down and they'd do a nigga right. Out here was a different story. I went in the shop looking for the dude who hooked me up last week and he done bounced, phone cut off and everything. The new cat looked sketchy as hell but we had that party so I tested it out.

Sitting in the barber chair I planned and ran through every way all the roads could intersect. The record in my head kept skipping and my first order of business quickly became finding a new barber. This nigga kept fuckin' up my train of thought by putting his stank pinky on my upper lip to balance the clippers. When he wasn't doing that he was completely disregarding all the personal-space boundaries every man is supposed to abide by no matter what. He was straddling my legs or pressing his meat up against my forearm. My head was on my shoulders; how hard was it to reach across and cut? I shifted so many times it was a wonder my shit wasn't fucked up by the time he was done. I'd go back inside the joint to get a trim or edge-up before I'd go back to this dude. The only reason he even got a tip was because I didn't fuck with a working man's paper. I told any and every one that. You always take care of the working man.

I still managed to walk up out that barber shop feeling clean as hell. Violated yes, but I was still ready to get my Denzel on. Know you can't tell a dude nothing when he got a fresh cut and edge-up hair smelling like Motions oil sheen.

I had Angelo run me past a flower shop. I wanted to get real flowers, not the ones from the grocery store that come in them flimsy bags like some penny goldfish. Twenty minutes and $135 later I climbed back in the car with a damn bush of purple orchids.

"Aww, Rah, you got me flowers." Angelo batted his eyes at me, laughing.

"Shut the hell up, and take me to the crib."

I'd been put up in a condo not far from his. His family owned the building so most of the tenants were connected or they came from stupid money. I kept to myself and they assumed I was a rapper or a basketball player, paying me no mind.

"Hey man, you look out and get me lots of cheerleader's numbers right?" The door man Ernesto grinned up at me. I just chuckled at him and shook my head as I walked past him into the building. Looking down at the flawless black marble flooring I checked my reflection outside the door. I could smell baked chicken with gravy and yams coming all up out the condo and my stomach growled.

"Oh, Rasheed, these are beautiful, baby!" Shiree gasped, her eyes brightening up at my gift.

I puffed out my chest and smiled. "I picked 'em out myself."

She closed her eyes and buried her nose in them and I let her have her moment before taking them out of her hand and pulling her in close.

She put her hands underneath my shirt and raked her nails along the skin on my sides. I loved that shit. My boxers and jeans were getting more uncomfortable by the second. Shiree had a way of looking at me. Her eyes would turn into these deep, loving pools of chocolate syrup. I know I ain't the most emotionally expressive person in the world but that look would make a nigga chest tight. I'd have to look away or drown on dry land from staring.

Shiree came to see me and apologized months after Michelle's confession. They'd thought Big gave her an STD so on some revenge shit they set her up with my pistol. Truth is, his dick game was wack and on top of that he was playin' her. She just went along for the money. She felt like shit for takin' part in it and even used some of her paper to get me a lawyer to help appeal my case. He did what all them legal liars do and took her money, but I appreciated her effort. She'd sat there goin' to pieces over me, and what they'd all done. Now, I'd tear through anyone with nothing but my bare hands if they fucked with her.

I nibbled her bottom lip and let it go. "I missed you."

She ran the tip of her tongue across mine. "You didn't miss me. You missed big Shirley." She rolled her eyes. "You betta tell her how much you missed her."

I hoped whatever she had in the oven was off or had a ways to go. As soon as she got that aggressive tone I got rock solid. There's nothing wrong with being a soft, yielding woman but nobody wants to be playin' keep-away with your grown ass all the time.

"Dick me down now, daddy." Go ahead, say it. I'll give you time to practice. Now, ask any man out there what the most beautiful sound to the human ear is. Remember you're asking a man, so it ain't a symphony in whatever minor or any of that other foolishness. Those words are it and the "daddy" at the end is optional.

I kissed her, sucking on her bottom lip hard. She tasted like Riesling and pineapples. I reached down and lifted her sundress, laughing when she ain't even have on panties.

"You think you slick, huh."

She shrugged in response and bit her bottom lip, waiting for me to continue. She was already slippery wet and ready. I parted her lips and watched her eyes barely flutter closed while my finger hovered over her clit, barely touching her.

"Go get me some peppermint tea and daddy'll take care of you."

She squealed and took off for the kitchen, clothes and ass cheeks flying everywhere.

I'd gotten off my shoes, pants, and boxers. My shirt was barely over my head when my eyes crossed and toes curled. Shiree dragged her nails across my bare ass with one hand and cupped my balls with the other. She had a mouthful of me and hot tea, as she slurped, tightening her lips around my dick, pulling me farther down her throat. I yanked my shirt over my head and watched her work. Knowing Shiree, she'd already had that shit on standby and it was beautiful.

I growled, pulling her up, bending her over the couch. Looking back at me with her head down on the back of the couch and her thumbnail in her mouth she gave me a little evil grin. She knew she was in trouble and loved it. I drank some of the tea, letting it warm the inside of my mouth before swallowing it. I didn't swallow the next sip. I leaned over her back so my dick was rock solid right in the crack of her ass and I slid a hot kiss down her spine. She moaned and pressed back into me. I took another sip, spread her ass open, and ran my tongue from her tailbone down to her asshole and dove in. She moaned like she was possessed, locking her ankles behind my back locking me in. Peppermint tea and ass eatin', be careful how and when you use that shit. If you've ever wondered what makes perfectly normal women turn into crazy, "kill your ass if you try to leave" psychos, there's your answer.

When the tea got down to room temperature that meant it was time to handle business. Shiree grabbed the back of the couch for leverage and threw all that ass back at me. I tensed and started thinking about how many grams it takes to make an ounce. How many ounces mak—

"You fuckin' me or am I fuckin' you huh?" she shot back at me, sounding all breathless.

I exhaled. My body back under control, I leaned down and pressed my chest against her back so she could feel my skin against hers. Grabbing her hips for leverage I pulled out and went in so slow and so deep she looked like she'd stopped breathing.

"I'm fuckin' you, baby," I told her quietly.

See, Shiree always fucked with these short-stroke, "no dick game" niggas she could out sex in the bedroom. All she needed was to sense a weak moment, and I'd have to remind her who was in charge less she go trying to pull a damn plastic dick out on a nigga. I have to admit, every now and again that shit did get to feeling good as all hell. But, I never slipped up though, to hell with that. I'd just pull some fuck-crobatics on her. Flip that ass over, give her one of them deep "I love you" kisses and go-go gadget drill-her until she'd tap out. Literally.

Chapter 16

All Over a Wet Pigeon

The spot Angelo found for the party was on some next-level shit. It looked like a meatpacking plant from the street view. But once you got inside it was perfect. Four themed levels broke up into smaller areas. It had pool tables, two areas that we were gonna use as dance floors, and a bar. I saw an investment opportunity. The place would make a killing as an after-hours spot. I made a note to check into the property owner.

I wasn't exactly sure what kind of turnout we'd have so I got there mad early to get everything set up. If Angelo did his homework like he was supposed to, we shouldn't have a problem. I kept it simple, balancing some black leather Giuseppe Zanottis with a blazer and some Balmain jeans. Shiree was all over me when I tried to get out the door so I know I looked good and smelled even better. She refused to not work and I loved that about her. Shiree wasn't the type to take handouts or live off a nigga. I refused to let her get back on a stage. We compromised and she found work doing hair and makeup for a major modeling agency. She had to be at a shoot tonight out at the beach with some dude who wore more makeup than she did. I let her do her thing, get that money.

Everybody who goes inside the way I did, usually come out broke. Not your boy. One day out in the yard I seen this dude scaring the hell out of a cat. He was a big, ugly somebody with one of those crazy brashes. A brash is a beard so long it could brush his ass. "Trying to collect cat piss," was what he said when he saw me staring him down. It was prison; people did all kinds of weird shit so I ain't ask why. The cat he was scaring to death was one I'd been feedin' scraps to. Since she liked me I knew what spots she liked to mark. I helped him set up bottle caps to collect piss with and he asked if I wanted to get high as his way of saying thanks. Me and this crazy white dude, who went by the name Scorpion, was tight after that.

Lo and behold him and his boys were making their own versions of powder by cuttin' down and refining the stuff that came in off the street. Cat piss was only one of the additives they used to tweak and mix shit down. They had a makeshift lab rigged up with butane lighter Bunsen burners, and soda bottles for beakers. I'd never seen anything like it. You walk up to a dude to buy an eight ball or whatever and then he turns around and asks you what you wanna feel? I remember standing there like, "Um, high."

There's levels to that shit like the levels to medicinal marijuana. There's clean high, which is your normal coke. Then there was the extreme left-field stuff like face melter, mind warp, wormhole, chest expander, and body rock. None of those were for amateurs. I'd sent some samples out to test the water and let's just say I'ma leave all that to the dudes inside. We don't need no more zombie apocalypse scares. Then you have lines like the phantom limb, where random body parts go numb or magically manifest. One cat swore up and down he had a damn tail. It was funny as hell but, I'm sorry prison is not the place to run around thinking you gotta ghost appendage attached to your ass. Heaven's gate was on some "so beautiful I'd never do it again" type shit. Have you seeing angels and talking to God.

Scorpion helped me tweak the fuck out of this one line though. I called my new baby Indican wet dream and she wasn't nothing but the truth.

"Rah, yous already here. Lookin' Ginsu sharp." Angelo walked in with a smug smile on his face. He was boasting like a boxer before the big fight, walking around the ring with his arms spread out yelling at the empty room.

"What you think, it's like Kitchen Stadium up in here or what? We's gonna flambé these bitches tonight Bobby Flay style."

The smile instantly fell off my face. "We gonna what? No. Don't ever say that again. Where the couches and them chaise things I asked for? We only got a couple of hours."

"My bad, dude. Honey used to keep me watching the damn Food Network . . ."

I glared, and looked for something, anything to throw at this kid.

"Okay, chaise lounges, I'm on it. Password wet dream."

Four hours later we were all set up and every major anybody who did anything started making their way in.

"Yo, what's up with me telling them a password and then you don't even make 'em use it?"

I didn't tell Angelo everything because just like a woman he'd ask too many inconsequential questions. I'd end up pissed off and not answering anyway, and we'd still end with the same outcome. I just sipped my Henny and Coke waiting for the crowd to peak, hoping Don Cerzulo would actually put in an appearance. Some of the finest women in Miami showed up fighting with each other to get our attention. I ain't gonna say I settled, but I could look at every last one of them and know they weren't worth half of my Shiree. She came to me when I was dirty, broke down, and hopeless. Stayed with me, gave me hope, and I refused to mess that up. I decided to text her to pass the time.

Hey, you. I stared at the screen. Secretly I was waiting to see exactly how long she'd take to respond.

Hey, baby. Is everything going okay?

When she replied immediately, I was relieved. If she was texting me then she damn sure wasn't fucking somebody else. Yeah, I put it down, treated her like my queen and all that but I'd done a lot of wrong in my time, told a lot of lies to a lot of women. It was hard for me to completely let my guard down. I was a changed dude, but I damn sure ain't want to go all in and throw on the blinders called love and then have someone runnin' game on my non-seeing ass. I tried to think of something cute that would make her smile.

Everything's good. Up here waitin' when I rather be home with my heart.

Again she hit me right back. Aww. Well your heart is still at work, baby. This shoot is running over. I'm on standby for touchups.

I read that shit twice and looked at my watch. It was damn near midnight. Shiree hadn't worked late in a minute. On second thought she hadn't even been flying out for any shoots with the girls. At one point it seemed like she was working late or hopping on a jet almost every other week. All that stopped once I got her locked down though . . . or so I thought.

My fingers were going a mile a minute. Why you ain't get somebody else to fill in? It's late. What time you gonna be home?

I waited and after five minutes I'd finished my drink and ordered another one. Angelo was all over the place like a Chinese spinning top and I was getting more irritated by the second. The first floor was packed, standing room only, and that was my cue. I signaled the DJ and the music lowered as I made my way up to the second floor. Reality nodded, opening the solid metal door that led to my showroom. Reality was one of the guys I'd recruited for the night's security. A dreaded, six feet six-ish, purple-black brick wall of a motherfucka controlled my door. If anyone tried to act stupid they'd get a Reality check.

The guests were all being told to consider using their password carefully. Once they came upstairs there was no going back downstairs or changing their mind. You'd be surprised how many people in this lifestyle hear something like that and push forward all gung-ho and shit. They'd seen and done everything so if you've got a novelty, you'd better use it to your fullest advantage. The first wave came in and stood under the black light, gripped in a state of frightened anticipation. To add some dramatic flair I'd found a Phantom of the Opera mask that covered half my face. The second floor was nothing like the club we had downstairs. Couches, chaise lounges, and oversized pillows were from one end of the room to the other. I opened a case covered in black velvet and the black light made the vials inside glow. One was incandescent pink and the other was bright blue. The room broke out in ooh's and aah's.

"Choose tonight's experience. Would you like to have a wet dream or become a wet dream?" I asked them, feeling like a damn ring master.

They came up and started making their selections. Wet dream was the prison favorite and the most hated. For a woman it was the equivalent of turning on every sexually arousable nerve ending in her body. That's how Shiree described it anyway. She said even her toes felt like they could actually cum if I touched 'em just right. It's a sexually explosive buildup that'd have you hangin' on a door humpin' the hell out of a doorknob. All the while it's feeling like you got ten niggas with ten dicks with lips on each dick going to town.

There honestly wasn't any difference between that pink shit and the blue one. As a businessman I just knew you always need an option, and it's always a plus if it's pink. Women tend to gravitate toward anything pink. So it honestly didn't matter who picked what.

"Come over here and play with me, sexy. I like the mask."

Grinning at my handy work I quickly peeled a topless Dominican chick off my chest, shaking my head at her. The no was more for the head in my pants than for her.

You stay down, boy. Yes, I seen them pretty-ass dark exotic nipples too but we can't play.

It was all going exactly as planned. I checked my phone and still no response from Shiree. Angelo was nowhere to be seen. Making my way up to the third deck I spotted him on a couch with two brunettes and shook my head. I specifically told him to wait until after we handled business. Of course Reality would hit me at that exact moment to let me know Don Cerzulo was on the way up. I made sure the third floor was completely empty before posting G and Fallon outside the door. Stuffing the mask behind the bar, I checked my reflection in the mirror.

Oh well, all or nothing, this is it.

"I don't think we've met, Don Cerzulo, I'm—"

"Not my son. Where is Angelo?" He dismissed me and looked around suspiciously.

"Angelo is downstairs, sir. I was going to partner with him but seeing as how he's in the middle of a naked orgy with the customers and we haven't done any business, I'd like to rethink my options. It seems as though you might be the better businessman?" I waited.

"You don't have anything I don't already have. Whatever it is I can get it."

"What I'm selling you don't have and can't get because I created it," I replied smugly, setting two vials of wet dream on the bar underneath the black light.

Don Cerzulo rubbed his chin and took a seat on the sofa facing the bar. He stared at them, frowning, tilting his head from side and then to the other. I wasn't sure what the protocol was for something like this so I went behind the bar to freshen up my drink while he stared or whatever.

"What the fuck kind of laser-light show cockamamie magic shamrock shit is this? You take me for a fucking fool?" Don Cerzulo's breath was a hot hiss into my ear.

I had to give him his props. He was quick and freakishly quiet on them old feet of his. His pistol was pressed hard up against my junk and I could feel a lonely tear burning in the corner of my eye.

"It ain't a joke. I learned to make it locked up in VA. My name is Rasheed White; your son fake killed me for street cred. Tomorrow, every dealer in the area is gonna be lookin' for me or wet dream because right now they on the second floor fucked up and fuckin', and I need my dick and a truckload of shit to sell them."

"Atta boy, no man alive'll lie on his Johnson. Fix me a gin and tonic. How much are we talkin' about?" Don Cerzulo dropped his gun and walked back over to the couch.

"Two mill for my time and the supplies and one major supplier. Guarantee I'll have your investment back to you with interest faster than a hummingbird fuck." I handed him his drink and took a seat, quickly sipping from mine to calm my jacked-up nerves.

"Gotta sample it. You do half first to make sure you ain't trying to poison me."

After the stunt he just pulled I wasn't about to tell him that we shouldn't be doing this shit together. But, Don

Cerzulo was not the kind of guy you hesitated around when it came to business; it made you look sketchy. I uncapped a vial and lifted it to my nose, inhaling quickly. The powder numbed my nostril, making my eyes water.

"Let me just tell you now, Don, shit hits harder than woodpecker lips, my dude."

I handed it to Don Cerzulo as the hairs on my head began to pulsate, sending throbbing vibrations down my back that made my eyes feel like they were dancing in my skull.

"We're gonna need to get a girl up in here, man. Trust me."

I stuck my head out the door with my body throbbing and I looked G and Fallon up and down. Fallon had scuff marks on his shoes and a ketchup stain on the bottom of his shirt. If he ain't care about his appearance, who knew what kind of women he'd come back with.

"G, go find me some girls." I relayed the quick order and popped back into the room, trying to stay as far away from Don Cerzulo as possible. I'd seen dudes do some fucked-up shit to each other inside, all because they touched and had a "it felt good" moment. No, sir, his old ass was not about to have me *Brokeback Mountain* up in this bitch. I made the mistake of looking in his direction and almost gagged. He was in the chair with his eyes closed, doing some kind of geriatric air humps. Sounding like a drunk gorilla.

The girls came in just in time and Don Cerzulo almost jumped out of the chair he was so excited. I busied myself on the other side of the bar, rubbing my junk along the counter with my eyes closed, thinking about Shiree. My phone vibrated in my pocket and the sensation traveled all the way up the back of my neck.

Do I ever ask you when your ass is coming home? No. So don't ask me.

That was her answer, damn near an hour later, and that's what she had to say. What the hell had she really been doing?

"Why you over here all by yourself, sexy face?"

I didn't even argue when she unzipped my jeans, wrapping her pretty lips all around me. And she was a hummer. A song came on downstairs and she got into it humming with the faint music. Even high as hell my conscience was fuckin' with me. I kept hearing Shiree's voice; it detracted from the mean sucking and slurping effects this chick was making.

"Yo, ma, you gotta stop." My words came out in a painful groan.

"Mmmm, Mr. Pretty Dick, does that mean you ready to fuck?"

She still hand my dick in a viselike grip and I gritted my teeth trying to hold back.

"I know you're not done already. What's the matter, your girl got wack head?" Don Cerzulo called out from over his shoulder. He had his chick bent over the couch. The chick on her knees in front of me turned to see who the hell was calling her head game wack. In the process of her turning her hair swept across me like a thousand fingers and that combined with her hand sent me over the edge. I exploded with a growl, clutching the counter behind me to keep my balance and she screamed.

"Eeew, you got it in my ear. Really? Arrrgh. It's in my ear!"

Don Cerzulo hooted, "Wet dream? You need to call it wet pigeon. I ain't wet pigeoned a broad since grade school. My partner, the wet pigeoner. I likes this kid; meet me here tomorrow, three p.m., two million."

All I could hear over my heart beating in my ears was Don Cerzulo telling his girl to get up so he could wet pigeon her, and Shiree, yelling.

Pulling my phone out of my pocket I squinted at the bright white letters that said Call in progress 00:6:48 and still counting. I didn't even bother lifting it up to my ear.

Chapter 17

Tell Me Somethin' Good

After my night with Devon I woke up practically singing. He seemed like such a good man and he was so easy to get along with. Even though he had no sense when it came to kids, I giggled at that haunted hayride fiasco. He even challenged Trey to an ice cream eating contest when he got off work. I'd have to run interference on that one, because the last thing I'd be doing is playing nurse to two bellyaches. I made his bed and straightened up wondering if I could ever think of it as *our* bed. It was kind of soon yes but, all these kinds of things made me think about having a real, normal life again. Not always running around scared of everything and everyone. I missed that and there was only one person keeping me from it and it wasn't Honey. She couldn't be my boogey-man forever.

Devon had already made breakfast and left for work. That one was still a jaw dropper. He got up and actually cooked real food from scratch, not some microwave heat-up crap. He'd brought me chocolate chip pancakes, turkey bacon, strawberries, and two little people covered from head to toe in flour. All I could see were Lataya's eyes. I was shocked they didn't have a fit and come screaming and kicking the door down when they woke up in a new place. Devon asked if they wanted to make Mommy breakfast and they were all in.

He'd called to tell me he rode past Momma's house and it looked like someone had already put the door back up. Mona or one of Momma's neighbors must've done it, I couldn't think of anyone else. The kids had enough clothes in the bags I always kept in my car to last for at least a month so I wasn't too worried about anything we had in the house. After lunch I decided to get the kids dressed and take them to see Momma. I was sure she'd enjoy having Trey there, and she probably secretly missed her "imposter crumb snatcher," too. She was still in the intensive care unit and giving all the male nurses hell, grabbing their asses and making kissy faces at them. When she wasn't doing that she was complaining: it was either too cold, or the food ain't have any flavor, the blanket was scratchy, the lady on the other side of the room sounded like she was getting more channels. It might be good for her to see a few familiar faces. Maybe she'd hurry up and get better.

"You just stick me in here like a potato plant, waiting for me to sprout roots to this bed," Momma whined pitifully as soon as we walked in.

"Hey, G-ma." Trey climbed up in her bed, geared up to show her his new iPad. That thing was Devon's idea not mine. Trey picked it up and Devon told him go for it, saying some mess about extra ones for the hospital. Yeah, well I hope he had an extra, extra one. I could just see it falling and cracking all over one of the many tiled floors in that house or outside on the sidewalk. But, he insisted and it'd been fused to Trey's hands ever since.

"Hey Grandma, suga'. I could just eat ya all up, nam nam nam."

She was making chomping noises and he was squealing, but still determined to show off his new present.

"What in the world is this? An i-what?"

I let them have their time and I wandered off to see if I could find Devon.

"No. I can't come see you. It's not because of anyone, it's because I don't want to. You'll survive I'm sure. I honestly don't care what she thinks."

I found Devon in a corner of the admittance desk having an intensely heated conversation.

I'd started to back away. I didn't want to get caught eavesdropping.

"Mommy, G-ma gave me money for the smack machine."

Trey slammed into my leg going a mile a minute about the snack machine? I was pretty sure that's what he meant. Normally I would have corrected him, but Lataya's car seat was getting heavy and I just wanted to disappear.

Devon called after me but I just wanted to get outside and get some fresh air. This shit was impossible; these men were damn impossible.

Was that a woman? And why was his ass whispering?

I walked out the front door trying to get my mind together. "We'll go get candy in a minute okay, Trey?"

I must have looked upset or something because he simply nodded, and he rarely did that. Devon would be out here in a minute and I needed to figure out what I'd say if I should ask anything, how to explain my reaction. It'd only been but a blink, here I was about to make myself look like one of those women who go all insane stalker over some good dick.

It was just a'ight dick anyway. Psssht. Whatever that shit was good.

Not in the mood for thinking I just took some breaths, cleared my mind. I'd read a pamphlet on his kitchen table that suggested you try breathing to alleviate stress, so here I was breathing instead of counting and I still felt stressed. At least counting down from ten kept me from thinking about all the other crazy shit going on in my head. So what if I never made it past eight. I just needed to slow my roll, not define anything; he did tell whoever she was he couldn't see her so that was a start.

And that's when I damn near had a real-live on-the-spot panic attack. We locked eyes as she walked past me. I couldn't believe she was alive even though I hadn't been sure she was dead to begin with.

"Hi, can't really talk. I've gotta get someone checked in," Towanna said and quickly walked by, dragging a young girl in handcuffs up the stairs toward the entrance.

The wind blew and I stood there staring at the back of her black windbreaker, slack-jawed and dazed. The girl stared back at me with demented crazy eyes and let out an eerie cackling sound of a laugh. I sighed. I really needed to figure out which pet cemetery or Indian burial ground they were sticking everyone in so I could go bless or whatever the hell you do to destroy those things. What was Towanna even doing in Virginia?

"Momeee, can we go to the smack machine now?" Trey piped up with his perfectly aggravating timing.

I walked back into Momma's room a complete flustered mess. Devon rushed in after me.

"It's so nice to see you two together all in love. I'm in love myself, with these murses," Momma announced with an ecstatic shimmy as she fanned herself peeking around for another nurse to harass. "Is it football season? 'Cause I've been watching tight ends all day. Whew, these male nurses running around here with these tight behinds, murses got my love oven getting moist and it ain't did that since—"

I turned to Devon. "Sweetie, can you please run Trey to the snack machine right quick before he asks again?"

He quickly obliged, happy to not have to hear whatever was about to come out of Momma's mouth.

"So you're feeling better, Momma White?" I sat down next to her on the hospital bed, noticing that for once she wasn't talking about predators, or body snatchers; she was her normal self. The woman I remembered meeting ages ago.

"Oh, I was lyin' here last night and I remembered so much, it was refreshing and hellishly scary. You ever rode a wild man or a rollercoaster backwards? It was like that." Momma nodded.

"It was like what, Momma, really?" I gawked at her and started blushing because I'd definitely ridden a wild man backwards, standing too.

"Child, I ever tell you what I did for the first three years after I had Rasheed?"

"No, ma'am. I don't even think Rah ever mentioned it."

She patted the pillow beside her. "That's because he ain't neva know. Get comfy."

Chapter 18

Momma's Maybe

Me and Ray always tried to find a way to see each other despite his parents foolishness. Even with the DNA test proving he was the daddy, his parents made him go through hell to get out the house to see me. One night he was walking me home. Sometimes it was just easier to visit him at work than to try to see him after hours. We heard all this noise. It was like a rusty trombone sounding off against an angry pirate. Hurt your ears something terrible. Frankie Diamonds was laying into some poor girl. He was stomping and beating her; blood was splattering all up against the side of that pretty Cadillac of his. Ray wasn't going to just stand by and watch something like that.

He marched over and asked Frankie what the problem was and of course Frankie put him off.

"You ain't gonna keep that nose if you keep sticking it in traps to see if they've snapped. This ain't got nothing to do you with you, young blood. Go tend to your woman before I decide to tend to her, too." Frankie Diamonds looked around Ray, blowing a kiss in my direction.

My baby whooped his ass right then and there. He went to help up the girl Frankie beat and she was pretty much at the point of just giving up. She wasn't going to *make it and she knew it. She told Ray where Frankie's clip was at in the car and he went for it. Came back across the street and showed me what had to be at least $30,000. Back then that was a lot of damn money. We decided we were gonna take that and move away together.*

A shout split the silence. "Them motherfucka's right there. They snatched my shit." Frankie's Cadillac pulled up at the end of the alley and we could hear him circle around. I took Rasheed; he was all I could carry and I ran like the devil was chasing me. I ran through front alleys, back alleys, slid through puddles, ducked around trash cans. I splashed through what I could only hope was mud or puddles.

"You'd better have a bank roll of bills strapped to that baby's ass or I'll kill everything you've ever known and that ain't a forecast, it's official," Frankie hissed at me as he climbed out of the Cadillac.

I wasn't fast enough and damn sure didn't hide well enough. Raising my chin and squaring up my shoulders I stepped out from behind the corner of the Dumpster where I'd been hiding.

"I don't have your money, so best you just g'on ahead and kill me then," I told him defiantly.

My head snapped around. I saw Frankie, brick, that dumpster, and then Frankie again. I could feel my cheek split open from the spot where his ring connected with the skin. He stood there in the alley with all of them diamonds glittering and glistening, sneering at me like I won't nothing but shit on the bottom of his shoe. Somebody'd gone and rubbed the lamp his daddy called a dick one day and this evil genie of a man floated into the world promising all of these riches and treasure, claiming he could make all your troubles go away. The only thing you had to sell was you.

He looked over at this tall, lanky black thang beside him. "What you think? Should I put her on the track, she look like she got thirty grand makin' snatch, plus my commission?"

They stared me up and down, assessing my street value while Rasheed whimpered in my arms.

"You down one ho anyway. Lexy ass is done for. Might as well make her work off that roll; the kid gonna be an issue. Dead that."

Even if Ray gave Frankie that money back I knew he'd still kill him, Rasheed, and Mona for taking it. Something like that wouldn't go unpunished and if word got out it'd make Frankie look weak. Police wouldn't do nothing about it except lock Ray up for stealing if I went to them. I did what I had to do to save my family.

"My sister can keep my baby. Put me on that track and I'll make you six figures. Please don't hurt anyone." I was out there begging for lives that ain't even know they were in danger, tears running down my face falling on Rasheed's. He stopped crying though.

"You make six figures and I'll give you my Caddy, throw in some girls and make you a damn partner shit." He laughed and jabbed the other guy with his elbow. "Tell Smoke where your sister stay and he'll take your brat to her. Understand one thing ho, my repumatation, yes you heard me right because I'm never wrong. My repumatation is imperial. I won't be known for peddlin' or maintainin' dirty sewer shit-stain pussy. Those are the kind of accusations I'd get if niggas saw or smelled yo' ripe alley cat lookin' ass right about now. I'm the hand of God as far as you're concerned, cross me and I

will smite thee. Your shift starts once you are cleaned up to my liking and you are on my clock."

That was the night Frankie the Ambassador Diamonds became my pimp, lover, husband, confidant, and my employer. When it was time to take me up out that alley and show me my new home he'd actually said out his mouth that I wasn't ready to ride in his car yet; that I'd funk and fuck up his interior. This nigga took every side street and back road through the city and I had to walk while he followed along beside me. He said it'd toughen up my feet, get me conditioned for long hours of standing. Teach me how to get out there and properly do that ho stroll.

It's a big deal when a pimp adds a new girl to his roster. All the other girls that want and chose to be there are instantly jealous and catty. There were eight women all cramped up in this small three-bedroom house. The master bedroom belonged to Frankie and the only way you got to sleep in there with him was when you were earning stupid money. It didn't make a lick of sense to me. If he had so much money why did he have us all up in this little-ass house and why would he want a ho that any dude could run up in on any given day? I never said that shit out loud though. Just kept it to myself.

Frankie had the girl he called his "bread winner" show me the ropes and explain how everything worked. His reasoning behind that was that if I was trained by a "bread winner" then maybe I'd become one. Royce was a pretty round-faced girl I heard him call her a black and tan. She had a nice brown skin complexion with long, shiny black hair. I didn't know what black and tans were but I was determined to figure it out one of those days.

"Hand jobs is ten dollars, blowjobs is twenty dollars, sex is fifty dollars. Always use a rubber and don't go

anywhere suspect with more guys than you can handle. Stay away from the other pimps or they'll think you're choosing. That means like you're looking for a new pimp. If you get locked up call Frankie, he gonna take it out cho' ass if he have to bail you out that's what happened to Lexy. Rule number one have Frankie's paper and rule number um, one don't get busted." She rattled off rules like she was reciting her bedtime prayers. I wanted to ask if both of the rules were number one because they were that important but I left it alone. Royce talked in a spaced out breathy little voice like she was in a galaxy far, far away.

Hours later I was out there with thoughts flying through my head, driving me crazy at around 145 mph. All I knew was that it was gonna be a helluva long way before I saw $30,000. My first hand job was easy as hell and after that I kept getting those left and right. Lacy walked over to ask my secret.

I shrugged. "I just stand there like y'all do and tell 'em it's ten dollars; ain't no secret."

She looked dumbfounded. "Ten dollars! Ho, is you crazy? Hand jobs are twenty dollars. Frankie is gonna have your ass if he finds out the only reason you makin' any money is because you out here giving discounts on your first damn day." She rolled her neck at me.

I almost popped her smart ass in the mouth for threatening to rat me out, and Royce for telling me the wrong prices. Spacey or not, she only did that shit because she was ruthless and wanted to stay the top earner. Showed me to never trust nobody no matter what. Just to show them hoes I wasn't playin' I waited until all they asses went to sleep and any nasty douche bottle left sitting in the bathroom got dipped in toilet water. Nasty-ass heffas ain't know better than I'd show their asses better.

After about a week I was the top earner and every-body except Lacy was up in the clinic with they snatch smelling like a sewer rat's ass. That week Frankie Diamonds took me to see Rasheed for the first time. He cried when I tried to hold him like he didn't know who I was and Mona clucked her tongue taking him back from me.

"Mona, you seen or heard anything about Ray?"

"He moved from what I heard, don't know where. His ass win the lottery or something?"

I smirked. "Yeah, or something." I couldn't believe he'd just leave without even looking for me or trying to help me. He didn't even have the nerve to face Frankie and here I was selling myself to pay back the money he was out enjoying? I changed the subject. "How you been doing though? You okay with the baby and everything?"

"Me and little man here is good. He get gassy at night and wake up fussy but Auntie Mona taking good care of you ain't she?" She cooed at my baby and he smiled up at her.

"Oh, sis, let me borrow about ten dollars. I'm gonna need to go get Rasheed some more formula."

I gave her ten out of the money I had to pay out to Frankie; it'd be nothing to make it back up. Frankie beeped and I kissed Mona's and Rasheed's cheeks.

After working for Frankie Diamonds for three years I finally decided to ask him how much I'd made him. He was sitting in the bathtub in the master bedroom at the house. It was one of the few times he actually stayed there during the week. The other girls were in the bedroom fighting over the clothes he'd brought us. He liked to keep us pitted against each other. Normally, I'd have already picked mine out and left the rest for them to fight over since I had the top spot. I had more pressing matters to deal with than cheap clothes.

"You ain't the tally keeper you the tail. You earn the tally and I run the tally wagon. When you hit your mark I'll give you your letter." Frankie smirked at me.

He tried to brush me off but I wasn't having it. I handed him my notebook wrapped in a towel so he couldn't complain about his hands being too wet to take it.

"I know, baby. You love your Diamond Ambassador pimp and you wrote me a poem or song or some other beautiful sonnettical form of self-expression and shit. I'm relaxing in my bath. I'll look at it later." Closing his eyes he laid his head back on the rolled-up towel on the ledge, mumbling, "Y'all hoes kill me thinking you worth a nigga every waking breath."

"That's because I am worth it. This year I started tracking every dick I've had to touch for a dollar. I've made you a total $115,200!" I screamed at him, throwing my notebook at his head.

You start to touch so many twenties and hundreds in a day and then you see a man with all these diamonds, watches, and furs. It makes you start to wonder what it all adds up to. The other girls didn't question shit because as long as they had their dope for the night or Frankie got them that bottle of whatever they liked to drink they were fine. My ass got out there every night. More sober than a got-damn saint. I seen what that shit did to Mona and I wasn't touchin' none of it.

There was a particular Friday night when I got out on that corner before sundown at six p.m. and didn't get in until the sun came up the next morning at seven. During those thirteen hours I made $975. That was in one day. Made me wonder where ol' Frankie really went when he stayed gone days and nights on end. He took me on a run with him once, to get dresses. He told me to go try shit on while he paid. I watched through the slats in the fitting room; he leaned 'cross that counter, running his mouth. When he was done, we were pulling around back and the bags went in the trunk. That register didn't ring, ching, or nothing. Our money wasn't even going toward us.

It had gotten dead quiet outside that bathroom, which meant all ears were probably glued to the door.

"Look here." Frankie sat up in the bathtub, adjusting the shower cap on his head. "What I tell you about trying to count higher than what you can hold in one night? Ho business is yo' business and dough business is mine. Unless you got receipts I don't know what the fuck you talking about. Matter of fact if you made that much and it ain't cross my palm"—he slapped the palm of his hand, spraying bubbles and strawberry-scented water into the air—"bitch, you betta go find my motherfuckin' money! Delusional ass. Hey, hey now! What the hell y'all give this ho to smoke before you . . ."

I didn't think about it. It was one of those things that you just see in your head over and over every day. Especially when you're laid up under some stranger and he's just sweating and gruntin' over top of you. Or someone's got you by the back of the head and they're mashing your face into they stank balls, for a measly fifty dollars. This is life day in and day out because a nigga says he'll kill you and everything you love.

One day I pulled that fantasy out of my head and made it happen. I turned to walk out of that bathroom knowing for a fact that I'd made this clown-ass poor excuse of a nigga well over $100,000. I'd lost my family behind it and sad to say for all that I barely had more than three grand to my name.

The curling irons sizzled when I knocked them off the edge of the sink into that bathtub. I could never put in words the way Frankie the Ambassador Diamonds smelled as he stewed in his own excrements in that tub. Burning flesh has a smell that's all its own. It's kind of like how bacon smells exactly like bacon, you can't describe it you just know it. He got fried to a crisp, knocked out the power in a four-block radius. And it all smelled like salvation to me.

I took his car keys and drove home to see my baby.

Chapter 19

Burn Bitches Like Bridges

(The Other Side of Miami)

There's only two times that a man is actually scared to walk into his own house. One is when you don't know who in there. That morning I'd stood in front of the door trying to perfect my game face before I walked in on that second moment—a pissed-off woman with Lord knows what as a weapon. I'd driven around the rest of the night hazy as fuck piecing together exactly what I thought she'd heard but the shit was fuzzy. There wasn't gonna be any lying my way out of this; she wasn't the one to play with like that.

Exhausted I gave up and went home when the sun started hurting my eyes. I'd gone up in there ready to face damn near anything except an empty house. Shiree sent my calls straight to voicemail so I blocked my number and started calling. She turned off her phone. I kicked myself for being so damn stupid. Last thing I remember was laying my ass across the bed fully clothed still buzzing from the long night.

Hissing woke me up. Shiree hissed in my face; her nose was so close to mine I actually jumped when I saw her.

"Shiree, baby," I started to explain, wanted to explain everything to her.

She held her finger up to my lip and shushed me. "You could have at least taken off your nut-stained jeans nigga. Don't even try to start a lie. Worried about me at work and you out doing you." She sneered.

I'd started to sit up; maybe I could reason with her or plead, beg her to stay, I didn't know. She laid her hand on my chest, motioning for me to lie back down. I ain't know if we was about to angry fuck or what. Tense as hell, I did as directed. My head wasn't flat on the pillow before she was floating a damn Mason jar right above my forehead.

She looked down at me out the corner of her eye. "Ah, ah, ah. Don't do that or you might make me spill it," she said in a calm quiet voice.

"What's going on, Shiree? What the hell is that?"

"Shhh. Acetic acid can eat through skin. You'd be amazed at what I have access to in the lab, Rasheed. I'd do worse to you, but karma is comin' around and it's gonna fuck you over better than I ever could. You've got me confused if you think I'm about to have this baby myself."

Baby? I ain't even know she was . . . was it mine? Of course it was mine. The cool glass bottom of the jar felt like a lethal iceberg resting on my forehead as Shiree removed her hand, letting it balance itself out. Holding my breath I watched her out the corner of my eye as she slowly backed away from the bed. I wanted to cuss at her ass so bad my lip twitched.

"I packed all my stuff while you were in your drugged-up, hoed-out coma. See how much the world loves you, when you and your pretty dick ain't so fuckin' pretty."

I heard her call out in a petty voice from the doorway but all my focus was on not breathing, blinking, or moving. Shit she was probably bluffing and that shit wasn't nothing more than bleach but I didn't want to take any chances with hit. The smoke detectors were going off and

I could smell smoke, even see it out the corner of my eye. If I ain't think of something quick that shit would have me coughing and it'd be a wrap.

I prayed every prayer I'd ever heard or read and I smacked the jar off my head, rolling to the side simultaneously. It shattered against the closet, sizzling and fizzing.

That crazy bitch really set a jar of acid on top of my fuckin' head!

I'd be mad about it later; first I had to figure out what the hell was smoking. The couch in the living room was completely engulfed in flames. All my clothes were up there my kicks, my dress shoes. I couldn't have slept that hard.

Grabbing the fire extinguisher out of the kitchen I got the fire put out. The fire department still showed up because all the smoke set off the alarms in the building. I lied and said a cigarette fell. Couldn't risk throwing her crazy ass under the bus out of spite; she was liable to throw the bus right back at me. After the fire department left I checked my voicemail and tried to find something clean to put on. She'd actually managed to fit every piece of clothing I owned on that damn couch. I was reduced to washin' the crotch of my jeans in the sink until I could roll out to buy some more.

That made me think of car keys. I panicked. Thankfully, they were still on the table by the front door. I checked my car and it didn't seem like she'd tampered with it so I was good. It felt like a piece of my damn heart was missing and it was my own fault. She ain't even want to hear anything I had to say. On top of all that she was havin' my baby. How far along was she? Man, Shiree couldn't get rid of it; that wasn't an option. She'd come around; she'd have to come back around and hear me out. I returned Angelo's call to get my mind off Shiree's craziness.

The phone didn't even ring a whole ring before he picked up.

"Angelo, what, was you sitting on top of your phone waiting for those chicks from the club to hit you back?" Hopefully he'd be able to get me out of this foul-ass mood I was in.

He shrieked in my ear, "You cut me out and cut a deal with my pop?"

Or not. I grimaced. It hadn't crossed my mind that Angelo would eventually find out and that he'd be pissed when he did. Shit, Shiree messed up my planning process. I'd have normally sat down and figured something like that out.

"You act like I can't still cut you in as a partner. Shit like this happens when you run off and get buck-naked with the natives when you're supposed to be in the skybox discussing politics. I keep telling you that it's all about opportunity and preparation."

"Opportunity and preparation? That's what it's about you say? Well, I'm prepared to find other opportunities and I hope you have a backup plan. We are no longer equals; you will bow."

The line went silent and I sat there trying to figure out what the hell to make out of that shit. Why did these Italians have to be on that damn emotionally dramatic shit? On the corner a dude would just be like, "Yo, I'm mad you cut me out of that deal. I ain't fuckin' wit' you no more watch your back." At the end of the day it was over and you knew exactly where you stood. *You will bow? What the fuck was he on with that?* I looked at the clock and jumped into action. Half the day was already gone and I still needed to meet Don Cerzulo.

The plan was to get there an hour early and park around back. That way I'd know if anyone sketchy showed up, or if anyone had eyes on the building I could hopefully see when they arrived and set up. Don Cerzulo walked up to my car and tapped on the window.

"You'd have to have been here yesterday to get a jump on me, wet pigeon." He cackled that old man version of a witch's cackle and I got out of the car laughing.

"I was just trying to make sure we were good. I don't do these kinds of large transactions often." I told him.

Don Cerzulo slapped me on the back hard before throwing his arm around my shoulder like we were old drinking buddies. "Well, Rasheed, today is your lucky day. Hey, Joey." Don Cerzulo whistled through his fingers and a heavyset guy in black sweats wobbled over. He was breathing heavy and I was hoping it was from carrying that heavy briefcase full of money, because it's not like he had that far to walk. He wheezed as he handed it over and then turned and wobbled back in the direction he came from. Don Cerzulo opened the briefcase and the smell of crisp, clean legal tender filled the air. He handed me a sheet of paper. I unfolded it, reading the neat handwriting before placing it in my pocket and nodding.

"Now you show us this works so I know it's not quack science and we're—"

Don Cerzulo stopped midsentence; he stood there with a circle of blood forming on the front of his white dress shirt. Since our backs were turned to his guys it would only be a matter of seconds before they figured out he'd been shot or before I got shot as well. Snatching the briefcase I jumped in and started my car as Don Cerzulo fell to his knees.

"He shot Don! Get him, he shot Don Cerzulo!"

I didn't shoot any damn Don Cerzulo. I just saw an opportunity and I'd taken his damn money. As soon as the thought crossed my mind I realized my own words had come back and bitten me in the ass. Angelo couldn't have shot his father over some petty business shit. Not only that but he was trying to make it look like I was the killer. *Angelo was trying to run me out of Miami.*

My phone went off and thinking it was a text from Angelo or Shiree, I flipped it open only to see a message saying my momma's house was in bad shape. Any other time Angelo would've had a fight on his hands. But I needed to go figure out what the hell was up with my momma. I didn't even think about it I just got on the nearest highway ramp and started heading north. It rang in my hand, I glanced at the number and started to ignore the call but I knew I couldn't.

"Yeah, this is me," I snarled into the phone.

"Right now I'm looking at a little blue marker on a screen. That little blue marker is heading north. Now, where could you possibly be going, Mr. White?" he barked into my ear.

Special Agent Harper was a poorly socialized evil Rott-weiler of a motherfucka who talked to anyone and everyone like they were plotting on his nasty-ass chewed-up lamb bone. And frowned like it, too.

I ain't have time to be a crook turned rook in the damn alphabet boys' chess game anymore. "I did what y'all asked. You got the deal on tape and on film ain't nobody ever got Don doing a deal."

"Wrong, you cocky son of a bitch! We got Don Cerzulo Campelli, the famous actor, handing you a got-damn piece of paper which could have been nothing more than a got-damn Kool-Aid recipe for all we know. The plan was simple. You get his trust, get inside, and get us his damn suppliers, find out if he's behind the SAG murders and director killings. Lucky for you the boys upstairs hit the kill switch on good old Donny before he could have you shot on spot as planned. We picked that bit of intel up from one of our informants who overheard the hit man complaining on a phone call at a gas station around three a.m."

Rolling my eyes at the phone, I scanned the rearview to see if my ass was being followed. If Angelo hadn't put the hit on Don Cerzulo then he and everyone would definitely think I'd killed his pops. There wasn't anything worse than a spoiled brat with an honest grudge.

Agent Harper finally decided to share why we were having this friendly little chat in the first place. "Your objective has changed. We need you to work an angle on Angelo. As Don's only son, he's most likely going to take over the family's cartel. I need clean bodies on him, clean suppliers—"

"You need to come back to reality. Y'all just made it look like I shot and robbed this dude's pops. Miami, hell all of Florida, will be lookin' to hem me up on sight. That shit is impossible."

"We didn't make it look like anything. If your ass hadn't picked up that briefcase, you wouldn't look like anything. No, son, you made you look guilty, and unless you want to go back inside with Scorpion and your buddies, I'd better see this blue marker on my screen busting a U-turn and heading back toward Miami. That paternity test you requested for your cooperation came back."

I could hear paper unfolding in the earpiece and I waited.

"The little girl, Paris born to Trenisha in prison is not your daughter."

The line went silent and I pulled over to the side in the emergency lane of the highway. I was so furious my insides were shaking. Fuck you Derrick and double fuck you Honey for whatever Angelo does now. Never in this lifetime did I ever see myself walking free with ties to my freedom.

I'd been in for about a year when they dragged me into solitary for no reason and sat me at a table. It was normal for Officer Reynolds to pull me away and do kinky shit on her breaks. I hadn't seen her in a minute and I was ready to wear her ass out something decent.

I'd stripped down to my boxers when the door flew open and in walks this big Magilla Gorilla nigga in a fresh black suit.

"This ain't that kind of party, son. Put your fuckin' pants on and have a seat. I ain't come here to fuck, suck, or stare at your ashy-ass knees."

I ain't never put my shit back on so fast, feeling like I'd just got caught by the principal trying to sneak behind the school with the class freak. A long brown file folder landed on the table in front of me with a loud slap.

"Go ahead, open it up," he commanded.

It was like looking at my entire life on film. There pictures of me as a shorty with moms. Some pics of mom dukes from way back with an old pimpish-looking moth-erfucka. I chuckled at that shit. This cat had a li'l curly mustache and pretty curls in his hair. Moms had never said nothing about whoever he was. Seein' me pause on that particular picture Magilla Gorilla started barking.

"That was Frankie the Ambassador Diamonds. Mur-dered in 1989, electrocuted in his bathtub. He was wanted for the murder of over thirty-eight women up and down the East Coast, and they almost had a solid case against him until he was murdered and robbed blind."

He continued and I flipped over a picture of the dude laid out on the coroners table. There were puckered blisters from his chest down and you could see the network of veins running under his skin in this eerie deep dark purple color.

"They couldn't find a single solitary one of his girls to question except your mother. Couldn't figure out why she had a dead pimp's car. Mona, your aunt, said she'd stolen it. Since they couldn't pin either one of them at the *scene for murder, your aunt with her theft record would have still gotten locked away for a long time. But, the judge was lenient because honestly Frankie won't shit so Mona got away with a warning."*

I'd flipped through a few more pictures and got a feeling in my gut I ain't like. "What does this have to do with me?"

"We've got more shit on you than a pig trying to keep cool fresh out of a pepper patch in summer. Last month we picked a woman up. Over the course of thirty years she's married and killed five men, clearing out their accounts every single time. For a reduced sentence she's pinned your mom in the Frankie Diamonds case, has a notebook of hers hidden away. She says it puts your mother under his charge, dated and everything to the day he died. Combine that with that Cadillac and even in her old age she's looking at some time."

My mouth dried out like I'd been sitting there holding a wad of toilet paper in it as I waited to hear the "but" or the "what." I didn't have to wait long.

"Your ex-girl Trenisha? She's managed to get out and align herself with one of the biggest coke dealers in Miami. We'll give you back your freedom, but the you sitting here right now has to die. After you've accomplished your goals, you go on with your new life far away from Virginia. And, well compensated for your time."

At the time it seemed like an easy out. Take water from a man until he's almost dead, hallucinating, sick, and dizzy from thirst. He can hear the slightest trickle of a stream. He won't care if there's garbage, syringes, and dead fish floating in that bitch. He's gonna follow the sound, fall to his knees, and drink. That deal was water, free water, and I'd been dying of thirst on the inside. Locked up, counting tiles, and going damn near insane.

A car whizzed by so close it made my shirt flap like a flag in its wake, snapping me out of my memories. Staring down at the cracked, broken concrete, scattered glass, and cigarette butts I considered my courses. Regardless of what them special assholes said it was never my complete intent to just forget about my son. I'd imagined waiting until he was older and better able to understand my absence. We'd sneak off on weekends when he was a teenager and I'd teach him about the world. Get him drunk. Just dumb shit that a locked-up nigga got time to sit and daydream about.

I looked at the text, wondering what could be going on with my momma. Her house phone and cell were tapped, I was sure of that. My cell was obviously tapped and Momma ain't know nothing about texting.

I was out because of Momma; without that case against her I probably wouldn't have done shit for those agents. They probably didn't have anything better to use against me other than her.

Climbing back into the driver's seat, I clicked the seat belt and sat there, staring at the road behind me in the rearview. *Nigga, you'd better haul ass. All of the FBI is about to rain a shit storm down on your ass and you ain't got a raincoat, umbrella, and you for damn sure ain't got toilet paper . . .*

The tires squealed and the tail lights illuminated a trail of rocks and dirt as I threw the car into sports mode and floored it. Throwing my cell out the window I started looking for the nearest rest area. It'd take them longer to find me if they couldn't trace me. Fuck stealing a car; somebody was about to sell me their shit.

Chapter 20

A Monster Is Still a Monster

When Momma had finished telling me her story I just stared at her in complete awe. I would have never guessed she'd been through and seen so much.

"Aww, Momma." I hugged her, clutching her side, unable to say anything more.

"Girl, don't aww me. If you wait for the walls to melt they'll show you all the secrets." Momma's voice had changed dramatically and she'd started talking like a little girl staring up at the TV in the corner in somewhat of a daze.

My brow puckered and I shook my head and sighed. News reporters were going crazy about a murder. Some crime boss or something of another named Don Cerzulo. He was a murderer, drug dealer, just more bad news if you asked me.

Here they go glamorizing the murder of someone dying by the sword he lived by. Typical bullshit.

I changed the channel to a soap opera and fluffed Momma's pillows. It was the Alzheimer's. The doctor had given me pamphlets to read and it said she'd come and go. One minute she could seem perfectly fine and the next she could be like she was right that very moment. My cell rang and I stepped outside, hopefully the office was calling me with some good news. Looking around for Devon and Trey I answered.

"This is Michelle."

They should have been back awhile ago. Devon was probably teaching him how to X-ray his foot or something crazy knowing him.

"Michelle Roberts?"

Frowning, I paused, afraid to answer to a name I didn't use anymore that definitely wasn't attached to this number.

"Michelle Roberts, my name is Special Agent Harper. I'm with the FBI. We have reason to believe Rasheed White is on his way to or already in Virginia."

I quickly leaned against the wall beside Momma's room, my hand over my mouth. I couldn't tell if I was gonna vomit or pass out. "No, Rasheed is dead," I whispered in a barely audible, shaky voice.

"No, ma'am, he's very much—"

Urgh! I swear I need to switch carriers. If I wasn't outside or standing on top of a got-damn cell tower I stayed dropping fucking calls. Why couldn't I just buy my own damn satellite? This couldn't be happening. It was all a bad dream and at any minute I'd wake up. Towanna decided to spring up on me and now this? It's a wonder I didn't march my ass up there to the insanity ward and check myself in. I debated whether it would be good to even mention something like this to Momma. Probably be best to wait until after I spoke to this special agent. I wiped the tears from my eyes and fixed my face.

Walking into her room I quickly blurted out, "Momma, sorry to cut this short but we've gotta go." I tried to sound as chipper as I could so she wouldn't get suspicious and ask too many questions.

Momma wasn't in her bed and Lataya wasn't in her car seat where I'd left her. I flipped the curtain, looking over on the other side of the room. There was a grizzled old woman lying in her bed with nothing but the sound of her oxygen pump. She barely turned to acknowledge me.

He's already here. I can feel it.

A single window was open next to Momma's bed and I picked Lataya's pink and red sock monkey up off the floor. My feet were saying to run outside, but my head was telling me Rasheed had them and he'd kill me if he saw me. If I took one step near the window or the door, I could feel my heart screaming from inside my chest, "I'm going to explode."

"I knew you'd be out here," Momma called out.

"Whew, momma, you don't even know—"

My chest felt like a mule had kicked me, caving it in, and my heart somersaulted at least five times. I screamed, and I screamed so loud it brought half the hospital down on that single room in less time than it'd take a SWAT team to raid a crack house. Someone pushed past me, grabbing Lataya's tiny limp body out of Momma's arms. They put her on Momma's hospital bed, yelling for doctors and intubation tubes and crash carts. A few nurses fought to get Momma restrained and out of the room. They pulled her past me and she looked at me but it was like she didn't really see me as she reached for me. Sobbing, I backed away from her and she started yelling at me.

"I baptized her, Mirna, just like you told me to. Ain't no man gonna ever hurt her. Ever."

Her eyes were wild and dazed. She didn't know who I was or where she was.

One of the nurses grabbed me by the shoulders and pressed me out of the room. I kept trying to look around her and over her shoulders, clutching that damn sock monkey to my chest pitifully.

"I'm her mother. I need to be in there," I begged her through my tears, but she just ignored me as they're trained to do.

I was left to wait miserably outside the door, feeling helpless and irresponsible.

"Michelle? Me and Trey were watching TV in my office I heard a code three to your mom's room?" Devon's voice was filled with concern and alarm.

He was holding Trey, trying to look over my shoulder and I couldn't get past the emotional bubble in my throat to even tell him what happened.

"Mommy, why you crying? Where's Taya? I got gummy bears for her out the smack machine." He held up the little yellow bag, shaking it at me.

Hearing Trey ask for her, and not knowing whether she was okay to even answer him shattered what little composure I had left. I bawled, throwing myself into Devon's chest.

"Nurse Denise," Devon called out over my head, "take Trey back to my office if you don't mind. Cartoons . . ."

"I shouldn't have left her in there. She seemed fine and was talking. The special agent called and I was looking through the door until he said Rasheed was here. I wasn't thinking, I just wasn't thinking."

My shoulders shook. My whole world shook from me crying so hard. The doctor walked toward the door, his expression unreadable. I tried to see where she was, if she was awake, and I couldn't see anything past all the nurses in the way. It felt like I couldn't breathe, like an elephant was sitting on my chest and my heart was exploding and then everything went black.

I opened my eyes and the room swam dizzily in front of me.

"Easy now, that stuff's got a kick." Devon's voice floated over to me.

I was lying in a hospital bed and my head was killing me. The hospital bed jarred my memory and all the misery I'd felt before surged back over me in an instant. I looked at him unable to ask but the question was evident.

"You got so upset; you were hyperventilating. I'm sorry. I just sedated you so you'd breathe, sweetheart."

He sounded so sincere. I didn't want to point out that this would be the second time I'd wakened in a hospital bed drugged by someone I was sleeping with. The "first-time award" goes to Larissa for using me as her voodoo lab rat while experimenting with cocaine and anal sex play.

"Chelle, Lataya," He shook his head unable to actually say the words. "She had a lot of water in her lungs. Her head had been held under in the sink for a while. Statistics show drowning is one of the most peaceful ways to go though. She didn't feel a thing . . ."

His voice droned on and on as the doctor in him took over and he tried to explain how peaceful death is. Like he'd drowned and knew firsthand. She didn't know what was happening to her or why and I wasn't there to protect her like I should have been. The hole in my heart opened up all over again and I started crying. I tried to wipe my nose and my hand wouldn't go any farther up than up to my chin.

"Why am I strapped to this bed?"

Devon gave me that pitying look that I'd seen one time too many. "You were talking about a secret agent calling you. The entire hospital heard you. It was a murder. I had to report it. They filed that on the report. Michelle." His voice took on a tone of seriousness. "I have to keep you for observation."

"Keep me for what? Where's Trey? Devon, let me go please, this isn't funny," I half whined, half pleaded with him. When he didn't look like he was going to even help me anger at everything welled up inside me. "For the record he was a special agent, and he said Rasheed isn't dead and he's on his way to Virginia."

Devon sat back in the chair beside my bed and put his chin on his thumb. He looked deep in thought.

"I looked this Rasheed White up while you were sleeping. I couldn't find so much as a birth certificate on him. Called and even got online looking for a Towanna James, Miami PD and Virginia, nothing. I even looked in your phone and there aren't any secret agent calls. I'm trying to figure out if you and Mrs. White are sharing a delusion. It would explain why you'd be at her house living out of suitcases and why you'd both share this Rasheed person. I can't help you unless you help me help you, Michelle."

A guttural animalistic wail escaped my lips and I yanked against the taught leashes on my wrists. He had to be joking. There was no way this could be happening.

"They erased it for some reason. I don't know. Where the fuck did my kids come from then?"

"I'm not even supposed to tell you that the real police are running Trey through their database of missing children. They wanted to take him. He's okay to stay with me. Denise has offered to help me watch him. I'll let you rest. I know it's been a rough day."

Chapter 21

Wheels of Steel

I didn't sleep as lightly as I used to. If I did I would have known this crazy little girl was in my room with a knife pressed to my throat. There was so much grief and so many drugs in my body I couldn't even feel afraid, and could barely feel the blade. My body was practically numb. Instead, I cried and pressed my throat farther onto it.

"You let her die," this girl spoke to me in a breathless whisper and her eyes only spoke of vague drugged sadness, pain, and death. They were Lataya's eyes and I didn't know if she was a ghost or an angel or a real person, but staring into them made me hurt even more..

"I didn't let anything. How do I live every day of my life loving and protecting someone else's child and then one day, just one day we're fine and she has pancake flour everywhere and then they wouldn't even let me hold her hand. She didn't have her sock monkey . . ."

The pain I felt at losing Lataya was like nothing I'd ever experienced and I let the dam that had been holding back all the helplessness and hurt break. I was flooded with drugged hazy thoughts of what Lataya might have felt, what she might have thought, the fact that she probably looked for me or reached out for me and I couldn't get to her haunted me. I closed my eyes and waited for that knife to cut into my throat.

"At least you got to hold her. Your life, for her life," she said in the faintest whisper.

Her voice was frightening and haunting, especially since I couldn't figure out if she was real.

I didn't care. I was tired of running and fighting. Always looking over my shoulder and not being able to trust anyone. It would be more like self assisted suicide than murder because in that second death sounded like a peaceful option.

"Take it because if you don't Rasheed will, since the agent said he's somewhere nearby." Exhausted I waited for the blade to tear through my neck. Trey would finally be safe. I'd put money into a college fund and a trust fund for him. He was his daddy's son after all, he could survive anything.

Voices stopped outside my door and I opened my eyes. I looked around as best as I could but my damn restraints only let me lean so far. She had to be in this bitch somewhere, unless I was dreaming. *That wasn't a dream, that was a straight up hellafied nightmare.* They were giving me so much shit to keep me "sane" it was making me crazy. Devon walked in staring intently at his clipboard.

"How are we feeling today sweetheart?" He asked.

"Did you see . . . anything on the news about kidnappings sweetie?" I asked smiling sarcastically. I'd started to ask about the girl with Taya's eyes and quickly changed my mind. No buddy, he already thought I was deranged. Even though she seemed kind of real and I think that knife felt real as hell. It was hard to say but my throat seemed to hurt from where the tip was pressed against it. There was no explaining how she'd gotten in and out without him seeing her.

"I did not. But, I did ask how you were feeling?"

I was beyond miserable. They gave me miserable flavorless food and I wouldn't eat it so they shoved IVs into me and fed me that way. I honestly just hoped Rah would just show up and prove to them all that I wasn't crazy. Even if he killed me, at least I'd die with everyone knowing I was a sane woman who did not kidnap her children. Devon would sit beside the bed and talk and talk. Whatever drugs they gave me kept me so mellow I could only look at him at times; blinking alone seemed to drain ounces of my energy. I didn't even know what day it was or how much time had passed.

On this particular day he was extremely chipper. The sound of his voice made me want to do nothing more than stab myself in the ears with anything I could get my hands on ear-hole size. They wondered why people lost their minds and lashed out? It was because of overzealous doctors who sat in your face and their very presence was a slap in the face. They made you remember passionate kisses and warm smiles, made you angry because they should have fought for you. Even if they were the only ones who believed you.

"Michelle, are you listening?" Devon sat there looking at me expectantly.

I shrugged in response since I had no idea what he'd said.

"Good, I'll have you escorted in as soon as everything's set up."

As soon as what was set up? I sat there staring at the closed door, trying to figure out what the hell was going on. Moments later Denise came in and sat me down in a wheelchair.

She spoke so quick and hushed I had to strain to understand her. "Your boy's doing fine, Michelle. I don't know what all's going on but I promise I'm looking out for him. He's at a homeschool my nieces run out of their place right now. They good people don't worry. If it was me and this shit happened I'd want somebody looking out. Shit, with the way they scoot folk in, out, and around on the fifth wing fuck that. I don't make enough money up in here to catch a charge over some uppity actress they check in for killin' folk who checks herself out before she even sees the doctor. Especially when regular folk like you catchin' the third degree. Anyway, he's been asking for you, and I told him you were at mommy daycare, resting up. So once you finish resting, he's waiting for you."

I had to look down at my hands in my lap so no one would see the teary smile on my face. Every now and again we still get angels to look out for us and I was so thankful for Denise's words. Devon refused to talk to me about anything relevant until I rewarded him by acknowledging any of my story as made up.

Denise wheeled me into a dim room. "Sorry boo-boo, I imagined strappin' you up but not like this," she said in a soft whisper, giving me a weak smile.

She strapped my forearms down onto the arms of the wheelchair and secured my ankles as well before turning to leave the room. The lights came up and I saw Momma sitting across from me in another room, strapped to a wheelchair as well. She stared at me through the thin pane of glass and seeing her for the first time since Lataya's death made me realize why I was strapped to the chair. Snarling, clawing, and growling, my hair flew wildly around my face, spittle hung off my lip as I looked at her through that glass. She'd taken Lataya, and now I was up in this hell because of her ass.

"Calm down, Michelle." Devon's voice sounded over-head on the intercom.

Chest heaving, I stared at the clinical pea-green tiled floor in front of me. Everything was pea green from the floor to the walls, even the toilet was that macabre shade of squished caterpillar, sea-sick green. As much as I hated looking at the tile, I refused to make eye contact with the woman across from me and I damn sure refused to cooperate with anything Devon planned.

"Chelle? I been wondering why I ain't seen you in a while." Reena's voice rang into the silence.

I stared blindly at the floor, trying to turn off my ears the same way I seemed to have turned off my eyes.

She isn't even sorry for what she did. Hell, she probably doesn't even know.

"Don't look like we going anywhere anytime soon, child." She paused like she was thinking or remembering something. "I ever tell you about the time I decided to become a madam?"

Chapter 22

Minding Madam Business

After everything blew over with Frankie I'd sold his car. Well, what I mean by that is I gave it to the Mexicans who ran the chop shop down the block. That was decent money to live off of for a while. At least until Mona came across Fink her ex. She called him an innovative misunderstood dreamer. He was a penitentiary pioneer. I called him that because every idea he had landed his ass in prison. Fink was definitely innovative. If that's what you call a fool that hides in a custodial closet at the bingo hall until everyone's gone so he can creep up on Mabel and Ms. Sarah countin' out the money. Only to be standing there holding the gun when his bowels creep up on him, fool was going through withdrawal so bad he had the shits. Police caught him in the bathroom of course they had to wait a good twenty-minutes or so until he was all clear. But you get my point.. He'd just gotten out again and he had Mona on some hard stuff. Couldn't tell you what because she had a cocktail of whatever you could think of depending on which day of the week it was.

I'd stomped into her filthy bedroom and stared down at the mattress on the floor. I picked a naked leg and started kicking. "Mona, wake your trifling ass up. Wake up, girl." I was screaming at the top of my lungs and wasn't nobody moving.

The rent was already a month late and I'd come up with the back end of it donating plasma and selling some of Rasheed's old clothes. It would have put us in the clear for a minute. Mona had found my cash by pulling out my bottom dresser drawer and looking underneath. What the hell she was doing down there I'll never know but she ran right through every dime. If we got put out we ain't have anywhere else to go. We ain't have any options left, no favors, no nothing. I'd used every last one, at least twice a month for something with Mona staying up in the house.

I decided that one time, I'd do the only thing I knew I would bring me quick money. I sat Rasheed on the floor in her room. "Watch Rasheed, Mona. You hear me?"

"Watching," was the muffled response I got back.

I started on the side of the track closest to downtown. That time of day the shipyard workers would be taking lunch breaks. It'd be easy to make a quick $500, $600.

My first customer was Tim Washington. He pulled up in an old blue pickup. It squeaked and rocked to a stop in front of me.

"What can I do you for, baby?"

"What can't you do for a hundred dollars?" he croaked out the window.

If you heard Tim Washington's voice and a croak coming backward out of a bullfrog's ass, I swear you wouldn't know the difference. I'd climbed up in that old toe-jam, corn-chip- oil refinery and sweat smelling truck and when he dropped trow I had a mind to charge him another hundred for having a third leg. There is such a thing as too big and if a woman ever said otherwise I'd let Tim say hello. That voice was the sound of his donkey dong pulling on his tonsils. Just think of the "camel through the eye of a needle" scripture. He gave me an extra fifty dollars for being a good needle.

I was climbing down out of his truck when he started looking all sheepish.

"Reena? I know that ain't little Ms. Top Seller herself. You stole my man from me and now you out here stealing my customers," Royce snapped at me.

"Your man? A pimp ain't no man for any woman, sweetie. He married to and respect money. You were just a way to get it."

She swung all that hair like she was about to do somethin' to somethin'. "That's why I'm married now anyway. Got me a good man."

I laughed in her face. "Royce? He so good, why the hell are you out here? And where is your married nah rock." I mocked her, throwing her words back at her when I didn't see a ring.

That's when I noticed Royce didn't have all that dazzle to her, not like she did a few years back. Her black and tan was looking a little more like ashy and burnt.

"He's rich, and he took my ring. He don't give me shit because he worried I'll shoot it up."

That had my full attention. "How rich, Royce?"

Her eyes got as wide around as footballs. "Filthy rich, Reena."

That shit gave me an idea so big I birthed the Northern Lights on the other side of the world. In order for it to work I'd have to keep Royce just high enough so she could function normally during the day. I'd started turning a couple extra tricks but I knew it'd be worth it in the end. Even ran into Lacy and offered her a percentage of everything overall if she cut me in on her earnings so I could keep Royce good. Royce's husband was used to her fien'ing or so high she couldn't see straight. Once we got her to a middle ground everything fell right where it was supposed to. She got the insurance policies changed over, the wills. She knew all the bank information. It was time.

I'd gone and seen this lady over at the African shop once when Rah had whooping cough and I couldn't afford a doctor. All I had to offer her was a peanut butter jar I'd started collecting change in. It won't even halfway full but she took it and cured him.

"Reena. Long time no see. How are you, my queen?" She greeted me soon as I walked in and I couldn't remember her name.

"I'm all right. um, you know it's been a while I'm sorry," I apologized because I should have known.

She laughed and waived me off, "You wouldn't pronounce it right even if you did remember it gal. Balifama tamunominini Bello, but call me Fama."

"You right, about that one. Girl that's a mouth full. I need something Fama, and I can pay. I'll pay extra if I need to." I strolled through, looking at the shelves by the counter. There was shea butter, black soap, coconut oil, nothing that I could use.

"What is this somet'ing?"

I put two hundred dollar bills on the counter and she snatched them up, making them disappear somewhere underneath the long sleeves of her tunic.

I made sure no one was standing down any of the tiny aisles before leaning across the counter and whispering, "I need to make a man die and it has to look like an accident."

"Hmmm. Are you sure?"

She'd just gotten $200 of my money. Hell yeah, I was sure. I nodded. "I'm very sure."

She went into the back and came out with a little box of powders and oils. My $200 bought me a bottle of oil that couldn't have held more than a thimble full of whatever she'd mixed up.

"Two drops in their bathwater for three nights; after that massage one drop on the soles of each foot. That's it."

That's it? Royce had a hard enough time remembering the instructions to boil a damn egg.

I gave Royce the bottle the next day and on the fourth day she gave it back.

"Did it work?" I asked her.

Me and Lacy were about to gnaw each other's hands off in anticipation.

Royce in all her splendid, ditzy wonder said, "I don't know. I didn't check. Was I supposed to check him or something? I mean, I just came to out here. I didn't think."

"Royce, where was your husband when you got out the bed this morning?" *I asked through my teeth.*

"In his bed and I got up and took my morning poo, and showered and had coffee, and put on my not going out - going out face, and I walked Kimpy our Kane Corso and then when I . . . Oh, I think it worked."

Don't forehead slap her, was the look Lacy was giving me.

"Don't you think it's going to seem strange that you got up, went in and out the house and did all that, and ain't call 911? Go home and call now please."

We waited to hear back from her and waited, and waited. A week passed and finally we went to catch the bus out to that old ritzy rich million dollar homes neighborhood. All the houses looked like castles and if I were Royce I'd have just kicked my damn habit. We went by the address on one of the forms she'd messed up when I was helping fill out the insurance paperwork at a restaurant. Something told me to keep one just in case, and I was glad I did. We walked up just in time to catch this heffa hopping into a shiny little Benz and speeding away.

We were leaving and I was scheming, looking to see what other eligible paychecks lived in the area. I looked over at Lacy. "I think we found another one and this time you are gonna do the marrying and hoodwinking."

Lacy took a little more work to refine. Royce already had all the beauty school guidance any single head could possibly hold. It would explain why her flighty ass couldn't retain much of anything else. I put Lacy on a diet, got her eating right so her skin would stay bright. She had high cheekbones and one of them beauty marks. That's what she called it. I'd call it a dern mole if you ask me. But, from the way fools acted when they saw her, she's the reason that model girl got famous, I'm telling you. The one with the big old big-ass mole on her face. I can't even remember her name.

Anyhow, we'd taken our money and gotten her hair permed and cut into one of those little bobs with the bang that's pointy and long on one side. It framed her face, accenting that big-ass mol . . . I mean beauty mark. I remember stepping back, looking at my baby-doll-faced perfection on many an occasion. No one would have ever guessed she'd gone from a hooker to a looker.

It took two years for her to woo that man and get married. But that was two years of extra money so we was off the street. We were enjoying gifts and all the luxuries that come with dating rich men. I had her treat this one the same as the last one. Slowly made sure she had all the details, got everything changed into her name. I wasn't worried about Lacy skipping out on me like Royce did. Lacy was loyal.

Another one down and unlike the first time Lacy actually came through; she only missed a couple of minor details but we still had a payout of hundreds of thousands each. We had a way to take a life with nothing pointing to foul play. It'd looked like he'd had a heart attack, no chemicals in his blood stream, absolutely nothing.

However, I wanted millions and so did she. Anyone who's ever gone fishing knows you've got to follow the tide and venture out if you want to catch bigger fish.

We went up north to Philadelphia, following the money flow. Rented out a place and in less than a week's time I had four girls working for me in exchange for a place to stay, protection, and bail money. I always remembered the look on Royce's face the day she took off with her millions. Lacy and me didn't have that look just yet though. No, if we actually went out and bought the mansion we wanted with the fleet of matching Mercedes we'd be broke.

It took me drawing her a pie chart on paper before she barely understood how millionaires got that way. A mansion cost millions and we only had hundreds of thousands. Million-dollar property came with a million-dollar property tax. She was addicted to all the diamonds, champagne, and flashy parties. I'd modified Frankie's business practice, only taking a fair percentage of my girls' money and Lacy was blowing through it like Kleenex.

We lived like this for years. The entire time my sister thought I'd just found a job out of state. I could never send her more than enough to scrape by with at a time. If she knew anything she'd have blown through it, or run her mouth in the streets and raised suspicion. We were making so much off the girls I started stashing money to keep Lacy from finding and running through it. When Lacy came and told me she'd run across a wealthy widower in the steel industry I was thanking my lucky stars. Then, I sat there and plucked every last one of those stars out of my unlucky sky. She came and told me the man's mother passed the very day before he was set to die. Lacy stuck me with his spoiled, miserable heathen of a child. I had no choice but to get rid of him. Told her she'd never pick her own mark again. That child was something that'd been on my conscious to this day.

We all packed up and went to Jersey near Alpine after that. A lot of good years were spent there. Think we had two or maybe three weddings in Jersey. Then there came a time when Lacy thought she was just too grand to be living with me and the girls. She even thought she could pick her next one. She pointed out five and I said no to them all, showing her who I liked instead, better targets. She went ahead anyway and I couldn't work with her anymore. Not like that.

"Dr. Harrington, how well did you like your stepmother? I don't think she goes by Lacy though. By the time she met your daddy she was probably calling herself Melanie Mal . . ."

Chapter 23

Psychics Get Called Crazy—Until They're Right

"Melanie Malia." Devon's voice was barely above a childlike whisper coming through the loud speaker. Static crackled through it and then the intercom went silent.

I didn't know what to think of Reena's story; the woman could have told me she was a royal cat burglar for the Queen of England and I wouldn't have batted an eye. None of it was gonna bring my little girl back though. All this story time and power-hour crazy house shit was pointless. I wasn't crazy; everybody including Reena was. The lights dimmed and I could barely make out the other side of the room. The panel window had gone dark, showing nothing, reflecting nothing. Reena was still there, singing at the top of her lungs. It was her rendition of "Amazing Grace" and "The Star-Spangled Banner."

"No one would know my stepmother's name, let alone her maiden name; how'd she do that?" Devon asked the question from behind me.

I shrugged. "Maybe because she obviously knows what she's talking about."

"No one could know what she's talking about. I didn't even find out myself until a little over a week ago. They'd told us she was suspected of murdering all her late husbands. They couldn't press any charges because there was no murder weapon, nothing linking the deaths except her being their widow. It hasn't gone public yet but it's only a matter of time."

He undid the straps on my hands and kneeled in front of me.

"I don't know what's going on, but the first thing you told me was don't trust the police, and I turned around and trusted their word about you, over you. I'm so, so sorry."

He put his head in my lap and I argued a vicious inner battle with myself.

It's not like we've known each other forever, he was just doing what he felt was right.

Leaning down I kissed his ear softly, saying, "I thought you were completely insane too when we first met. On that, we are even. But just so you know, I do get to drug you at least once in this lifetime and you can't be mad."

He smiled up at me as he unlatched my ankles.

"You can drug me whenever you want and I wouldn't complain. Let's get your clothes and get you out of here. We can go get Trey and then you can rest."

"So by letting me go without the police or anyone's permission, that doesn't make me a criminal does it?" The last thing I needed was more drama to explain later down the road; wake up and my whole identity was gone, except for this one visit to the psych ward.

"I wrote everything up before I even came down to get you. You are fine and clear to go, per the doctor's orders. "

Clearing my throat I hesitated. "Have, um, arrangements been made for Lataya yet?"

Devon got that clinical look that he used to break any news he felt would be negative. "I made all the arrangements and took care of everything; it's scheduled for tomorrow. I wasn't sure how to tell you, or not to tell you."

"Just get me to Trey. I'm ready to get out of here."

We rode out to an area near Campostella; it was mostly Section-8 housing and a few overlooked trailer parks. It definitely wouldn't have been the top of my list of choice areas to send Trey to on a day-to-day basis. Devon went inside to get him while I waited in the car, on high alert. I'd been around Rah and his boys enough in the beginning to know what corner boys looked like. They weren't anything to worry about unless you bothered them. I was, however, worried about that agent who had called me. I knew I hadn't dreamed or imagined that phone call. I'd checked my phone and just like Devon said an incoming call didn't even register during that time frame.

Something was going on and I didn't understand what or why, but I felt uneasy and anxious knowing Rah could be anywhere. Trey came outside and I got out giving him the biggest watery squeezy hug. He eventually whined to get in the back so he could finish watching his movie on his iPad.

"Chelle, you hungry?" Devon put his hand on my knee and squeezed.

"Can I have cake?" Trey yelled from the backseat.

I wasn't but I tried to perk up just a little for Trey since he hadn't seen me in a week. "I think Ruby Tuesday's has cupcakes. Devon, does Ruby Tuesday's have cupcakes?" I asked in the most serious tone like it was up for major discussion.

"Well, since I'm driving to Ruby Tuesday's, I think they have cupcakes." He screamed and Trey screamed.

"Mommy, can we save Taya cupcake too?"

I knew it was coming, he'd ask and I'd start crying.

Devon's squeezed my knee. "We can do Ruby Tuesday's another night, Michelle."

Shaking my head at him, I wiped my nose and my eyes on my sleeve.

"Trey, baby, do you remember when we had that talk about heaven and Daddy—"

"Michelle, can he have his cupcake first?" Devon tried to stop me.

Before I could finish asking, Trey answered, "I 'member, Mommy, and G-ma told me that she was gonna have to send Taya to heaven. When the walls melt away you can see all the secrets. Did Taya go to heaven already?"

We pulled into the restaurant parking lot and me and Devon were staring at each other not knowing what to make of Trey's words. Some minutes later we were all inside seated in our booth. Trey insisted on sitting by himself like a big boy. I was just trying to keep it together. I let him have his way for once, so long as he promised to behave.

"No. You know you wanted this dick." Some teenagers behind us were making me rethink the seat and the restaurant all together. There was so much coughing, snickering, and inappropriate chatter going on.

Frowning, I leaned over and turned Trey's headphones up on his movie.

I fiddled with the straw in my soda, debating something that had been floating around in my mind.

I nudged him with my shoulder, not looking up. "Devon, I have a question."

Nudging me back he responded, "I have an answer."

I stopped using my straw to pop bubbles in my soda and decided it was time to woman up. Looking him in the eye I said what was on my mind. "I heard you on the phone at the hospital, with a woman that day after I came out of Reena's room. Who were you talking to?"

Devon frowned with a look that could have been confusion or, maybe, he was a bit taken aback. He'd started to answer when our waiter came back over. I was about to ask for a new seat when I realized it wasn't our waiter.

He slid into the booth next to Trey. One of his hands was underneath the lapel of his jacket. He stared at Trey for a moment in a look of joy or shock before turning to me with those memorable embers of anger and hatred still burning in his eyes.

"Hey, Michelle, how've you been? No letters, no postcards, no forwarding address. It's like you were trying to move on without a nigga. Scream or draw attention and it's happening."

He nodded down at Trey, who'd barely glanced at him. He was a toddler the last time he'd seen Rah. I never showed him pictures because I wanted him to forget, in the event they ever met again, like now. I wanted Rah to see his son, growing up without him, unaware of him as his father. Trey was watching his owl movie for the fifth time in a row, not paying any mind to the adults at the table.

Rah put his arm around Trey, sliding off his headphones, tapping at his iPad. "What you got there, li'l man?" Rah asked Trey, his voice cracking, choked up with emotion.

"My iPad," Trey whispered.

Rasheed started tapping on the screen. He put his head against Trey's. "You know what that word says?" he asked Trey, sniffing quietly.

Trey shook his head up and down and his eyes got wide. "That's 'daddy.' My daddy is in heaven and—"

"What are you doing here?" I quickly snapped at him destroying their bittersweet moment. The last thing I needed was for Trey to get talkative.

"I'm trying to find my moms. A little birdie pointed me in the direction of that fancy mental hospital. Imagine how exciting it was to see my favorite person in the passenger seat at the light beside me, when I was tryin' to find it."

"No. You just high as fuck and technically both y'all were fighting over this d-i-c-k," the guy behind me bellowed and laughed.

The teens in the booth were getting loud and a few restaurant guests were casting annoyed and disgruntled glances their way. I was praying it would be enough of a distraction to get a manager or a waiter over.

"Big!" Rah jumped up, looking over our heads but his hand was still too close to his gun.

Damn, is that Big Baby? Guess they're just gonna have themselves a reunion up—

Devon nudged me and I looked down. I took his cue and slowly reached underneath the table, blindly feeling for his hand. He handed me the car keys.

"If I can take him you go," Devon mumbled, his lips barely moving.

"Hold up, Rasheed? Dawg." The guy in the booth who had been making all that noise behind me addressed Rah, sounding excited.

"I know that ain't no motherfuckin' Rasheed, triflin', hoing, nasty, druggy, dopin' ass."

I didn't recognize the hoarse, raspy woman's voice coming from directly behind me.

I looked at Devon dumbfounded; he shrugged in return. Neither of us could see over the high-rested back of the booth seats but I was able to lean just enough to see through a small gap between the booth walls. The raspy voice was Shiree.

"You left me to run back to Big Baby? Really? Did you get rid of the baby too? I actually loved your ass." Rasheed actually sounded hurt. I stared at him in awe, no this fool was not still making damn babies.

"Oh so, nigga, you loved her ass, huh?"

I mouthed the words "oh no" to Devon. I knew that voice just as well as I knew my own. That was Honey and she did not by any means need to see me up in here with Trey having dinner without Lataya. I tried to peek and get a glimpse of her but there was no way to do it without drawing attention to myself. The sound of her voice jarred me back to that night in my hospital room but the sedatives they'd given me were so strong I could barely remember it now. It felt like a dream and the girl I'd seen and heard didn't even look like Honey. She might have been a cousin or someone I didn't know if she was ever even there. But, Honey was right here right now and God help me because I didn't even have the one person she wanted back from me.

"Look you high as fuck, we don't need to handle this right here, just let it go girl," Big said.

From all the stories Rasheed's momma had told me, I was pretty sure she had a million and one "oh, shit" and "oh, no" moments. It explained why her hair had grayed all the hell out. I couldn't help wondering if it was a gradual change or if after one too many the whole thing just sprouts.

"Nah, this is exactly who I need to be handling. This is why it all started. So this is where it's ending. Right here, right the fuck now. Because even though I'm the one who got locked up behind yo' ass, had your baby, and then got you out of prison, you're gonna stand here and say you loved her?" Honey shrieked at Rasheed.

Please just don't let anyone come around this corner, look down, and see me. I'd rather take a gun and shoot myself than have to say what happened out loud if anyone asks where the baby's at right now. It would just be too much for me to answer.

It was as if the director had yelled "action" and we were dropped smack in the middle of a bad Western. The cold metallic clink of guns cocking behind our heads was unmistakable. Customers started running out of the place. The most I could do was hope that we got out of there with a mild flesh wound. If you've ever heard an M-80 go off in the middle of a packed hallway in between classes, that's what a gunshot in a restaurant sounds like. The sound hurt my ears and Trey cried out, throwing his hands over his before crawling under the table and into my lap. It was akin to raindrops on unsuspecting ants. The people and staff who hadn't started fleeing ran ducking and screaming, scattered in various directions toward exits.

"Pull a gun on me over a kid who ain't even mine? That's that bullshit. Get y'all asses the fuck up, take me to see my momma."

We rushed out of the restaurant to the sound of sirens wailing in the distance.

Chapter 24

Hit the Brakes Like Errrrrrrrrrrr

We drove in silence, me sitting in the back with Trey. I wanted them to have as little contact as physically possible. The less the better; he'd just accepted the fact that his daddy was in heaven. I couldn't just *Pet Cemetary* Rasheed back into his life even though everyone seemed to keep jumping back into mine.

Devon led us in through the admin entrance so Rasheed wouldn't get asked for ID and go on a shooting spree to get to his mom. I couldn't figure out where the hell the special agent was now who had called me earlier. If they had so much intelligence out there and they were that worried why weren't they watching the hospital the moment his momma was brought in?

We followed Devon up through the back entrance and I was hoping he had some kind of plan. None of the nurses were aware that we were walking hostages. How the hell do you blink a distress message at someone?

"Every now and again, I'll have high-profile patients or people who need to get in or out without a ton of publicity. They'll be in an area where the rules will need to be altered a little. I'll have your mother brought up to the 5th floor you'll be fine; the staff is used to it."

Devon's words reassured Rasheed, simultaneously squashing any hope I had for a random act of assistance. Rah paced the length of floor until his mother was just outside.

"Is that my momma? Why she strapped down like that? Let her in," Rasheed growled at the door like a wounded bear.

"She's dangerous and unstable. She might not know who you are."

"Man, fuck outta here with that. That's my mom; she knows me."

Devon nodded and she was rolled in, he then dismissed the nurses. It was a bittersweet reunion. Rasheed was teary-eyed trying to hug his momma; she was doped up and strapped to the bed.

"Rasheed? Boy, they'd told me you passed on. Second saddest day of my life. Where've you been, what happened?"

"Yo, take her out of that shit. She don't need to be in no shit like that," Rasheed barked at Devon and he obliged, undoing the straps and letting her free.

"Why they do this to you, Momma? Was it because of me? Is this because of something I did? I ain't dead. Look, I'm right here. This ain't because of me is it?" he asked her pitifully. He sounded like a scared and worried little boy, talking to his momma. Like my old Rasheed, not the angry shell of a man I'd gotten used to dealing with.

"No, my love, this is all me. Sometimes my memories are as crystal clear right in front of me happening right now, and I can't tell the difference between what's now and what's past. Everything look like it's supposed to and feels real as you and right as rain baby. Other times I can't remember how to brush my own teeth unless somebody shows me where or what a toothbrush is first."

He looked at Devon like he wanted an explanation and he explained, "She'll need to be in an institution or a full-care senior living facility. We had one slip-up here where she didn't take her meds and"—he hesitated—"she drowned Michelle's daughter in the sink in her bedroom."

Actually hearing the words out loud to describe what had transpired made tears fall down my cheeks. Rasheed looked at me and seemed completely bewildered as to how something like that could happen. I didn't have an answer.

Rasheed pulled his phone out of his pocket. "Yo, this is me." He answered and paused, his face getting darker and angrier by the second.

"How did you get this number? It's a prepaid phone," he demanded angrily.

"What do you mean mixed up the swabs? You was only supposed to swab one?"

My eyebrow went up on that. The tone of his voice had gone to furious in a matter of a few words. I didn't even want to know what the person on the other line had said but I had a feeling I was about to find out.

He slid the phone into his pocket and stared at me like he didn't know me, like he'd never seen me before and he still hated me.

"Life or death, were you cheating on me before Trey was born, Michelle?"

Shocked as hell, I quickly shook my head back and forth. "I don't know who just told you that but they're lying. I never did anything."

"You never did anything when? You was doing shit with that bitch remember? So, I'm gonna ask again and I'm gonna let you think about it. Because, my people swabbed Trey and Paris, he ain't mine and her swab . . . Aw fuck! Ma."

It was as if the realization of what happened didn't hit him until he was saying it out of his own mouth. I'd already been feeling what was just now hitting him head-on. Even though the part about Trey not being his was all new to me.

"Momma, what did you do? What did I do, Honey aww fuck Desi . . ." He fell to his knees crying, crippled by pain and reality.

I'd never seen him or any man cry like that. It made me want to put my arms around him and kiss his shaking shoulders. What he was feeling he didn't deserve, none of us did; at least Honey wouldn't have to find out. Not one time had I ever cheated on Rah with another man.

Oh, shit. Ris, what the fuck did you do?

I felt like I was about to throw up as I thought about Ris underneath me and what I thought was Keyshawn behind me. How mortified I was when I realized he was just watching. Thankfully that one time it was Lania with a strap but she hated Rasheed and if it meant blind-folding me and getting me knocked up. There was no way I'd ever know who the hell it was with unless he came out and told me. Trey was still my Trey, it just meant I didn't have to worry about Reena's mental health history affecting him and—

All the air left my lungs in a sickening sharp thud. I wanted to vomit and breathe at the same time. Crashing to my knees, clutching my stomach, I gasped for air. He'd gotten up and out of nowhere stormed over hitting me with the butt of the pistol.

Devon roared and charged Rasheed, knocking him off his feet and they both sprawled across the floor in a tangle of limbs and angry grunts and growls. Trey started crying. The only thing going through my mind in those seconds other than trying to breathe was trying to get to Trey and shielding him.

The gun exploded again and again. The sound was deafening and, slightly dazed, I looked around examining everyone looking for visible signs of blood or pain. My eyes swept over them all: Reena, Devon, Rasheed, Trey. It was chaos and everyone seemed to be midmotion screaming or saying something. Blood started seeping through the hole in Rasheed's shirt in his chest and he fell to his knees. Trey ran to Reena. Devon and I examined each other, breathing sighs of relief when neither one of us were shot. I watched Rasheed take his last breath, for real. I felt for his pulse and everything.

We were sitting out front waiting on the police to get there. Devon felt it'd be best to bring Reena out for the fresh air. I honestly couldn't care one way or the other. All of this just needed to be over so I could figure out what else I needed to do for Taya's service.

"That was my baby who got shot wasn't it?" she asked in a tiny voice.

"Yes, that was Rasheed." I answered her cautiously, scared of what she was about to do or how she'd react to the news.

She turned and looked at me as if she'd just seen me for the first time all day. "Michelle? Where the hell you been? I ever tell you how I met Rasheed's father?"

Not in the mood for any more of her stories I held up my hand and said, "I think you have."

She frowned, and went back to la-la land.

Devon had gone all quiet and pensive on me and Reena just sat there staring off into space. He seemed like he had a mindful of questions to ask but settled on staring down at the pavement instead.

The police pulled up and we were swarmed with activity.

"Someone called; I need to see the person who committed the homicide," a rough voice called out.

I glanced at Devon and he had the same confused look that I did. Homicide? How could he possibly call it that without hearing our side of the story? We looked up in unison as a tall man with the presence of an ominous thundercloud approached us. Everything about him from his suit up to the top of his head reeked of this darkness.

Devon began to step forward and I pressed ahead of him. "I shot him. He'd taken us against our will and I was struggling with him for his gun."

He gave me a gruff nod. "Glad you've decided to cooperate." His hand pressed at the small of my back, pushing me toward a black sedan. "It'll make it easier to request a less severe form of punishment for that actress you shot back at that restaurant. Hopefully she won't press charges."

Actress! Nobody shot an actress. What the hell?

The car door slammed curtly in my face with the ending of that statement. Impossible, they had it all wrong. One of the witnesses must have seen or reported something inaccurately. Reaching for the handle, dread was all that met my fingertips in the sensation of smooth, molded leather. There were no handles in the back seat and a Plexiglas divider cut off access to the front seats. The man who led me to the car was speaking to Devon, who was holding Trey. They'd turned and he was making hand gestures, pointing toward the hospital. Pounding my fists against the window I screamed and yelled. It had to be some kind of reinforced glass.

The car shifted as someone got into the driver's seat. I was so busy trying to get Devon's attention I didn't see who it was. The Plexiglas distorted my view of the other side. I clawed at the plastic divider, growled, screamed, and kicked at it, but just like that damn window I didn't even put a scratch on it. Feeling like a complete idiot I remembered my cell and jerked it out of my pocket. I had 8 percent of a charge left. That would be enough to make a call or send a short text but not both. I tapped a quick message to Devon.

They think I shot some actress. Need a lawyer.

I almost snapped that pretty piece of shit phone in half when it vibrated.

Message send failure. No service.

The car rolled for what seemed like forever. It finally stopped moving and I tried to get my bearings. We'd stopped in front of storage rental area. The driver walked over and opened my door.

"We've been ordered to shoot on site if you run."

Nodding my understanding I timidly climbed out of the back seat. He led me over to a storage unit. The metal door slid up with a loud clanking sound that shook me all the way down to my core. It was a sound that rang of last words or last rights. I peered inside waiting to see my executioner in there. The only thing visible was a single fold-out metal chair beside what looked like an old card table.

"Sit, this won't take long." The driver spoke in a curt tone.

The sound of the door sliding down in place made claustrophobia set in instantly. The space was small and dank. Mildew and mold seemed to be the scent of the evening. It made me think of spiders, brown recluses, and black widows. My skin was starting to crawl and I tried to focus on anything but what could or couldn't be in that space.

Thankfully the door slid up just as I was about to lose all my nerve, get up, and start banging on it. He didn't introduce himself or even say anything. Simply strolled in and slid it across the table: thick green paper with fine printed handwriting in blue ink.

"What is this?" I stared at it, straining my eyes to read the wording, afraid to touch it.

"Sign it. It's an agreement." He paused, waiting for me to read it. I didn't move. "It says you murdered Rasheed because we asked you to. We paid you with money from our fund and even gave you the gun he was shot with.

There are bank transfer slips, six overall backdated to various points in time. When I give the okay, the money will go into your account and it will look like it's always been there. It's the only way I can help you."

It sounded like the losing end of a deal to me.

"I don't understand who are you; what fund am I getting paid from?"

If something went wrong or anything I'd be signing something saying I conspired to murder Rasheed. There was no way, a judge or court anywhere would let me off with that.

"We can't help you otherwise. It's a sinking ship and you're standing on the bow, Michelle. This is your life-saver."

My hand shook as I scribbled a barely legible version of my name. He clicked open his briefcase, placing the papers that determined my future inside.

"Tell no one. I'll be in touch."

Chapter 25

Secret Agent Man

It was about time spring started showing its ass. I was getting restless with all the cold, gray doom and gloom. You could see all the signs, fresh buds, melting ice, and twitter-pated squirrels. Spring was becoming my new favorite time of year. The air was losing the brisk chill from winter and we were getting some of the warmer days everyone yearned for minus the humidity and the bugs.

It'd been four months since Lataya's funeral. It was the only thing about those events that I chose to mark on my calendar. She wasn't my baby, but in my heart that little girl would always be my baby. I'd like to think that being with me even for that short time was heaven before heaven for her.

Devon had been stressing and having a multitude of fits. It seemed like every day he'd get a call from this lawyer or that lawyer with a detail or another bit of information on the case concerning his step-mother. It was hard on his family and tearing him apart. I had no idea Devon owned the hospital and every day he was being asked to furnish a financial record for this holding or financial evidence backing that holding. I'd gone online and done some research. I tried to explain they were doing it to all the families not just him. Every dime she extorted had to be accounted for.

The case was becoming so intricate that he was looking into another facility to move Reena to, and I didn't blame him one bit. Things finally seemed calm enough for me to start working a little more. I took on a manager to help makes decisions on major closings but an absent owner would be a broke owner. I tried to step in on major closings when I could or at least help with properties that they were having problems moving. Too much turbulence and my ass would get airsick so I tried to stay put as much as possible.

I'd just landed and was trying to remember where I'd parked my car in the garage. I'd closed on a $4.5 million waterfront property that we hadn't been able to move for a year and was damn excited. The seller was threatening to find a new agent and we'd moved it just in time. My phone died on the flight and I cursed when I didn't see my car charger in the car.

Not having my cell was like leaving the house without a shirt on. Frustrated I slammed the hell out the car door cursing silently. Those silent curses turned into shouts when my damn car wouldn't start. Opening the glove compartment to get my AAA card a tiny black laminated card fell to the floor on the passenger side. I picked it up and read the silver letters with my lunch slowly making its way up throat.

You are activated. Instructions will follow.

Everything stopped moving. The armpits of my blouse and blazer jacket were instantly soaked.

Activated? What the hell was I going to have to do?

A yellow cab squealed to a stop behind my car and I almost fainted from the sound. Dust flew up and engine exhaust hit my nose. The purr of the engine echoed through the garage. I swiveled to look out the back window as the cab driver leaned over and yelled out the window in a heavy accent.

"You get in, now."

He nodded toward the back seat, his black leather fedora bobbing on his head.

I reluctantly got in and he sped off. Arabian music was blaring out of the speakers as we bounced out of the airport garage. I could feel myself getting nauseous as nerves built on top of nerves.

This wasn't the kind of person I was. What the fuck had I signed? Why the fuck did I sign that shit? I didn't even read it; I just scribbled my name because the man in the suit said do it. My dumb-ass didn't even ask him for identification.

I couldn't call Devon. I couldn't call the police. I'd felt better with a gun pointed at my head; at least then I knew what the outcome to that would be. He flew down Military Highway and I noted landmarks, car dealerships, IHOP. We got on the interstate going toward downtown Norfolk. He stopped in front of an old office building on Granby Street.

"You're here," he shouted to me over the music.

I looked around trying to figure out where "here" was. I got out and stood staring at the crumbled front of the building, trying to figure out if I was supposed to just go in or what. The doors swung open and a young woman in a black pantsuit came toward me.

"Michelle, follow me." She turned and walked back inside without waiting.

"What am I doing?" I asked her shakily.

"You've been activated. Follow me for your objective briefing," she replied matter-of-factly.

She led me through the building, up a stairwell, and across a mezzanine. I followed shakily, not sure if I'd make it without falling out first. We walked up another stairwell and we got onto a service elevator. She stood in front of me and I debated trying to hit her on the back of the head like I'd seen in movies. Knocking her out and running. Something wasn't right. I looked to see what button she pressed and in that moment she stepped off through the front elevator door and my ears went super sonar a split second too late as the back service door of the elevator opened behind me.

Someone grabbed me and instinctively I slammed the heel of my pump down. The joy I felt at the yelp of pain I'd elicited was short-lived as I whirled around my hand poised mid-throat chop.

"What the fuck, Devon? You scared the fuckin' fuck out of me!" I screamed in his face, punching his arm.

The elevator stopped and the doors in front of me opened onto the main floor of a breathtaking hotel suite. I gasped in awe, my hands flying up to cover my mouth. There were vases of bright yellow calla lilies, pink and white tiger lilies, and birds of paradise, all over the suite.

Devon sucked in his bottom lip turning bright red. "The plan was scoop you up, kiss your neck, and ask if you were ready to be debriefed. Then um, debrief you as in get the panties, but you went all *Charlie's Angels* on me," he mumbled sheepishly, as he escorted me off the elevator. "It just all worked out so perfect in my head . . ."

"Aww, baby." I grabbed his face in my hands and kissed him.

Devon tried to talk against my lips. "Statistics show relationships that start off dramatically—"

"Boy, I know your ass ain't up in here quotin' lines from the movie *Speed*." I kissed his nose sweetly. "I've had enough drama in one lifetime that you don't need to do none of this, not this. I don't mean the room. I like this part, the room is good. But, all that other stuff . . ." I shook my head. "I can do without that."

He smiled, nuzzling my nose with his. I was thankful when he didn't nuzzle any lower because all that adrenaline and running around had me wanting a shower. As if he read my mind he took my hand and smiled, walking not to the bathroom but toward the bed. I started to say something until I saw the Olympic-sized Jacuzzi bathtub not three steps away. But he didn't go to the bath; he went past that.

"Baby? Umm." I pointed and pouted sadly at the inviting water.

"You're not dirty enough for a bath yet." He responded in that authoritative seductive voice of his and I instantly got chills.

It's one thing to have a man who knows what the hell he's doing in the bedroom but you've got a beast of a completely different nature when he ain't scared to experiment. My legs were straddling his face and I'd just gotten his sleep magic number down. So I was working it. Sucking and simultaneously stroking him to the damn finish line. He had the dick game down but, I couldn't lie, the head game still needed work. He needed to learn my sleep magic number. That's when you know exactly how, where, and how many times to lick, suck, or flick. Some might need a nipple twist or their clit sucked hard; some women don't like it sucked they like it rubbed. Whatever it is, you know exactly what the magic number is before that head game puts your boo to sleep. Well, he ain't know all that.

I knew he was in the final stretch. His stomach was flexing and I could feel him swelling in my hand and in my mouth, when I started vibrating. Not a small vibrating, but I almost shot up off him and backed back down. He'd gone and bought a big-ass dildo. I mean like one that I would have gone and bought myself if he was gonna be gone on a long business trip. I tried to scoot back on it because it was feeling super nice and then "pop."

Oh no, he didn't. I know we'd had the ass discussion. It was off limits.

My ass was plugged and it was vibrating and my clit was still vibrating, and it wasn't bad it was just so much vibrating that I couldn't tell if I liked it all at once. So I licked my pinky and slid it in. See how much he liked it. One second I was holding the dick and voila it went from being magically delicious to feeling magically delicious.

"Oh, you wanna play in asses?" He roared, "You forget that I'm the nigga?"

Each word was accented with a pussy-clenching, sheet-tangling, mattress-shifting, power pump that slid me across the bed. It was the worst best punishment ever.

"Damn! Yes, you are. I'm sorry." I moaned and whined.

Devon stroked my pussy with the determination of a man with OCD methodically stroking a cat. They'd be long and rhythmically deep. I agreed with him, apologized, and probably thanked him in advance until he'd find those bittersweet spots that'd make my legs tremble. All I could do at that point was hold on and then everything stopped. Exasperated, I clawed his thighs with my nails. Devon grabbed my wrists and leaned forward, pinning them above my head. He kissed me and I moaned against his lips, wiggling my hips, trying to get him to move.

"Tell me what you want," he directed.

When I merely frowned up at him not answering, he pulsed in between my legs, making my walls clench in reflex and my eyes cross. Devon made me aware that no matter what happened on a day-to-day basis, when we got down to us, man to woman, skin to skin, it was okay to want or even like for someone else to be in control. I didn't have to pretend to be unbreakable or invincible. Although sometimes I just liked pretending so he'd try to break me.

"I want you. I don't want anybody but you, baby," I whispered helplessly. I was lost and loving every bit of it.

"Good, now you've earned your bath and when you're done maybe I'll give you the present I bought you." He grinned and I wondered what the hell he was up to. It was too damn early for a ring. It'd better not be a damn ring. I watched his thigh muscles flex as he kneeled to adjust the water and turn on the jets in the tub. Trey was with Denise so I knew he was in good hands, but I didn't know about this whole surprise business. I hated surprises. People never seemed to give you exactly what you wanted or expected. The room was beyond nice; it was on some all out honeymoon suite type shit. At the moment the last thing I wanted to do was have a Twix moment on this nigga because he'd popped out a promise, engagement, or even a damn friendship ring.

Devon brought me a glass of moscato once I'd eased myself into the water. He'd remembered that I didn't really like champagne. I was so nervous I downed the glass. You definitely shouldn't drink in hot tubs it makes the smallest amount of alcohol go straight to your head.

"Okay, no peeking. I promise you'll love me for it." He handed me a damp wash cloth.

Laying it over my eyes I put my head back with a sigh. The jets were loud so I strained to hear what he was doing. A glass touched my lips and I took a sip rolling my eyes at his attempt to get me drunk. *Okay, more moscato.* He pressed up against me removing the washcloth. I was instantly teleported back to the hospital. My heart had to have skipped at least five solid beats. She was right there pressed up against me, the girl with Lataya's eyes. The back of the Jacuzzi scraped my back and water splashed everywhere as I panicked and tried to climb out. I was scared to take my eyes off of her to see where Devon was. Her hand quickly flew up covering my mouth and she smiled shaking her head at me.

Where was Devon did he set me up? Was he hurt?

Chapter 26

Twisted Sister

"Hi, Michelle. Did you miss me?" she asked.

It was Honey's voice, I was dead certain of that but it wasn't her face. I squinted at her like a Monet but aside from her eyes I just couldn't see the baby-faced bitch I knew. Devon moaned from somewhere behind me, it sounded like the bed. Honey grinned at the sound.

"Oops, I might have drugged y'alls wine a little bit. See after Rah oh, wait, they think you shot me, huh? Hmm, wonder how that happened? Well, either way it hurt like a mothafucka. I was tryin' to get a refill on my oxy when I'm in the E.R. and I overhear a nurse on her break talkin' all quiet to who? Your boo, Dr. Harrington on the phone. He's telling her how he's tryin' to find a girlfriend for his girlfriend." Honey explained.

I was starting to feel sluggish and woozy as she talked. So she was Devon's damn surprise. Ugh. He had the worst taste in surprises; I didn't want or need a woman in our relationship.

"Honey? If it's even you. Why would you hurt him, he hasn't done anything to you?"

She didn't answer me, she slowly backed away taking enough bubbles with her to cover her body. She was staring at me the entire time. My eyes were starting to feel lazy, not sleepy, just lazy.

"Michelle? I'm not gonna kill you. You'll wish you were dead by the time I'm finished though. When you an' Larissa decided how and what would happen to everybody around you, it was like playin' God and shit right? You ever tried china white? I think we gonna stay here until you love china white more than you love life."

What the fuck was china white? I tried to think of every damn drug I'd ever heard of or seen Ris do or deal with. Honey climbed out of the Jacuzzi gracing me with a view of her full bare ass. She had a stripper's ass, and then there they were on her left shoulder the letters Honey. It was definitely her. A new surge of adrenaline and fear coursed through me and I tried to get up off the seat before she came back from wherever she was. Devon was laid out across the bed, I could barely see his chest rising and falling. There wasn't anything close that I could use for a weapon except . . .

Grabbing the champagne flute I slipped it into the water and snapped the cup off the stem against the edge. I'd accidentally broken enough of those things doing dishes to be a wine glass breaking pro. I ran my thumb across the jagged glass pick I'd created. It could work. Honey came sashaying back from the direction of the bathroom.

"Just in case you wanna' try some sneaky shit. I brought my l'ila friend," she announced with a fake accent and a giggle waving a small gun. "Now, come here."

I refused to let the only weapon I had go, it was no match for a gun but she wouldn't have that gun in her hand forever. My legs felt like rubber as I tried to stand up. I used my imbalance as a reason to turn my back to her and I slid the washcloth over my glass shank. She walked over just as I managed to climb up and sit on the edge of the tub, guess I was moving too slow for her.

"Look at me, Michelle. It's time to start your new life," she instructed.

I refused, scared she was about to stick the barrel of the gun to my forehead or in between my lips. I sat there naked and shivering shaking my head no. She pointed the gun at me and my nostrils flared as I weighed my options. Reluctantly I did as told and she blew some kind of powder into my face. I coughed and gasped for air, rubbing my eyes and blinking. She started speaking but her voice sounded like she was in a different room and it was strange but I felt happy as fuck. Like there was nothing wrong at all. I couldn't remember where I was or why but I honestly didn't care, everything was good.

"That was scopolamine or devil's breath. You won't remember none of this. Now, we are going to have ourselves some fun."

I watched everything from somewhere inside my body. It was like I wasn't in control of what I was doing; I just gladly did as I was told. Honey scampered away and came back. She laid out all these syringes, pills and powders in front of me and I smiled down at them. She laughed at me and I laughed with her.

"We are gonna play a game. We'll start with the pills you'll work your way up until you get to the syringes. There's one for you and your boo, Krokodile. It's paint thinner, kinda like heroine tears your skin to shit so we'll save it for last. Um, this should be heroine, or it's morphine I don't remember. But, when your man wakes up you'll pick a needle, walk over like nothing's wrong and give him a shot. Okay?" she asked.

"Alrighty. But, what do I win?" I asked.

"You win a fucked up drug habit, and we'll ride to your bank and you'll withdraw some money for me after that you'll go get your son so I can take him with me. He won't want to be with your broke drugged up ass now will he? Isn't that how everyone thought about me?"

"Yes, that is how we thought." I giggled like we were discussing an episode of *Love and Hip Hop* and not my son.

"Okay, let's do some pills or something my ass gettin' bored as fuck."

Honey took two and handed me two; I did what she did and swallowed them drinking from the moscato bottle nearby. She threw a robe at me and I slid it over my body enjoying the feel of the cotton gliding over my skin. Devon moaned over on the bed so I did as instructed and reached down picking up a syringe filled with this brownish tinged fluid. I watched him in the setting sun and waiting excited to have a mission. Honey swayed on her feet and I giggled at her. Devon shifted and I rushed toward him smiling, he was waking up and Honey took off in the direction of the bathroom.

"Don't worry. I think this one is the cracker bill . . . crocodile . . . heroine. This one is heroine." I called out to her straddling Devon.

He opened his eyes as the needle jabbed into the skin of his neck, I started to press the end of the syringe smiling brightly all the while.

"Nothing's wrong." I told him, just as I was instructed.

Frowning, he swatted me off of him with a growl.

"What the hell are you doing?" He touched his fingers to his neck.

"Nothing's wrong," I couldn't think of anything else to say it was as if I needed a script.

Devon rushed past me toward the bathroom and I followed behind him.

"Aww, what the fuck?" he cursed.

I looked around him, Honey was on her knees in front of the toilet. Well, more like her head was in the toilet. From the looks of it the pills she'd taken didn't mix well with whatever was in the bottle of moscato. She went to vomit, passed out, hitting her head on the way down, she drowned with her face in the toilet bowl.

I had the worst headache of my life the next day. We didn't say anything to the police about her drugging me. Devon carefully put everything in her bag and luckily for her they didn't mention any of that in their reports to the media. It looked like an accident and they left it at that. I remembered bits and pieces of what she'd said and I'd laid him out decent for finding a random female to come through in the first place.

As an apology Devon finally let me have my way and he agreed to let me do teeniest bit of redecorating in his "asylum" portion of the hospital. I told him that after having firsthand experience as an actual guest and an actual million-dollar broker, I was beyond qualified to help make the place a little more antidepressant.

"Devon, I'm not even crazy and I wanted to kill myself after only a week up in here." I laughed.

"That is sea-foam green and it's statistically relaxing," he retorted.

"Mmm hmm, just like your 'statistically dramatic' date that almost put you in the ER? Humph, relaxing my ass."

My first order of business was repainting and redoing the floors. No more of that putrid green, period. We were putting lounge chairs and couches in the visiting areas; no more of that sitting in the cafeteria shit. You treat people like children in a mess hall and they'd act that way. Plain and simple. I'd found some nice landscape portraits of fields and flowers, dreamy stuff that depressed people would feel uplifted looking at. Overseeing the process was a headache as always. I had to keep the patients quarantined to one area, work in another, and keep Devon calm.

"Ms. Michelle?" one of the painters called out. "All this needs to be redone; the wall is chipping."

I wouldn't be able to get that kind of job past Devon. He'd have a fit. Maybe if we did it in pieces. This old place should have been redecorated and primped ages ago. I gave the painter the go-ahead, telling Devon's ass take the day off; his pacing combined with the, spot, and corner checking was getting on every last one of our nerves. I was pretty sure I caught him with a leveler over a picture.

We'd found a nice place that would take Reena and we decided to split the cost of her stay equally. On nicer days they let their patients go outdoors for a few hours and I'd decided to personally see if she was settling in okay before we left her in their care. Devon walked with me. Reena was sitting on one of the cement benches beside the rosebushes this place had. I wanted to nudge or punch him and say "see, they have rosebushes." Men don't know anything about what the hell would cheer up a depressed anybody.

"Reena, it's your lucky day," one of the nurses called out from the hospital entrance waving. "Your sister is here to see you."

She approached us, wearing a dramatically huge black Kentucky Derby straw hat, and I shielded my eyes, smiling brightly. The sun was glimmering off all these gold bangles, bands, rings, and such.

I extended my hand.

Let me find out Mona can clean up?

When she gripped it in a firm handshake I immediately snapped it back as she pulled off that hat.

"What in the hell? What the kind of bullshit is this? What are you doing here?" I huffed at her.

All the patients who were outside, started screaming or skipping and singing at the sound of my outburst. One of them even had the nerve to start skipping around us singing ring around the damn roses.

I grabbed Shiree's ass around the neck and held her in a straight-up choke hold. All the gold bangles on her wrist clanged in protest as she waved wildly, flaying her arms, trying to grab me. I wasn't about to get played or taken down by her or anyone else. Not after Honey came and zombie voodoo blasted me in the damn face at the hotel and especially not after I'd just seen Shiree's ass cozied up with Big Baby and Honey. Then the heffa had the nerve, Rah said he was in love with her ass, too. Oh, no, we were not having this conversation any other way than how I had her ass.

Devon was telling me to calm down, the orderlies were trying to get me to calm down, Shiree was trying to get out my damn arms.

"You had the nerve date him or whatever after me and then show up here? You set Ris up? You probably set Honey up that day at the restaurant didn't you?"

"I wanted to pay my respects to Ms. White; it ain't got shit to do with you," Shiree squeaked from under my arm.

Hearing her name Reena floated over like the world wasn't in chaos all around her. "Michelle, where you been, girl? I ever tell you how I met Rasheed daddy?" she asked.

I rolled my eyes and tightened my grip. "Yes, you have," I snapped. Nobody was trying to hear that mess right now, especially not me.

"No, I always skip the beginning. Let me tell you the beginning, baby."

Chapter 27

Summer, 1986

"Look, how many times do I have to tell you to leave my damn son alone?"

"But it's his baby, I swear. I wouldn't lie about something like this." I pleaded pathetically but she wasn't trying to hear a word I had to say.

This definitely wasn't what I was hoping for given my circumstances. I'd caught two busses and walked Lord knows how many blocks just to get over here. The sun felt like it was damn near sitting on the back of my neck the entire way and I only had enough cash on me for bus fare back. I'd stared some poor little Jamaican dude down so hard he'd actually backed up into his shop out of the doorway. Shit, my mind wasn't even on the cash register; if I stole anything up out of there it'd be beef patties and an ice-cold Ting soda.

"I swear, if your little trifling hoing ass isn't wobbling off my porch in the next three seconds I'll go get Big Bertha. She ain't as nice and she's way louder than I am."

I hurried up and got my "nine and some change, sweaty, hot, an' ready to burst" pregnant behind up out of there. Mrs. Tessa did not play when it came to three things: her son, the lottery, or her shotgun also known as Big Bertha.

I'd met Ray when he was interning up at the free clinic on Twenty-eighth Street. No, I was not up in there for *no crazy shit. I was actually volunteering. All the crazy shit happened after that. My sister Mona and I had been on our own for nearly as long as l could remember. Our oldest sister, Mirna, had gotten all sanctified leaving us to do for ourselves. She'd been putting in overtime turning out this deacon's son and once she'd gotten him on lockdown she acted like she ain't want anything to do with any us anymore. She packed all her stuff and moved out to be with him, turning her nose up at us like we was beyond God's reach in the process. Mona did what she had to in order to keep us decent and to keep the roof over our heads. Sometimes that meant doing things that some folk might consider immoral or scandalous but it made do.*

See, our momma had left us for Mr. Johnson. No, not a man named Johnson, but the Johnson or should I just be obvious and say she left us for some dick? Mona had broken it down to me once but at the time I was too young to understand. It was around ten or eleven at night on my seventh birthday. I had a habit of crawling up under the bathroom sink whenever I was upset. There are some things you never forget, they stay with you, and the feeling stays with you for a lifetime. Like the first time I ever smelled a full pack of crayons, Christmas Day. But every box smells like Christmas after that. Everything from the night of my seventh birthday is still fresh in my head too.

On that particular night I remember waking up to the sound of clapping. Curious about what was going on, I slowly parted the peach vinyl curtain that draped from the bottom of the sink to the floor. My nose wasn't but a hair's breath away from some man's bare, wrinkly, hairy, sweaty, hanging man danglys right in front of my damn face as he slid in and out of my momma.

I instantly felt sick to my stomach and lightheaded. If Mona hadn't come knocking on the door, I might have passed out landing face first into a threesome with my own mother. Ugh. Nothin' would ever take those memories away; they're an oil stain on the concrete driveway of my brain. To this day the color peach was a tainted, sinful, filthy color and I couldn't stand the cloying, flowery scent of Anais Anais perfume.

"Reena, Momma has a problem," Mona tried explaining later as she held me in her lap, rocking me back and forth. Mona had realized I was upset when Momma finally came home and didn't have a birthday cake or a single present. I'd run off upset and she knew exactly where to find me, unlike my sorry-ass momma.

The problem was Momma was always good for tripping over her heart and landing all the fuck up in some man's lap. When the last "daddy stunt double" she brought home said he wasn't really feeling kids, well, Momma was so caught up in the rapture of love that she tucked tail and ran right on up out of there with his ass. They just rode off into the damn darkness like it was nothing. I say "darkness" because that's what happens when the light bill doesn't get paid; there ain't no sunsets to look forward to. After she left we were introduced to Mr. Late, Final Notice, Overdue, Collections, and best of all good old Mr. Eviction Notice.

My sister Mona was nineteen and working part time at the shirt factory in between losing her damn mind the winter that I met Ray and I was going on seventeen. He was hell-bent on making something out of his life and at that point I was just hell-bent.

I was volunteering or more like "voluntold" to work at the free clinic as punishment for shoplifting. It was one of those drab gray winter days where the sun sits like a block of ice in the sky, and the wind's so cold it makes your lips burn. I'd been pissed all week about Mona selling my pea coat at the flea market that Sunday. If I weren't trying to keep my record clear over that *shoplifting shit, I would've whooped her ass and gotten myself a new one off that five-finger discount.*

Inside the clinic I took up my usual position behind the reception counter ready to read and reread the articles in my Ebony magazine. It must have been too much for me to ask for a peaceful day. Glancing up I cringed as a woman staggered in through the door toward the front desk where I sat. Before I could even open my mouth to ask her what she needed, he walked, no, let me rephrase that, he glided in not far behind her. I'd heard about pimps bringing in their girls for the free STD treatments but I'd never actually seen or dealt with one. The entire concept of giving up hard-earned money to someone else for no reason completely baffled me anyway.

His floor-length mink fluttered around him in a fur cloud as he sauntered toward me with a smirk on his face. There were so many diamonds on him I damn near had to squint as the lights shimmered off of them in various directions.

He leaned onto the receptionist desk like he owned it, a tea-tree stick hanging out from the corner of his mouth. He was so close my eyes started to water from the pungent minty scent as he chewed it casually.

"Let me tell you how you're doing today." His voice was smoother than a baby's ass and equally as soft as he continued. "You finer than fine china, eating off paper plates every night. I already know I'm right, because wrong ain't an option. You been misguided, because somebody sold you a blank map to life, when all you really need is someone to map your life out. Let me get you off this road to nowhere and into show-where. Ho-where. Ho territory making that prime ho fare."

This fool couldn't be serious. "I think your lady friend over there needs help." Frowning, I gave a quick nod toward her. She was leaning against the wall looking worse by the minute.

He didn't even glance in her direction. "Business first, ass last. That's rule number one."

"Well, I don't think she's interested in doing any kind of business so you can check in or leave." Ray's voice was a deep road block in Frankie's map.

"You know you're addressing Frankie the Ambassador Diamonds, young blood?" Frankie straightened slowly, his jaw flexing around the chew stick.

"I know who I'm talking to, but your title doesn't mean anything to anyone outside of the broken women you exploit."

Frankie Diamonds stared straight past Ray as if he didn't even exist. He flung the lapels of his coat behind him and marched toward the door, angrily yanking the girl up by the arm on his way out.

Up until that point Ray had all but ignored me anytime we were stuck working together. He was quiet and stayed lost in his head, but there was always something about him that stood out from all the idiots who cat-called at me all day. He was a Venus flytrap in a garden of geraniums and I just had to know if I put my finger next to him . . . near him . . . on him . . . would he snap. And, snap he did.

It was as if I'd been sleepwalking through life ever since the day Momma left us, and being with Ray was electrifying. He was that feeling you get when you dream you're falling and you jerk yourself awake. I wasn't about to tell him that though, couldn't have him thinking he had me all wrapped around his little, middle, and index fingers. Even though he did. Truth was I didn't have to tell him anything. Anyone looking at us could see it written all over our faces and in our body language. Our souls were mirrors of the other and it was seen and felt no matter what we did. You'd think working in a damn clinic with mounds of birth control at our disposal we'd use it, and we did. But it only takes that one time to get caught up in the moment, and it's a wrap.

His parents eventually found out through the gossip grapevine of nosey-ass neighbors and store owners that we were seeing each other and they had him moved into a new intern position. They'd been molding him to follow in their footsteps and they damn sure weren't about to let him get mixed up with anyone that might get him off track; especially, not with someone like me. Ray managed to sneak across town to see me throughout my entire pregnancy. He was probably more excited about the baby than I was.

The problem with young, stupid love is that you never realize you're being young and stupid while you're in it.

When I finally went into labor it was a muggy summer day in August. Mona was in jail for breaking and entering and my damn water broke while I was on a bus of all places. When Ray got to the hospital I'd already put his name on the paperwork and dozed off. Not long after he'd arrived a roar started in the hospital lobby that burst into my hospital room in the form of two angry parents.

"What the hell is this, Ray?" his momma fumed; her face was damn near bright red she was so mad.

Ray was seated in a chair in the corner holding an ice pack to his neck.

"Son? Answer your damn mother. How could you go against what we said? We forbade you to deal with this girl, and now look at the mess you're in." Ray's daddy was pacing back and forth, his long legs covering the length of the entire room in three steps before he was turning to repeat the process.

I couldn't take it anymore; my body hurt and I was dead-ass tired. They acted like I wasn't the one who had just done all the fuckin' work.

"*Excuse me; Ray is still a little fuzzy from his head hittin' the floor. He kinda passed out a few minutes ago. If the two of you would please stop yelling and just sit down, the nurse will be back in a few minutes and you can meet your grandbabies: Rasheed, Rayshon, and Rosalyn.*"

Chapter 28

Momma's Maybe, Daddy's Baby

It was as if a game of freeze tag had ended and everyone could move again.

"Michelle, can you let my sister go please?"

"Sister?"

"Michelle, let me fuckin' go," she squeaked.

I tightened my grip. "So why you ain't say anything to her at Ruby Tuesday's when she was sitting behind us, Devon? She was right there, squakin' at Rasheed, remember?" I asked him sarcastically.

Devon took a step toward me with his hands out and I tightened up. The orderlies were all over the place corralling the crazies, but I kept an eye out for one just in case.

Devon sputtered nervously, "I honestly didn't see her, didn't recognize her voice or anything, Michelle. They were behind us remember. You're tripping right now."

"You really wanna call me crazy again, boy?" I gave him that look that said when and if we got home it was goin' down, and not the type of going down that he'd appreciate.

Shiree tapped my arm. "Chelle, he probably ain't know it was me; my ass had laryngitis. I swear on my life. I was up in there coughing and everything. You had to have heard me."

"I really didn't know. I swear I ain't know it was her, Michelle." Devon said looking at me pitifully.

I looked down at Shiree, in her tight sundress, there was nowhere to hide a weapon except for up in her snatch.

I wouldn't even put that past these trifling-ass heffas these days.

I let Shiree go, throwing her away from me so she'd lose her balance and she fell into Devon. They were both scowling at me and in turn I scowled right the hell back.

Devon looked between me and Shiree and started laughing. "She gotta be a keeper if she can whoop my sister's mean ass."

Reena wandered back off and was busy humming back into her rosebush.

Shiree watched Momma walk away. "Sounds like old Reena was getting it in." She laughed and asked, "What she say all them damn babies names was?"

"Rasheed, Rayshon, and Rosalyn; damn, even I caught that and I had you in a choke hold. She was stuck on them Rs, must've had a Reese's. I think they're wrooooong. I don't like any of 'em. But that's just me." I laughed.

Shiree hit *the* ground. Devon swayed where he stood. I was the only one laughing.

Uh oh. Whatever it is, it ain't gonna be good.

"My first name is Rayshon. My dad raised me, Shiree, went to Grandma's. I remember him and Melanie arguing about another little girl he had that went there too, but I never met her. I went to Great Uncle Lowell," Devon whispered.

The orderlies helped Shiree sit up and she looked a myriad of emotions that I could never begin or even want to understand or explain.

"First thunderstorm. I can hear it already. Y'all hear that? 'How sweet the sound . . .'" Reena asked in a singsong voice, before bellowing out her haunting, memorable rendition of "Amazing Grace."

We all looked up; there wasn't a single cloud in the damn sky.

We were all sitting around the kitchen table silently, with grim, somber faces. No one really wanted to say what the others were thinking or feeling. It was as if we'd drank and partied, finally waking up hung over. Each of us in bed with someone we knew but didn't really know, remembering what we'd done or did with and to each other. Reena was a mouse trapped in a maze of memories. She'd find her way out only to go get lost again.

"Why did she keep Rasheed and not us?" Devon wondered out loud.

Remembering the Frankie Diamonds story, I answered him. "They got chased and split up she could only carry one of you, so I think your daddy grabbed you two."

The Cliffs Notes, minus the gruesome details. That's what I gave them and they still looked down at the table like I'd stepped on their favorite pet cricket. Shiree was even harder to read and I could understand why. She literally loved and lost her brother.

I wasn't even trying to wrap my head around my relationship with Devon or Rayshon or whatever. Ugh, I shuddered whenever I said or thought of that name. I'd decided to call it a night after the pizza came for Trey. I put on my house sweats, did the movie and pizza thing with my little man, and then we were out.

I woke up in the middle of the night, sweating and out of breath. I was having a nightmare that Devon was Rasheed and he was trying to kill me. Out of habit I turned to Devon and realized I'd fallen asleep with Trey. I quietly climbed out of Trey's little bed and stretched my stiff, sore back.

"I can rub that for you."

I turned around slowly. "How did you get in here, Towanna?" I asked her quietly.

"You didn't answer my calls, didn't return any of my texts. I had to make sure you were good." She shrugged and picked at her fingernails.

"Towanna, where's Devon?"

"On the couch, exactly where he was when I came in," she replied calmly, too calmly.

"Stop playing with me; you know what the hell I'm asking you. Is he alive?"

"For now. I'm not the one who's going to determine how long he lives. You are. So come along; we don't need to get cliché about this shit either."

"What about Trey? What am I—"

"He'll be safer here. So give him a kiss and let's go."

We walked right out the front door. Past Devon who was passed out drunk on the couch and everything. The only good thing was I still slept in full preparation mode sometimes. My phone was in my pants pocket and I looked for any chance to call or text for help.

So much for my macho man super protection; and what's the point of the damn house alarm if he's not going to use it? Worse than Key's ass.

We drove for about an hour until she finally stopped at the Chesapeake Bay Bridge. The water was pitch black beneath and the night wind whistled in cold sheets against the side of her SUV. I was too scared to ask why we were there or what she was about to do with me. I just stared at the stars; every now and again a stark white seagull would appear and dive below.

"Get out of the car, Michelle. It's time to get this shit over with."

She got out, walked around, and opened my door.

"Whatever this is, I don't want to do it. I'm serious. I really don't want to. You're right, I'm wrong."

"I'm not the one trying to prove anything. It's your ass. Get the fuck down here and stop acting like a little punk-ass bitch. You done let that nigga twist your mind all the fuck up like that? The dick can't be that damn good."

I climbed out the truck, slamming the door and I walked up to her, yelling the entire way. "Are we really standing in the middle of this fucking bridge having a damn argument over . . . over I don't even know what it's over? So leave my man and his dick up out ya mouth, Towanna."

"Okay now we're getting somewhere. So he's your man now?"

"Yes, he's my man, Towanna. You mad or somethin'? Is that why we here?"

She ignored me and kept going with the questions, her nostrils flaring and eyes raging. "Does he love you?"

She would ask me that after the day we just had.

"What happened? We ain't so quick when it counts anymore. Does he love you as much as I love you?"

I actually laughed and loud, too. "Towanna, you might need to go get checked out your damn self. The hell are you talking about? No one came to the house that night, there were no cars, you were sleep on the couch. It was just you wasn't it? You tortured me for Rah's money."

"Right, you right." She pulled out her pistol.

My phone vibrated in my pocket.

We have what we need. Get down.

That text turned me into a human panic button and I was suddenly the one pressed for information.

"Towanna, did you kill your partner that night?

She curled her lip in a smirk. "Fuck no. The hell would you—"

"Towanna, shut up and just answer the damn questions. Is your mom's name Lacy?"

"Da fuck? Huh?"

I clenched my fist and literally groaned out loud. "Tell me, hurry up. What is it?"

She started looking at me sideways; she obviously didn't understand but I didn't need her to understand. We didn't have time for the theatrics right now. My eyes were all over the place, scared a helicopter was going to rise up beside us at any minute spraying saltwater everywhere. Lightning lit the sky up and I almost came up out my skin.

"My mom's name is Royce," Towanna finally called out suspiciously narrowing her eyes.

I ran toward her, waving my arms before throwing myself at her, knocking her to the ground. The sky split open in a crack of lightning and a roar of thunder and down came the rain.

Towanna looked at me like I'd sprouted a nose in the middle of my forehead. "Woman, have you lost your damn mind? What in the world?" she asked me.

"Why does everybody keep asking me that shit?" I smiled down at her.

And then I passed out.

Chapter 29

Orders Are Meant to Be Followed

Iodine, ultraviolet lights, and ointment: I could smell it everywhere and feel it on the backs of my eyelids prying them open. People were walking and talking around me in hushed whispers. The last thing I could remember was looking down at Towanna in the rain and then this. I had no idea where I was, where she was or where . . .

I sat up and pain ran through the entire left side of my body. There was no pinpointing where it began or ended. It felt like the skin was tearing and pulling from the front of my stomach to the back of my ribcage.

"She's awake," I heard someone say on the other side of a white curtain.

"How are you feeling, Michelle?" A nurse approached me and checked my vitals.

"I don't know, tell me what happened and I'll figure out how I feel as opposed to that."

"Well, you were brought in with a gunshot wound to the abdomen. The police report says you tried to kill yourself. Did you know you were pregnant when you attempted this, Michelle?"

I sat there with my head cocked to the side as if I'd gotten water in my ear and I were waiting on that one drop to drip its way out. I didn't move, I didn't blink, and I didn't make a sound.

I was what? I was what? I did what?

Even after I told them not to shoot, throwing myself on this woman like she was a fucking live grenade, they did anyway. And when I got hit, they called it self-inflicted and on top of that I was . . .

Not ready to think about that part of the equation yet. Let's stick with A and B: did the FBI or whoever just shoot me and make it look like I shot myself, and where is Towanna?

"Do you have anything to say, Ms. Roberts?" the nurse asked, raising an eyebrow.

"What hospital is this? Where are Devon and my son?"

"Excuse me, I—"

"It's a simple question. What hospital am I in?" I shouted.

The chatter stopped. The makeshift curtain flew open. A bear of a man appeared holding a soiled Dunkin' Donuts coffee cup. I tried to focus and not to stare at the graying box-fade shaped thing growing off his head.

He spoke in a brusque voice. "Okay, Michelle, calm down. I'm Special Agent—"

"About to get fucked up if you don't tell me that what this nurse just told me is a bunch of bullshit."

He drew in a long breath. "You were given an order, a directive. You failed and this is your fault, your punishment, your fuckup. I'm Agent Harper."

"Have you told anyone that I'm here?"

"Not yet, we need you to corroborate the story before we set you out in the world with it. You're stuck here until you cooperate."

"And Towanna?"

"She's being questioned."

"What if I told you that you have the wrong person? Do you think I'd throw myself in front of a bullet for no damn reason?"

Agents I didn't even know were out there poked their heads in at that moment. Looking, listening, ready to hear what I had to say. But, not until I knew Towanna was okay.

They brought Towanna in and she nodded, assuring me that she was okay.

"Okay, Michelle. We can't just have people sitting around without an explanation. This is your show; all eyes are on you right now."

"Melanie Malia took out five genteel wealthy men, one of whom was none other than Momma White's baby daddy Ray and, on top of that, she somehow got Devon and Shiree in the process. When Momma White told me the story she said it happened twice. I had to do some research into Lacy's cases."

"What are the names of all the husbands, Agent Harper?"

"Renner, Clark, Kellam, Latharium, Ponce, and Harrington." Agent Harper rattled them off one by one.

"There's a man in the area by the name of Marcus Latharium Bello; he was good friends with Rasheed, goes by Big Baby. He's the only Bello I know and Rah told me they grew up together, how Big just showed up one, day no parents, he just appeared. I never thought about the story until now. Mr. Latharium's son. Momma helped Lacy get rid of him by giving that little boy to the African lady at the shop, kind of a repayment thing. When Lacy picked Ray, Momma refused to do it again."

A few agents had some light bulbs go off and began writing down what I was saying. Good, because I was starting to get tired.

"He has some massage something or another's popping up all over the place. Check into him and his stuff he's probably hiding whatever it is that Lacy used in plain sight."

There was a rush of excited voices and they exchanged glances.

"I asked to redecorate Devon's hospital after he checked me in, no thanks to you morons. A nurse had mentioned stuff happening on the 5th wing. Devon checks out. I couldn't find anything on him. The only thing you'll find there is that area, his lab, which also houses the electro-shock therapy units. Every now and again he has elite and VIPs come and go without check-in or special clearances but that's expected when they're high-profile celebrities and don't want the press finding out about it.

"And, Towanna. I didn't forget about you. Your momma married three times I think? But remind these good people who she is and who her second husband was."

"They already know. My mom's name is Royce; she didn't know she was pregnant when she did what she did to my dad. Don Cerzulo is my stepfather. May he rest in peace, even though me and him weren't that close."

And then a light bulb went off in my head. "So that's why you're helping them, because you just tie the whole family together, huh? Then when I came in the picture they were all like find out what I know so that when a time like right the fuck now came they'd have whatever they needed to get me to help fit everybody the hell together."

"But, Michelle, that's why nothing really happened and I didn't even have anybody up in the house to hurt you. Angelo didn't even come to the house. I'd asked one of the agents to swab Lataya and for whatever reason he did them both. When these dudes killed Ennis . . ."

"He drew a weapon on an armed agent and refused to stand down, ma'am."

I didn't see who said it but that explained poor Ennis.

Towanna sneered at one of the men and went on, "I just wanted to know if you knew anything ASAP so I could be done with the shit. So I staged that whole thing to try to make you talk. That's all, and then you ran all the way out here."

I was starting to feel weak and nauseated. Connecting all these dots to all these different people was really starting to wear me out. The FBI and CIA had tracked down and traced everyone connected to Lacy in some way, shape, or form. I guess the world really does revolve around money. I still had to know something.

"One last question and then I'm done. The agreement I signed said that I killed Rasheed. What did yours say?"

"That's classified, Roberts," several agents blurted out at once.

"It's okay, Towanna, I already know. It said you killed Lania and Keyshawn, didn't it?" I asked her anyway despite their warnings.

Towanna looked down at the floor quickly but not before I could see the tears in her eyes, confirming my suspicion.

"That's enough, Roberts. Conditions of your agreements are confidential and need-to-know only. You are relieved and needed no further."

"Well, we might as well show our hands then." I addressed everyone in the room, taking turns looking at them one by one. Some of them looked away, some met my stare with indifference or defiance as I continued, "It doesn't make any sense acting all shy now. Not when we all know who's using who. Tell me again, my options were to sign or what? Sink, right?"

Done with my tirade, I was finally feeling winded and my side was aching. I had to get a point across even if they didn't give a fuck about me making it. They scowled and Towanna stood there clammed up looking pensive and hurt. Drained, I lay my head back, empathizing with the pain I knew she was feeling.

"And for the damn record, my last name is Laurel. I've changed it since you don't seem to get up-to-date information. And, you're welcome."

Chapter 30

I Am Relieved

"You sure you wanna do this, Michelle?" Devon whined, looking at me with the stank face.

We were lying in bed enjoying the peace and quiet. Trey wouldn't be home until Sunday and me and my man had ourselves a date. Devon rolled on his stomach sticking his head under the pillow, ostrich style. I quit fiddling with the button of his pajama top I was wearing and rolled my eyes. Trey might as well have been in the bed with me; the man was acting just like him when he ain't wanna get up in the morning.

"Boy, stop. It ain't gonna be that bad." I smacked his ass.

Biting my nail I grinned at that bad boy as it bounced in the matching bottoms to my top. I was about to reach over and smack it again.

"Stop smackin' my ass, woman." His voice was muffled under the pillow.

"Huh? What did you say, baby? I can't understand you when you're speaking ostrich," I teased him.

He threw the pillow and snatched me down in its place and I yelped. Giggling, I stared up and him through my lashes.

"Guess we need to work on that language barrier then. 'Cause, I can understand yo' ostrich perfectly fine." He mocked me, "Harder, baby, get it, get it, choke—"

What in the hell, is that what I sound like? Good Lawd.
Slamming my finger up against his lips I shushed his
ass. "What I say or don't say in the heat of the moment is
not to be repeated. Ever. I made a list of stuff you need to
get before our date night. So we need to get up."

There was too much on my to-do list today and ass was
not one them. At least not now, definitely after, but now
we had shit to do.

"But a double date though?"

"What's wrong with a double date? It'll be fun and I like
Nurse Denise."

"How you even know she swing that way? She might
just be shy or a late bloomer or something. I know you
can't tell because I'm so ruggedly sexy and shit now, but I
too was a late bloomer. You might mess around and have
her out there embarrassed and shit."

*Just keep your mouth shut, Chelle. We ain't even
gonna touch this one. We can't be talking about the same
Nurse Denise I got eye-molested by. Her brazen ass.
Thick as fawck ain't a late bloomer, shit if he was Ris.
Change the channel, Chelle.*

"Look, I think Denise is cute and I also think she and
Towanna would make a cute couple. Besides when's the
last time you took me out on a date, Devon?"

"Um. The, uh. We go on dates," he eventually sputtered.

I gave him the side eye. "The secret agent hotel doesn't
count, bae."

I'd had lunch with Towanna at least once a week since
the night I took a bullet for her. I'd told her that she was
gonna have to let me shoot her for GP now. It was only
fair. We couldn't be best friends otherwise. She'd laughed
her ass off that day, reminding me that I'd already shot
her. Not sure how on earth that little detail had slipped
my mind. I never told Devon about losing the baby. There
was no point in upsetting him over something he couldn't

have controlled or changed. He would have been hurt for no reason, banning Towanna from our lives when I still would have gotten over it as I did.

The Feds finally caught up with Big Baby. Turned out he did have that concoction that connected Lacy to all five of those deaths. He'd been remaking it up in his shop in Miami. Shiree was taking it the hardest. Devon said she'd actually miscarried not long after finding out Rasheed was her brother and I was hoping my manhandling her ain't have anything to do with it. He said it was stress related, but on second thought I think she might have gotten rid of the baby all together. She'd only come by the house once and that was to say good-bye. She said she was staying in Miami, and then possibly going to Cali.

Trey didn't bat an eyelash, pout, or anything when I'd dropped him off at Denise's nephews on Friday evening. It felt good to have some little boys around his age he could play with. He'd been so excited and it was all he'd talked about all week. I'd never seen that child struggle with anything more than when it came time to figure out which toys he wanted to take. You'd think I'd asked him to only take items that would keep him alive on a deserted island of children.

Mommy was excited too. This was going to be the first night in I couldn't remember how long that I was going to have a grown-up dinner and dancing date night with no drama and no bullshit.

I'd gone to at least three different stores and finally ended up around the corner, spending around $450 at Pier One on candles, wine glasses, and vases. I wanted to have a real nice evening before we went out with wine and talking. It would give Denise and Towanna a chance to warm up to each other. I figured given the rare chance they didn't like each other, they would have an escape before we got to the Melting Pot.

"Look, I don't want you hookin' me up with none of your dude's Nurse Ratched friends," Towanna complained, moping into her Cobb salad.

Reaching over I smacked her elbow.

"This one ain't ratched, trust me. She's cute, thick, an' Towanna wanna thicky, dimpled hippy girl . . ." I bobbed back and forth singing to her in my seat.

"Yeah, All right. What's her Facebook?"

That was all I needed. She started grinning sheepishly into her plate. Clapping my hands I tapped my feet on the floor squealing in delight like I'd just scored myself a touchdown.

"Don't worry 'bout all that. I already showed her your picture. She's all in. It's a double date. We goin' to the Melting Pot. Saturday, fool. So dress cute, pretty please. None of this T-shirt business," I warned, waving my hand over her with my face all furled up.

"Damn. I ain't give her the stamp of approval or nothin'. And what the hell's wrong with my T-shirt? Makes my arms look good. Gun show all day, baby."

Everyone was supposed to be at the house at six p.m. and I'd made our reservations at the restaurant for a late dinner at nine. That would be more than enough time for the two of them to sit around chat and play the interview game. Since this was Denise's night and I didn't wanna upstage her date night, I kept my attire simple with a fitted above-the-knee cream-colored dress and yellow pumps for flair. I pinned my hair up because Devon always liked to call himself messing something up. This was just for him. I'd told Devon if he played nice tonight, I'd let him have his fun losing all my damn bobby pins between carpet and the bed later.

I turned the TV on to one of the Music Choice channels that played a variety of R&B. The entire house smelled like the crisp bamboo and citrus cilantro from candles I'd gotten earlier. He did it on purpose, and my head almost rolled off my shoulders. Devon zipped past me into the kitchen. Dolce & Gabbana all over his baahdy, probably even on the top of his freshly shaved head knowing him. My nose followed my favorite smell until he came into my line of sight and I damn near jumped the man.

"Negro, where the hell are your clothes? They're gonna be in a few minutes and you ain't even dressed?"

He bopped over, smiling wickedly. "You have to give me something if you want me to wear clothes tonight. I just said I'd shower and be nice."

I smirked at him. "Fine then, walk your ass around naked. They ain't gonna care. I'm the one getting the show."

Why I thought I'd get away with that answer I had no idea. I was trying to take the wine out the fridge . . . and then I was pressed hard up against the fridge. My eyes narrowed impishly. Devon was already hard up against my stomach. He was being so bad. But getting so, so good. One night he was going in, or so he thought. Moaning to himself, wiggling his ass, for all I could tell he was eating the sheets. The bad head had to stop. I grabbed his face, put his mouth right where it needed to be. Then I took one of his fingers, put it up to my lips, and we played what I liked to call mirror, mirror. Everything I did to that finger he did to my lady finger and nothing else. At that moment he was about to hit my sleep magic number all on his own. He'd started off licking every inch of my pussy. I alternated between holding his head and the top of the fridge for balance.

The doorbell rang and I swear I wanted to cry in frustration. He slid me down, sitting me on the floor, and we butted foreheads. My eyes instantly watered as I fought a sneeze. Pinching the bridge of my nose I glowered at him, trying to figure out where he was even bending to in the first place. He chuckled and I climbed back into my heels . . .

When the hell did he take off . . .

"See, I told you they'd be here; where the hell is my thong? You couldn't have just pushed it to the side? When the hell did you even take it off? Go get me one out the laundry room!"

When the doorbell rang again I hurried to answer it.

"Hey, y'all. Sorry, I was trying to open the wine."

You know how people come in and sit at your counter in the kitchen or your kitchen table. Well, that's what I'd planned for the start so we could have finger foods and chat. Bruschetta with tomato and cheese was laid out, different kinds of dip to pair with different kind of wine. I turned to get the wine and wine glasses and ta-da there's my wonderful thong sitting in the kitchen sink! Hoping that neither of them had seen it I took a plate out the cabinet when . . .

Devon's still in the damn laundry room!

"Excuse me for a second," I said politely, "I just need to go in here and see if Devon's shirt is dry."

"Um, Chelle. You ain't wash our glasses in the sink with them thongs did you?" Towanna asked with a sarcastic grin on her face.

I could feel the red creeping up my neck. Oh, that was so embarrassing. Sliding my hips through the smallest crack I could possibly make in the door, without letting in any light, I exhaled when I was finally all the way in the room.

"Took you long enough," Devon whispered from directly behind me before picking me up and sitting me on top of the cool laundry of the washing machine. I was struggling with every shred of self-control to maintain my composure and be the adult.

"We can't, they are gonna hear us. You need to get your ass dressed." I grabbed a mismatched sock and shirt from under my butt, handing them to him. "We gotta go out there. This is rude; stop being rude." I slapped his arm.

"They gonna hear you making all that damn noise, not me. They can have their date and we'll have ours. You done already took your panties off for me remember?"

"No, I didn't. You did that—"

Devon knew I'd have argued with him all night in there if he let me. He shut me up the best way he knew how and I answered with my teeth all in the side of his neck.

Chapter 31

Which Witch is Which?

We were seated at the restaurant having our first course of fondue. The waiter stood beside the table mixing everything in the little broiler on the tabletop burner. It was everyone's first experience except for Devon. I shot him a look, daring him to compare my night to another date and he'd be reliving the laundry room experience with his hand. He clammed up quick.

From what I could tell Towanna and Denise were or weren't getting along. They were both kind of take-charge so it was like watching a couple of rams go head-to-head. Devon started getting annoyed around the third course but I thought it was hilarious. I was digging around in my oversized purse, trying to find my phone so I could take a picture. I felt like the worst parent in the world when I found Trey's iPad. He'd specifically asked to take it and I'd forgotten to give it to him. He was obviously having a good time if my phone wasn't getting blown up about it though.

Speaking of phone, I couldn't find it anywhere. There was so much going on I prayed I'd just put it down somewhere at the house. I must have hit something because the iPad came on at a screen called notepad. It was the screen where Rasheed typed to Trey before he'd died. I shut it off and stuffed it back into my purse. My appetite was instantly gone and I sat there rigid as a board.

"Bae, you okay?" Devon put his arm around my shoulders, looking over at me concerned but I couldn't speak past the lump in my throat.

"You're cold, here." He took his jacket off, draping it around me.

Towanna tried to get my attention. "Chelle, what's the matter? We can leave if y'all ready to go."

I didn't want to leave, and I didn't want to stay. I felt feverish but the minute I went to remove the jacket I felt cold again and pulled it back around me. I nodded. I was ready to go.

Denise was trying to call and check on Trey for me since I didn't have my phone. When she couldn't get a call to go out with a full signal, my favorite friends, fear and trepidation, paid a visit.

"Towanna? Remember when we were in that hospital?" I barely whispered my question.

She was sitting behind Devon on the driver side of the SUV and I barely looked over my shoulder to acknowledge her response. Devon and Denise looked back and forth trying to figure out what was going on. Towanna nodded ever so slightly.

"I had all these questions. There were so many things I didn't understand. I asked those people question after question. Lania and Keyshawn, they weren't on your agreement were they?" There was so much sadness and regret in my voice.

Devon frowned over at me in between glancing anxiously at the road. "Michelle, what's all this about? What the hell has gotten in to you all of a sudden?"

We were slowing to a stop at a red light and I saw the only chance I had. I grabbed the syringe I'd felt in Devon's jacket pocket at dinner and pulling the top off I reached back, stabbing Towanna in the leg.

The pistol in her hand fell to the floor and Denise screamed at the sight of the gun. I was surprised the glass didn't shatter. Devon stomped on the brakes. Towanna stared at me in shock, her eyes taking on that drugged, glazed look.

Grabbing the pistol from her lap I turned it on Devon. Denise continued screaming like the gun was actually pointed at her.

"Denise, I'll shoot you to shut you up at this point so please . . ." I threatened her, thankful for the immediate silence.

"Devon, you're a psychiatrist with a damn chemistry lab in your asylum. You have people come and go at all hours of whatever on that floor. Rich people who could actually afford cocaine if they wanted it. You keep no record of who comes or goes or when they come or go. I've already dealt with one dealer. I'm not doing this shit again."

The light turned green and he looked at me, hesitating. I pointed the gun, instructing him to drive.

"What you want me to do, baby?" he asked quietly.

I almost didn't know what to say. My throat got this scratchy feeling like I was growing a baby cactus in it and for a second I couldn't speak.

"You're gonna have to turn yourself in. They're not gonna stop until they have you."

He nodded, but of course it couldn't have been that easy; he wasn't nodding at me.

Do all of these motherfuckas' carry emergency knock-out needles in their damn pockets?

I cringed, waiting for the pinch and paralysis that never came. Thank sweet baby Jesus in a manger, even after threatening her with a pistol Denise stuck Devon instead of me. I straddled his lap and pressed the brake, putting the car in park.

"Find Towanna's phone. I know they called or sent her a text. I need to know where to take him."

Just like my phone the day Devon checked it, there were no missed special agent calls or texts. I cursed silently trying.

"How long does that stuff last, Denise?"

"It depends. It could be twenty minutes up to an hour."

I did the only thing I could think of. Hell it worked last time. I hauled ass toward the Chesapeake Bay Bridge. It wasn't super early a.m. like the last time but there was barely a car out there. I stopped in the middle and Denise helped me drag Devon out and then we got Towanna.

"Okay, now you get back in and stay down. I got my ass shot last time."

Her eyes got huge and she went MIA inside the truck.

I pulled out the pistol and fired into the air three times and waited. Every fiber in my being was clenched with the memory of the last time I was up here. You get shot one time you remember that feeling. It's not like a tattoo needle or piercing, it definitely ain't something you forget.

Squad cars came rolling up with the lights on, sirens blaring and I was beyond relieved. Devon was still out but Towanna was moaning. A spotlight turned on, blinding me and I shielded my eyes.

"Drop the gun. Get down on the ground, with your hands behind your head."

"I need to see Agent Harper." I called out nervously, dropping the gun, and the spotlight immediately shut off.

I was grabbed and thrown into the back of a car. I could see police officer's going to Devon and Towanna. They yanked Denise out the truck ass first. I slammed my head back against the seat and waited impatiently.

"You were relieved, Roberts; what in God's name are you doing here?" Harper blasted his question at the side of the car I sat in. The windows possibly rattled.

"Rasheed left a note on Trey's iPad. Then you guys sent Towanna the message; when I figured it out, I brought him in."

Harper exhaled loudly, leaning up against the side of the car. He was staring at the flurry of activity across the bridge where they had Devon. He'd finally come out of his stupor and was being put into the back of car across the way. Harper opened my door, letting me out the squad car.

"Don't discharge another damn firearm in public. You'd better go make up with that man 'cause he look some kind of pissed off right now. You were relieved, Michelle, and we meant it."

If I wasn't mistaken, either Harper had given me tender smile or a heartburn, vexed scowl. It's not like there were varying degrees of emotion to the man's face.

Chapter 32

An Equal Sign
=

Ain't Nothing but Stacked Up Minuses

Devon wouldn't speak to me let alone look at me after the officers released him from the squad car. He'd stood there with his eyes mysteriously hooded by his dark lashes, feeling withdrawn and distant. In the entire time we'd been together I'd never seen him so angry and cold. I just kept waiting for him to turn around and blind me with that disarming boyish smile or wink at me, but nothing happened. Standing in jaw-gaping wide-eyed disbelief, I watched as he got in the Land Cruiser and with a stony voice suggested that one of "my girls" drop me off at the house. It was as if my best friend had sped off and left me holding the sack on the day of the championship three-legged race. I'd just felt the other end of betrayal's double-edged blade.

Denise had called one of her nieces to pick up her and Towanna and they'd agreed to let me ride with them. The girls had all decided that drinks were in order after what they declared from beginning to end as "the official hell date of the year." I was outnumbered and outvoted. As bad as I wanted to curl up in a ball and cry it would just have to wait until later. Of course they'd pick a strip club of all places.

I was sitting in Liquid Blue all the way out Newport News far from where I really wanted to be. My head hurt and my eyes hurt. I was squinting against all these bright blue neon lights that just followed me and magnified whenever I close my eyes. Towanna's buying so of course the shot of the night was her signature drink, Pixy Stix. After about four of those things I just felt like I was gonna be Pixy Sick. All I could think about was how mad Devon looked and how horrible I felt for trying to turn him in. I mean in the time I'd known the man, granted he did put me in his asylum but he still took really good care of me. It was more than Rasheed or Ris or anyone had ever done for me. He'd never cheated on me or lied to me and the one time that I should have trusted him, I took him to the Feds and straight up turned his ass in.

There couldn't have been any way possible for me to feel like the world's biggest douche. Until someone thought it'd make me feel better if I got a lap dance. Dynasty spun my barstool around and climbed, yes, climbed on top of me. She'd started grinding all over me and I couldn't breathe because, one, I had Dynasty's double Ds up my nose, and two, I'd started crying. Yes, ladies and gentlemen, there I was having a complete emotional breakdown in the middle of the strip club. Ass, titties, liquor, and tears . . .

Towanna, the guilty party, pulled me into the ladies' room.

"Don't cry, man. Everything'll be fine." She patted my back, trying her best to console me.

It was atrocious. I'd started doing this uncontrollable hiccupping thing like I couldn't breathe but I was still trying to talk at the same time. Through hiccupping and sobs I'd managed to ask Towanna why she was even pulling her gun in the first place.

"Um, because your name was originally on my agreement. I was supposed to kill you on that bridge; you jumped in front of your own bullet and lived because you asked my mom's name. They figured you knew more than you should. Remember the agent said you tried to commit suicide. I thought you'd gotten a call or something, you invite me on this date with a chick I can barely stand and midway through you go all Stepford wife, then we get in the truck and you go in with the questions—"

"That's because I was thinking Devon's name was on your agreement. Rasheed wrote 'Don Cerzulo told Daddy see Doc in Trey's iPad. I sat there piecing everything together and when we got in the truck and Denise's phone didn't work I thought you were going to kill him. I'd just as well take him in and I fucked the fuck up . . ." I started crying all over again.

It was a total misunderstanding, except you know neither of them drugged and then literally drug me to the law enforcement. Towanna was just a lot more forgiving about it all than Devon was.

He sat in the darkened living room in nothing but his sweat pant bottoms when Denise dropped me off at three a.m. I was still wearing my dress from our date night. An empty cocktail glass was sitting on the coffee table in front of him as he sat with his forearms resting on his knees.

I stood in the doorway debating what to say while I closed it behind me. I settled on keeping it simple. "Hey."

He didn't look up or anything at the sound of my voice. "I think you and Trey should find a place for a little while. Might be best that way." He was frowning at the floor in front of him.

Tears clouded my vision, welled up and burned so hot I wouldn't see my own hand if it were right in front of my face even if I'd wanted to. I blinked and they rolled down my cheeks. There was nothing for me to say. If he wanted me gone I'd leave. There wasn't a single thing I could think of to make up for my fuckup of mammoth proportions.

I got my and Trey's things together as quickly as possible. I put his key on the table beside the door and just like that I left. Now, I knew Devon was missing from me the moment; he wouldn't smile for me anymore. It's actually fucked up because in these movies we grow up with, the guy chases his woman down yelling about how much he loves her. And, it's usually right about now that he'd do that shit. Because sometimes they have to watch you leave to realize they really want you to stay.

Well, some shit just doesn't go down like it does in movies. Checking my rearview only made me cry harder and it only made my heart feel like a worthless block of sorrow sitting in my chest when I didn't see him there. My phone, which had been in the bottom of my purse all along, was painfully silent.

My chest almost exploded when it rang. Seeing Denise's number I was so let down I didn't answer. Towanna called and I still didn't answer. I just didn't feel like being bothered right that second. We could chat and I'd let them know what went down later. I needed to find a damn hotel. I almost threw my phone out the window when Towanna called a second time.

"Yes, Towanna?" I answered in a watery voice.

"You good? I'm worried about you."

"I'm good, I promise," I lied.

My eyes were so puffy and swollen I could barely see the road. I'd passed at least five hotels but I was so depressed I kept driving just for the sake of having something to do.

Towanna's voice was whisper soft. "You can always come to me."

"What's your address?"

Exhausted I actually just wound up finally parking in a Wendy's parking lot and reclining the seat. My intent was to only close my eyes for a couple of minutes.

There was a loud tapping on my window, and I blinked and shielded my eyes against the intrusion.

"License and registration please?" The officer waited beside my car.

"I'm not driving, sir," I called out, looking at him, confused.

"Are you intoxicated? I will have to write you a ticket for public intoxication as well as disruptive conduct and . . ."

I looked at the clock, and winced. I didn't mean to sleep until almost eleven a.m. Annoyed, I got my shit out. It must have been end of the month and these idiots were trying to meet their damn quotas and shit. Handing him my information I rolled my eyes and sat back as he walked to his car. He finally came back and handed me my ID and registration and the damn ticket.

Leaning down beside my window he said, "Okay, I'm just issuing a warning this time. This is her, boys."

Two men hopped out the back of his squad car and climbed into the back of my car. I'd gotten lazy and comfortable; the old me would have been ready for something like this.

No, the old you wouldn't have been out here for something like this to happen.

"Drive."

I could feel him staring at me, watching my every move. It's akin to when you're outside and people peek at you through the curtains. That feeling you're in a room and the hairs in your ear vibrate and stand up on the back of your neck.

"We haven't been formally introduced have we?"

I looked up into the rearview and found myself gazing into eyes the turbulent color of the underside of thundercloud. For some reason, I couldn't help feeling as though I'd seen them somewhere before.

Chapter 33

Sins of the Father

I stared at this silver-eyed stranger and my mind clicked. He sent champagne to Keyshawn at Liv.

Glancing back in the rearview as I drove without directions I asked him, "I'm sorry, but are you sure we haven't met before?"

"I'm sure we have not met. Pay attention to the road please. So in case you's wondering I'm Angelo Testa. Rasheed got some vital info out of my father and killed him. His name was Don Cerzulo. Now, I need you to take me to Rasheed; that info was extremely important. Otherwise, I'll use you and your son to flush him out."

This might not be a good time to tell him neither of those is possible. How do I keep ending up in these impossible, impossible-ass situations? Koala's fingerprints look similar to humans. They're almost identical.

"Rasheed is in the hospital with his momma, but I have the info. Look in my purse, it's on the iPad. He typed it so he wouldn't forget. I didn't know what it was or I would have erased it. Trust me."

Angelo gave me a suspicious glance before digging through my purse. I dropped my phone into my lap, tempted to text Towanna but I didn't know what to say just yet. I couldn't risk reaching down to put my phone on vibrate and drawing attention to it. So I let it be.

"It's a phone number with the name 'Doc.' I'm setting up a pickup at your house, what's the address? That way if there's any funny business and this shit isn't real, you'll suffer."

I glanced down at my phone and gave him Towanna's address, then quickly sent what was probably the worst shorthand text in history: omw2 ur plc wt angelo 2mt drg dealr b rdy

Angelo called and set up his deal and I drove toward Towanna's, praying the entire way. When she didn't respond I almost cried. I was pretty sure I'd died and hell was reliving your last moment thinking you were still alive. Because, when we pulled up to the house and I saw the empty driveway I died over and over again. If I'd left Angelo would have known I was lying about where I was taking him and his supplier. He probably would have shot me on the spot so I committed to my lie and pulled into the empty driveway.

I was so busy looking for Towanna's car that when I finally saw Devon's Land Cruiser pulling up on the opposite side of the street I gasped out loud and if I'd had my gun I'd have shot it at him.

"There's your man," I told Angelo, pointing at Devon's truck. I was seething with the most irrational anger. *I bet he didn't even know I'd be here either. Probably feels stupid, too.* I'd started climbing out the car and walking over without a second thought, barely glancing at the black car pulling up in the driveway. Devon got out of the truck. I took one look at his face and almost turned around and ran back across the street.

"Dad? What are you doing out here?" he shouted across the street.

Confused, I spun around and there was this handsome older clone of Devon standing at my car. It wasn't Towanna who had pulled up; it was a black Lexus. I'd walked right past him. At that moment Towanna did pull up, along with the FBI. Angelo was yelling about his narc sister turning on family as they put him into a car.

"Devon, I thought your dad was dead." I looked at him still completely puzzled by everything I'd just seen.

His face was a complete mask of upset. "I never said that, it's something else you assumed and ran with instead of asking me. I said my great uncle raised me. Pops fell in love and took off with Melanie, her case if for murdering her first five of husband's he was the sixth. They were too busy globetrottin' and shit to deal with us. He might as well have been dead though. I didn't want him or her in my life after that."

Getting anywhere with this man seemed damn near ridiculous no matter how hard I tried. Everything I'd accused him of and put him through was all because of his damn father, and because I was too stubborn and foolish to trust a trustworthy person.

I grabbed his hands and he reluctantly let me hold them; he looked everywhere but down at me.

"Devon, you can't make me realize that I need you and then take you away from me. You're the one who said you can fix anything, so help me fix this." My voice broke and tears ran down my cheeks but I didn't hide them. "I can't love you by myself. I didn't want to fall all by myself. You were supposed to fall too." I dropped my head against his shoulder and cried. I'd been refusing to let anyone in for this very reason and then he came along and—

"I did." Devon's voice was a raspy whisper as he lifted my chin and stared into my eyes. "I did fall too, and I do love you. Baby, please stop crying." He leaned down and kissed my cheeks.

"I'll probably have to get you an autographed R2-D2 jersey to make up for it, huh?" I asked him in a pitiful voice.

"Get me a what, woman?" He looked down at me with the sweetest confused face.

I shrugged. "That football guy you like for the Redskins, RPG. I'll get you an autographed jersey to hang on your wall," I explained.

He made an exasperated sound and started laughing. I didn't get the joke.

"Chelle, it's RG3. And after I figure out what's going on with all this"—he pointed toward his father being put into a car—"I know something even better than can um, hang from my wall," he replied, winking down at me.

"Glad you answered your Bat-Signal, playboy," Towanna called out as she came across the street grinning like a damn fool.

For the first time since all the commotion started I noticed the letters FBI on her shirt.

"You've got to be playing. This whole time, Towanna, really?" I stared at her.

She nodded and kept grinning. "Yes, the entire time. Let's go have a drink and I'll tell you all about it. Feels like I ain't seen you in forever."

"Shots fired, shots fired," Towanna's radio blared.

Devon pushed me into the Land Cruiser and Towanna drew her gun. No one, and I repeat no one saw the shooter that took Angelo out as he was being put into the cruiser.

Chapter 34

Always Share Your Nightmares So They Can't Come True?

(Three Years Later)

Most people loved summer. Not me, and especially not in Virginia. The heat and humidity alone could make your boobs and butt combust into sweat the second you stepped outside. My favorite time of year quickly became early fall. Fall was supposed to be a time of year when the clouds brought to mind marshmallows and hot cocoa with a splash of Kahlúa. The crunch of leaves on the ground sounded like cute boots and comfy sweaters. Yet, there was nothing fall-like or cozy about sitting directly underneath the "cook your forehead" hot sun on a Wednesday afternoon during one of Virginia's Indian summers.

Someone had a grill going nearby and the smell of charcoal and hotdogs in the air reminded me of summer on the Fourth of July. We were sitting Indian style in a soft patch of clovers near the swings. I was glad I'd just worn an old comfortable pair of jeans and one of my Old Navy tees. All these confused-ass heffas in workout gear had taken up all the benches in the shade. All they were doing was sitting around eating snacks and talking on their cells. Not one of them looked like they were trying to scoot over or leave anytime soon.

"Show me which one you're thinking about. I wanna see if her ears bleed." Towanna leaned over, nudging me with her elbow, laughing. Denise sat behind her, arms wrapped around her waist, smiling over her shoulder. Funny how they couldn't stand each other as Towanna put it.

Some people like to get close to you just so they can say they were close. They really don't care about your dreams or what makes you, you. They just want to be able to tell people on the outside that their asses were part of your inner circle.

Thankfully Special Agent Towanna James wasn't one of those people. After everything that'd happened I never thought I'd let anyone get near me again but, I'd found genuine friendship with her and real love and happiness with Devon. They both had ways of making me laugh and the drama that used to be my life seemed worlds away. Well, except for my usual drama.

"Trey, you'd better put that down. I'm watchin' you," I warned, giving him a stern look and in turn focusing that same gaze on his counterpart. "Paris, little girl. Ah . . . no. If I have to get up and come over there. Don't put that on him. See, that's why he hit you. Trey, pick her doll up. I said I was watching you. Both of y'all just stop, nobody touch nothing. Go play on the slide over there or something."

He gave me a big grin before he went bouncing toward the slide.

Blowing out an exasperated breath, I fanned myself. For a parent, even playing was hard work. I felt akin to child wrangler out here. All I needed was a bullwhip and a megaphone.

"Towanna, I swear that boy is the devil sometimes. He is fa' sho his daddy's child, because that kind of foolishness is not of me." I shook my head. "No, I didn't make all that."

"Stop frowning at the boy, Chelle, he's behaving." Devon plucked a dandelion, tossing it at me. He was sitting on the opposite side of me. Giggling I tossed it back. I'd never told him what Rasheed had typed into Trey's iPad before I'd deleted it. I debated ever telling Trey. But, I needed to learn a lesson from Reena and not turn into an old woman withholding a century of secrets in my head. Secrets like, "Don't be like Daddy." I had reasons for what I did, and like Devon always said, if I'd asked instead of jumping without looking well . . .

Towanna snickered. "Yeah, he's a boy, Chelle, that's what they do. They terrorize little sisters and when they grow up they become their bodyguards and best friends. I grew up with two older brothers remember? Trust me, I'd know. It could be worse; he could be stealing Paris's tiaras calling himself the Queen Bitch. Snappin' and twistin'." She chuckled.

"Heavens no." I sucked my teeth and let out an exasperated breath on that one.

"I'll just be glad when the terror, tease, and fight phase is over all—" I'd barely gotten the words out before little Ms. Lataya Paris II came launching her little self up into my lap.

I was stuck trying to find her head out the sudden crash of upside down bright pink and white dress and limbs. She'd face planted and all I could see were little legs sticking from in between mine. I finally managed to pluck her out without getting kicked in the process and she was crying and screaming at the top of her lungs, damn near splitting my eardrums in the process. Of course Trey wasn't far behind, proudly carrying a got-damn baby python. I grabbed Paris and hopped up, screaming my own head off.

"Trey, what in the hell? Put that thing down before it bites your ass. Have you lost your mind, boy?" I looked over at Devon to handle what was also suddenly on his feet beside me.

"Hell, no. I don't do snakes," he shouted, throwing his hands up.

"Calm down, y'all, it's just a garden snake. A baby one at that. They're harmless." Towanna went all nature woman on our asses. She got up and took the ungodly spawn of Satan boa constrictor from Trey.

I backed up with Paris in my arms. "If you come over here, on my life I'll get in that car and leave all of y'all asses out here." Just then a large black bat looking something or another hovered suspiciously near me and I went Mayweather on it. Bobbing and weaving, sidestepping and shrieking all with Paris squealing in my arms.

"Um, it's just a butterfly, Chelle. The two of y'all are a mess. We will never go camping."

"Camping is anti-evolutionary anyway. I don't give a damn. It's a bug. I don't do snakes, bugs, critters, creatures, creepers; anyone who knows me knows that shit. I have nightmares about them things crawling on me and I can't get them off. I'm telling you about it now so it can't happen again."

"And, I have nightmares about my wife trying to kill me and holding a gun to my head and drugging me and turning me into the FBI."

Denise, Towanna, and I gasped in unison and I immediately started blinking back tears and smiling. This fool was on one knee holding up a ring.

"I'm telling you about it now, so it can't happen again. Emphasis on wife. I think we've traced our family trees and learned enough about each other. I want you and the silly, crazy, somewhat controlling woman you are more than just my baby momma," he added in a hushed whisper.

Denise took Paris from me because I was about to fall all to pieces as I said yes.

He wasn't gonna ever let me forget that whole drugging, FBI thing either. Devon stood up, pulling me close, and I could hear Trey groaning as he stomped off behind Towanna and Denise so they could set their anaconda free at the edge of the park. I smiled into Devon's face and pressed my nose against his.

"You sure your auntie twice removed on your momma side ain't run a brothel off Hampton Boulevard in 1986? I'm just askin'."

ORDER FORM
URBAN BOOKS, LLC
97 N18th Street
Wyandanch, NY 11798

Name (please print):_____

Address: _____

City/State: _____

Zip: _____

QTY	TITLES	PRICE
	16 On The Block	$14.95
	A Girl From Flint	$14.95
	A Pimp's Life	$14.95
	Baltimore Chronicles	$14.95
	Baltimore Chronicles 2	$14.95
	Betrayal	$14.95
	Black Diamond	$14.95
	Black Diamond 2	$14.95
	Black Friday	$14.95
	Both Sides Of The Fence	$14.95
	Both Sides Of The Fence 2	$14.95
	California Connection	$14.95

Shipping and handling-add $3.50 for 1st book, then $1.75 for each additional book.

Please send a check payable to:

Urban Books, LLC

Please allow 4-6 weeks for delivery

ORDER FORM
URBAN BOOKS, LLC
97 N18th Street
Wyandanch, NY 11798

Name (please print): _____

Address: _____

City/State: _____

Zip: _____

QTY	TITLES	PRICE
	California Connection 2	$14.95
	Cheesecake And Teardrops	$14.95
	Congratulations	$14.95
	Crazy In Love	$14.95
	Cyber Case	$14.95
	Denim Diaries	$14.95
	Diary Of A Mad First Lady	$14.95
	Diary Of A Stalker	$14.95
	Diary Of A Street Diva	$14.95
	Diary Of A Young Girl	$14.95
	Dirty Money	$14.95
	Dirty To The Grave	$14.95

Shipping and handling-add $3.50 for 1st book, then $1.75 for each additional book.
Please send a check payable to:
Urban Books, LLC
Please allow 4-6 weeks for delivery

ORDER FORM
URBAN BOOKS, LLC
97 N18th Street
Wyandanch, NY 11798

Name (please print):_____

Address: _____

City/State: _____

Zip: _____

QTY	TITLES	PRICE
	Gunz And Roses	$14.95
	Happily Ever Now	$14.95
	Hell Has No Fury	$14.95
	Hush	$14.95
	If It Isn't love	$14.95
	Kiss Kiss Bang Bang	$14.95
	Last Breath	$14.95
	Little Black Girl Lost	$14.95
	Little Black Girl Lost 2	$14.95
	Little Black Girl Lost 3	$14.95
	Little Black Girl Lost 4	$14.95
	Little Black Girl Lost 5	$14.95

Shipping and handling-add $3.50 for 1st book, then $1.75 for each additional book.
Please send a check payable to:
Urban Books, LLC
Please allow 4-6 weeks for delivery

ORDER FORM
URBAN BOOKS, LLC
97 N18th Street
Wyandanch, NY 11798

Name (please print):_____

Address: _____

City/State: _____

Zip: _____

QT		

Ship   for
each
Pleas

Pleas